Amanda

Copyright © 2005 Pamela P. Conrad
All rights reserved.
ISBN: 1-4196-0907-6

To order additional copies, please contact us.
BookSurge, LLC
www.booksurge.com
1-866-308-6235
orders@booksurge.com

PAMELA P. CONRAD

AMANDA

A REVISED EDITION

2005

Amanda

*To My Husband Gary Whose Encouragement And Support
Helped Me To Believe In Myself As A Writer*

CHAPTER ONE

The train belched smoke one more time before coming to a halt. Amanda's stomach churned from the continual rocking, lurching movements of the train. Dear God! She still had to find the stagecoach and possibly endure another two day's ride. If she were not sure that what she had to go back to wasn't worse than what she was going to, she would turn back now. Even the unknown pits of hell couldn't be worse than what she had left.

"Mama, I'm thirsty," a small voice complained, as it had been for hours. Controlling her irritation, Amanda reminded herself that it wasn't the child's fault for complaining because she was miserable and uncomfortable.

"Yes, sweetheart, we'll find some water. Let's get our bags together." Miserable barbarians. No one was around to carry the bags. Amanda, acutely aware of the weight of the two heavy bags, trudged to the door of the car.

"Melinda, get the satchel," she ordered the child.

"It's too heavy," Melinda complained.

"Get it," she snapped. (You must not scream. It will make your voice harsh and unladylike – her stepmother's rule number five-hundred-twenty three or so.)

Mother and child stumbled off the train. No smiling black porter to help with the bags. No polite conductor to tip his hat. Just as well. This train's conductor also stoked the furnace, so he smelled of coal, smoke, sweat and tobacco. She could see no one on the loading platform.

"Sit here in the shade, sweetheart, on the bags. I'll find someone to ask directions from," Amanda told Melinda.

"I'm hungry, Mama," that for the hundredth time.

"Yes, I know. I know," she uttered it absently, not reassuringly. She looked around. An old man sitting on the far end of the platform studiously chewed tobacco and stared at them. Amanda approached him.

"Pardon me, can you tell me where the stagecoach depot is?"

After spitting expertly into the dirt, the man said, "Harlan."

"I'm sorry, I didn't hear you."

The man squinted up. "Harlan," he shouted. She must have still looked puzzled, because he elaborated, "Town. About fifteen mile down the road."

"It isn't here?"

"Nope. Harlan." The man looked down and terminated the conversation.

Amanda whirled around and stomped back to Melinda.

"I'm thirsty, Mama."

Amanda sighed and sat on the other suitcase. What a ridiculous sight she must make! She wanted to cry and cry and climb on to her Papa's lap.

But there was no Papa here. And tears would not feed her or her child. Food. Where to get it? She never though such a basic need could be so difficult to fulfill. She remembered Rosies' honey cakes and strawberries and cream.

Enough! That was done forever. Aha! A general store. Perhaps there. She saw no hotel where there might be a restaurant. Restaurant. The further she traveled west the more ridiculous that name became. Definitely not the chandeliered palaces Papa and John-Paul had taken her to.

She pointed to the pump at the horse trough. "We'll get some water there."

Melinda ran to the trough and tilted her head so her mouth was under the pump, wetting some of her golden, albeit dirty, locks of hair in the trough. Amanda pumped the water. (Always maintain your delicate manners when eating and drinking. Rule number seventy.) Amanda ducked her head under the water when Melinda had had her fill and slurped up the water and rinsed her face off. Then she splashed some water on Melinda's small round face and gave her a quick cat wash.

"Stay here with the bags and I'll find something to eat."

It wasn't as though the chubby little five-year-old could actually protect the bags, but Amanda had to be relieved of her whining for at least a few minutes. She had not realized having the constant care of her daughter could be so trying. There had always been Rosie or Elizabeth to take her away whenever Amanda tired of here. Amanda grimaced. Skinny, pockmarked, sinister Elizabeth. The bruises and cuts on Melinda's little body. Dead God, Amanda prayed, forgive me for not seeing it sooner.

The store was dusty and crowded. A wizened old man sat on a stool by a barrel. Amanda marveled at the way his hair, skin, and clothes blended into the dusty atmosphere of the store.

"Kin I hep ya?" The voice was even cracked and gray.

"Yes, I..." She spotted a barrel of apples and one of crackers. "I'd like two, no, four, of the apples and a small bag of crackers."

The old man shuffled around, filling Amanda's order. It wasn't much, but maybe there was a place at Harlan to eat.

"Fifteen cents," the gray voice croaked.

As she counted the change, Amanda asked, " Is there

somewhere I can rent a horse and buggy to take me to Harlan to catch the stage?"

"Nope, but I'm going that way and can offer ya a ride," a deep, burly voice answered.

Amanda turned to the voice. A large man with dark, longish hair and a short curly beard peered at her with large dark eyes. He could have been thirty or fifty. It was impossible to tell.

"No, thank you," she replied coldly. "I don't accept rides from strangers."

The man looked at her. He wore a star saying "Sheriff" on his dirty shirt. He shrugged. "Okay. But it's a long walk."

He ambled out of the store. Amanda made her decision in a split-second. Fifteen miles was a very long walk, and if he was the local law officer, well, then, he was probably trustworthy, she reasoned. She grabbed the groceries and ran out of the store.

"Officer!" she called. The man went on walking. "Oh, Sheriff!" He stopped and turned. "I was, uh, rude. I hope your generous offer still stands." She gave him the smile that had wounded many a stout heart at the dances back home.

"Wagon's over there," the deep voice growled.

"My bags are at the train depot."

"Put'em in the back of the wagon." He walked toward the wagon.

Incredible! He wasn't even gentleman enough to offer to help with the bags. Perhaps he just forgot. Amanda waited briefly, but it was apparent he wasn't going to help. Amanda ran to the station.

"Mama, I need to go bad," Melinda greeted her. Where? Nothing in sight.

"Go under the platform."

"Mama!" Even the five-year-old was shocked.

"Go!" Did one really become uncivilized so quickly?

The child's biological urgency overcame her modesty and she scrambled under the station. Amanda struggled to the wagon with her burdens. Melinda raced to catch up with her. Amanda needed to relieve herself, too, but couldn't very well follow her daughter's example. The sheriff sat on the seat of the wagon, waiting. He reached over to help Melinda up as Amanda hoisted her to the seat, but didn't do the same for Amanda. She heard something in her skirt rip as she fell into the seat. The sheriff clicked to the horses and the menagerie was on its way.

***

An odd ride. And hot. Amanda had lost her bonnet and gloves on the train yesterday and how the broiling mid-day sun was frying her pale skin to a crisp. Thank heaven Melinda had her bonnet yet. The child had munched on the apples and crackers and then fallen asleep. She had leaned against the sheriff, who, surprisingly, had not objected. Amanda surprised herself by just letting the child alone. The sheriff did not speak one word the whole trip. Amanda felt no obligation to make social conversation. (Social conversation, rule number ninety-one: Men like women who can indulge in small talk, but never get too serious or argumentative.) But that was for gentlemen, and this sheriff was definitely no gentleman.

When they reached Harlan and the stage depot, the sheriff pulled the wagon to a stop and sat in the seat and waited. Amanda hesitated only a moment, and then fairly leaped out of the wagon, discarding all dignity.

"Come, Melinda," she barked at the just awakening child.

Gently the sheriff lifted the small head from his shoulder and pushed back her hair. She smiled up at him in confusion, and then finally woke up enough to remember where she was and joined her mother. Amanda did not wait for the sheriff to even offer to get the bags. She dragged the heavy things off the wagon and into the depot. She felt the eyes of the sheriff staring after her.

The depot did not have a restaurant but it did have an old cook who, with one look at Melinda's pleading face, fried some bacon and eggs. Amanda thanked him politely and tried not to wolf it down like Melinda. Two weeks ago she would have meticulously correct the child's manners. Perhaps her stepmother had been right. We are animals unless we are constantly reminded how to behave.

She tried to clean up herself and Melinda as well as she could at the makeshift washstand. They didn't have time to change their clothes as the stage came rumbling in. Amanda's heart sank as she paid their fare. Her money was dwindling fast. Perhaps she could get an advance on her salary. Her salary. She had never earned any money in her life and already she was spending what she hadn't yet earned. And what she would earn in a year, she had once spent on one dress for a Christmas party back home.

If the train had been rough, the stagecoach was ten times rougher. But in spite of the discomfort, Amanda found her head drooping and soon she was in a fitful sleep, with dreams of fiery red Indians, huge black mammies, and her pockmarked sister-in-law. She saw flashes of the events that led to her flight – the surreptitious hoarding of the money she had begged from her brother-in-law and even stolen from the egg money in the cookie jar. Then the flight away, every minute the cold fear they would be discovered. She had chosen her destination carefully. Once within this territory, she was comparatively safe. No extradition agreements had even been made with the other states, and women had the right to own property, raise their own children, and even vote! Her brother-in-law was at least good for something, even if it was only his law books and newspapers.

She awoke abruptly. The stage had stopped. No town around.

"Just a rock-slide. Have it cleared in a few minutes. You can get out and stretch your legs a spell," the driver informed them.

"Thank you, I think we will," she answered. The man helped her out of the confined, dusty quarters of the coach.

What a strange land this was. Her home would be lush and green this time of year. The trees would be in full blossom and the smell of flowers would fill every breath. And the fields would be rich dark brown where the plow had turned them. But here. Rocks. The land bred rocks. Hard, granite rocks. And a few pine trees and cottonwood. And sagebrush. That is what she smelled. The pungent sagebrush overpowered the few pathetic flowers and scrubby pines. The green-gray color dominated the endless stretches of nothing she had seen from the train. She could still see the range of mountains to the west that she had seen for a couple of days now. They seemed much closer now then before.

"Mama, I'm thirsty," Melinda had been strangely quiet since they had gotten onto the stage. Perhaps she was too exhausted to fight it anymore.

"I am, too," Amanda surprised herself by saying. She went to the driver, who was clearing the last of the rocks out of the way. "Excuse me, do we have any water?"

"Canteen on the seat of the coach," he said.

She hesitated at the bottom of the coach. Climbing up there in a skirt was not going to be easy. She bunched her skirt above her knees, got a firm foothold, and pulled herself up. She snatched up the canteen lying on the seat and jumped back down. Her agility pleased her. She hadn't done any climbing in ten years. When she was twelve, her stepmother had ordered no more climbing trees or running races with the "poor white trash" that lived over the hill. Amanda was a lady, or so she had been continuously told.

She and Melinda took a long drink straight from the canteen, without a cup. Reluctantly, Amanda admitted to herself that being uncivilized might not be proper, but at certain times it was exquisitely expedient. She handed the canteen back to the driver as he ordered them back into the coach. She was glad there were no other passengers. She wanted to be alone right now.

"This here's the agent's place, ma'am." Amanda started at the driver's voice. She had fallen asleep again. She had expected a longer ride.

She stepped down out of the stagecoach. As the driver helped Melinda and got their bags, Amanda surveyed the scene. The "Place" had the aspect of a ranch, with fences, horses, some cattle, and a barn and corrals. There was a larger building up the hill, and a team of horses tied outside that looked familiar. The Sheriff's. Amanda was surprised, but she was sure it was the same team. She had always had an excellent eye for horses, another point of pride her father had always had in her.

A short, sandy-haired man emerged from the building. He hesitated a minute and examined the new arrival. Then he approached Amanda. He limped slightly on his left leg.

"Mrs. White?" He had a whine to his voice. Inexplicably, Amanda felt irritated.

"Yes. Mr. Kinney?" She extended her hand, uncouthly ungloved. She become even more irritated as the agent shook her hand by taking it in both of his sweaty palms. Amanda quickly withdrew hers.

"Yes, I'm Mr. Kinney," the reservation agent. "Washington had written me of your pending arrival. I must say, I am surprised at your youth. I expected a much older woman. I wish to extend my sincere welcome. Oh, this must be your little daughter. She is as pretty as her mother," he exclaimed, cupping Melinda's chin with his skinny fingers. Melinda promptly took shelter behind her mother's skirts.

"Mr. Kinney, we have had a long, hard trip. I would appreciate it if…"

"Of, course, of course," he interrupted. "You'll want to eat something before you go to your quarters. Come inside and I'll have my cook prepare something for you." He put his fingers between his teeth and whistled shrilly. In response, an old, incredibly shriveled and dirty Indian emerged from behind the building and shuffled up to the agent. Amanda recoiled slightly from him.

"Take the bags and put them in the wagon," Mr. Kinney ordered him. Then, smiling, turned to Amanda. "The school compound is a few miles away from here. That's where your quarters are, also. We found it was wiser not to have the school too close. The children have no sense of honesty, you understand, and the temptation to steal from the reservation store is too much for them. Sheriff MacGregor has generously offered to take you out to the school."

She would have to endure another rider with the scruffy, taciturn sheriff. If she had known he was coming here, she could have saved herself the stage fare. Why hadn't he said something about it to her?

The Sheriff sat in the corner of the small store, feet propped up on the potbelly stove, chair leaned against the wall and hat drawn over his eyes. He didn't move or acknowledge their entrance. He annoyed Amanda, although she wasn't sure why.

"My quarters are behind the store here," Kinney indicate the door back to the left.

The store was small and dusty and what few things that were out on the shelves and counters were dusty. Even at a brief glance, Amanda could tell they were of very poor quality.

When the door was opened, Amanda's eyes widened in surprise. It was obviously a dining room but not what she had expected. A heavy oak table sat in the middle, surrounded by six chairs. A sideboard and hutch contained lovely blue china. Three places had been set. The washstand had two clean, fresh towels next to it. All was clean and neat and civilized. Amanda was suddenly very aware of her gown's very dusty condition. She wished she and Melinda had brushed the dust off their clothes.

Kinney gave his shrill whistle again. A young Indian woman brought two covered dishes and put them beside Mr. Kinney. She was dressed in a neat but faded red dress with her black hair done neatly in two braids. She kept her eyes down and never looked at either Amanda or Mr. Kinney. Amanda guessed her age to be about sixteen, although it was difficult to tell. Amanda had never been around Indians, and these tended to all look like the other, and they seemed to be either very young or very old.

As Amanda and Melinda gorged themselves on the meat, potatoes and gravy, corn and beans, Mr. Kinney kept up a running dialogue on Amanda's position and duties.

"You are officially, of course, only the school teacher for the young Indians. But you'll have to be more. They need a firm hand. You will have to be like a warden. Don't let them get the upper hand. If things get truly bad, just tell me and I'll deal with them. Don't expect the little bastards, sorry, excuse my language, don't expect them to really learn anything. Basically, they are a stupid lot. Can't seem to catch on too much of anything. Just let them know who's boss. Your quarters are separate from the school. You can do what you want with the place there. I've taken the liberty of laying in a few basic supplies. They will be charged again your account here, of course."

"Thank you," Amanda replied.

Mr. Kinney looked at her sharply, as though debating if she were being sarcastic. Amanda wasn't sure herself. The tone of the litany was disturbing, not to mention the singsong whine Mr. Kinney delivered it in. All the while the girl was bringing food back and forth. She finished by clearing the plates and bringing in pie and coffee. Her serving efficiency was excellent, she noted. Rosie herself could not have done much better. Melinda had silently devoured every bite just like her mother.

"Excuse me, but I think my daughter needs the, uh, necessary room. Could you tell me where it is?" Amanda interjected. She had ceased to really hear what Kinney was saying.

"Huh? Oh, yeah. Down the hill," he said.

Amanda took Melinda's hand.

"Mama," Melinda asked as they walked toward the outhouse. "Mama, what's a bastard?"

Amanda stopped and looked down at Melinda in surprise. She may not have been listening too closely, but her little daughter obviously had been.

"It's a bad word," she said abruptly.

"I know. But what does it mean?"

"You're too young to know."

The rest of the walk was in silence.

When they returned, the agent was standing outside, smoking a huge cigar. The sheriff was in the wagon. Amanda was evidently being dismissed.

"Your, uh, students should show up tomorrow. I've sent a message to the chiefs. They know they have to send their youngsters. Not sure how many there'll be, though. Good Luck." He took her had again to shake it.

Amanda decided that the less she had to do with Mr. Kinney, the better. She didn't wait for Sheriff MacGregor to offer any assistance, but lifted Melinda into the wagon and swung herself up, making sure this time that her skirts were tightly around her, so as not to tear them again.

The road to the school was really just a trail, probably used by horses more than wagons. The wagon bumped along. Amanda kept her eyes glued to the land ahead of them, politely refraining from curious questions. This sheriff revolted her, but also intrigued her. What was a sheriff doing on the reservation? And what, for heaven's sake, was he driving a wagon for? She thought all western sheriffs rode gallant horses and carried a gun slung on their hips. She stole a surreptious glance at his side. No gun. She did notice that a shotgun lay under the seat. And the man was definitely no dashing figure. Slovenly, that's what he was.

"There's the school," the sheriff said at last.

She couldn't see any building. The sheriff pointed to the hill. Amanda sat up straight, startled. It had never occurred to her that the school and the residence would be anything less than what she had attended when she was in school – the proper brick schoolhouse with the proper brick home with it. Even in some of the towns she had been in, since coming to this desolate country, there had been nice schoolhouses. But this! This was just a hole dug into the foothills. It was fit for foxes and badgers, not people. A hole in the earth. That's what she had exchanged her mansion for. Sheriff MacGregor jumped out of the wagon and lifted Melinda down. Amanda sat frozen to the seat.

"Mrs. White?" The Sheriff asked.

She looked down unseeing at the sheriff, not even seeing his proffered hand of assistance to help her down. Then she pulled her skirts around her and climbed down unaided. She walked slowly to the "house." The door, for some eccentric reason she couldn't begin to fathom, was not built straight into the hill, but built as sort of an entryway so the door faced southeast instead of due east. This meant, she noticed as she ducked into the hole, that the place did not even get the full benefit of the morning sun. She stood rooted to the spot, trying to adjust her eyes to the dimness. She didn't even feel the sheriff ease past her. He managed to find a lantern and light it. When the full light hit the place, Amanda wanted to run, anywhere, just anywhere but here. She could never live in such a confined, dark place. She closed her eyes tightly to regain her composure. She would not lose her dignity in front of this white trash that had brought her here. When she opened her eyes, she became aware of the intense curiosity with which she was being surveyed by the sheriff.

"Oh, Mama, it's as tiny as a dollhouse!" Melinda squealed. Evidently the child had already forgotten the huge room and soft bed she had had but a short six weeks ago.

Amanda took a deep breath, determined to survey the scene with a practical eye. The room measured about eight feet by eight feet. There was a cot in the corner of the room with one blanket thrown over it. She would have to do something about finding a place for Melinda to sleep. A large box evidently contained the "supplies" of the irritating Mr. Kinney, and another box contained pots, pans, plates, and other sundry sort of things. A washstand leaned then unsteadily against the wall. Atop lay an incredibly dirt washbowl. A three-legged table with a three-legged stool stood in the middle of the room where the sheriff had found the lamp.

"This is evidently the living quarters," Amanda said with as much dignity as if she were being shown the White House. "Where, if I may bother you for but a moment more, Sheriff MacGregor, is the school?"

The sheriff looked at her, and then ducked out of the hovel. "This way."

They walked about fifteen feet from the cave and came to another sod entranceway, facing southeast, the same as the "house." She knew she could not expect much when she entered with the lamp, as the sheriff and Melinda waited outside. It was about the same size as the house. A box of books lay in the corner and a few other unopened boxes were scattered around. Two rickety benches leaned against he walls. That was it. The room had the same dark, close feel about it.

"Mommy, where's the necessary room?" Melinda inquired as Amanda came out of the school. Amanda looked at the sheriff. "Where is it?"

He looked at her blankly. "The what?"

Amanda hesitated. He really was a barbarian. Well, simple minds needed simple language. "The outhouse," she said bluntly.

"Oh, there isn't one," he replied. Amanda instructed Melinda to go behind the rocks. Melinda took off like a little jackrabbit.

"I'll get my things from your wagon and let you get on your way," she told him.

Stiff-backed, with measure tread, she walked to the wagon. Not even waiting for any assistance, she reached for the heavy suitcase and dragged it off the wagon. She then turned and yanked off the satchel. The sheriff picked up the suitcase and watched her with that strange look in his eyes. She put the satchel in the doorway and indicated for the sheriff to put the suitcase there also. She would not invite this man into her "home" again. She reached out her hand delicately to him.

"Thank you, Sheriff, for bringing us here," she said politely. "I'm sure you have more pressing business to attend to then my settling in."

He took her hand and held it briefly. His hand was large and strong, but he did not try to crush her hand like so many large men would have done. She felt uncomfortable. Then he let go and left quickly. He was gone so fast Amanda hardly realized that she was alone.

Very alone. As she stood in front of the sod entryway, she knew how absolutely alone. As vestiges of the civilization and life she had known had been left by the wayside of her journey of the past six weeks. Now she was going to live in a sod hut. The warm sun beat down on her bare face, its warmth having an almost hypnotic effect on her tired body. Suddenly a cool breeze slid by, lifting and swirling her blue cotton skirts and her coal black hair. It chilled her as much as the sun had warmed her and she shivered.

"Mommy, I'm hungry," Melinda cried.

Melinda, Melinda, Amanda thought, are you ever anything else but hungry?

"Yes, I know," she caressed Melinda's golden locks, the only true legacy the child had from her father, although his gold had turned to gray before Melinda ever was born. Amanda shivered as another breeze blew through her. "Let's go inside, honey," she told Melinda. Together, they entered the hovel.

She marched into the cave and began determinedly taking the supplies out of the box. Flour, sugar, coffee, baking soda, bacon. As she took out each item she began to move slower and slower. She arranged the boxes and tins in a neat row on the three-legged table. She eyed them critically. Then began rearranging them, concentrating on each one to be sure it was square with the one next to it. She saw nothing of her surroundings – not the fact that the small shaft of light was fading from the doorway, nor the fact that the light from the lamp was flickering as it ran out of kerosene, and not the strange look on the face of the child with the golden hair. Amanda saw the tins of food, but she also saw her father's face, the face white against the sheets of the deathbed framed with the black hair and beard. His voice, rasping from the diseased lungs, while the bony, once strong hands, gripped hers, rasping.

"Mandy, my darling Mandy, I've betrayed you. I didn't give you that beautiful world we wanted. Mandy, forgive me," he had said.

She had said she did, she had said she understood, but she had not really understood. She was still bitter. It was all his fault, all of it. All of – this.

She looked up and brought herself back to where she was. But all she felt was confusion. She was surrounded by darkness. It was black as a hole in hell. What happened? Where was she? Melinda? A surge of panic rose in her, making her body shiver and her voice quake.

"Melinda, where are you?"

"On the bed, Mommy," a small, surprisingly calm, voice replied. "The lamp went out."

Amanda groped her way to the bed, and encircled the small body with her arms, as much to comfort herself as the child. If it had not been for her precious daughter, she would probably have escaped her asylum back east with a simple suicide.

"You're not afraid of the dark, are you, sweetheart?" she asked solicitously.

"No, Mommy."

"Most children are. You're very brave, sweetheart."

"Dark is better."

That's a strange thing for a child to say, she thought. "Why is it better?"

"Because, Mommy, then nobody can find me."

Curious as to the child's reason behind the strange idea, Amanda asked," Why don't you want anyone to find you?"

"Then they can't hurt me."

"Did someone hurt you?

"Aunt Elizabeth and Uncle Aaron, sometimes," Melinda's voice was getting faint. But Amanda's heart was racing. Then she hadn't just imagined it. "What happened, sweetheart?"

Melinda buried her head into Amanda's skirt, gripping them with her small hands. "I can't tell. I'm not supposed to tell."

"You can tell me, sweetheart. Aunt Elizabeth and Uncle Aaron will never hurt you again. I promise. They are far, far away." She stroked Melinda's hair, wanting to cry, yet knowing now if she did, she would never know. Melinda would never be able to tell her.

Between the crying and the shivering, Melinda told her. "Aunt Elizabeth would get mad at me and hit me. Once I fell down and she kicked me down the stairs. She told me I was ugly, and a bastard child." So that was why Melinda had noted that part of the conversation with Mr. Kinney. "And then Uncle Aaron and Aunt Elizabeth would fight. Uncle Aaron would come to my room, and .." She stopped and gripped Amanda's skirts tighter.

"Go ahead and tell Mommy. Uncle Aaron isn't here anymore." Amanda was afraid of what she was going to hear. She was afraid not to hear it. She was afraid because of the horrors the child had experienced. She was afraid because she knew, in the final judgment, it was her fault that his small person had to endure these horrors.

Melinda sighed. "Uncle Aaron would come to my room, and make me take off my clothes, and then he would do bad things to me, Mommy. They would hurt, Mommy. Why did he hurt me, Mommy?"

And then she began uncontrolled sobbing, sobbing so loud she didn't hear her mother's crying. Amanda held Melinda tightly and rocked her. But Amanda stopped crying after awhile. Her hurt and fear were replaced with a cold, violent anger. It was her fault that she had let this happen. She could not undo the last five years. But Aaron and Elizabeth would pay, somehow. She hated them. She hated them and the world they lived in and their self-righteous hypocrisy. "Amanda," Elizabeth would say every Sunday morning while putting on her faded pea-green bonnet, " a proper Christian attends church every Sunday. "

Dear God, were these Christians? "Then I am not one," Amanda muttered to herself. "I will not belong, then. Whatever I was in that world, I am no more." She continued to rock the child and herself until they fell asleep. The silky darkness of the hut protected them from the cold, unpredictable winds of the outside. Both slept deep, dreamless sleeps, purged of their fears of yesterday and bone-weary from the long trip.

AMANDA

A strong shaft of sunlight bouncing against the wall of the entryway awoke Amanda. Melinda still slept curled next to her mother. They had both managed to squeeze onto the small cot. Amanda's eyes opened slowly. Her feet felt like lead. But the hunger pains in her stomach and the demands of her bladder forced her to move. Gently she shifted Melinda so not to wake her. On her way to and from relieving herself, she meditated. There was a lot to do here, and a lot she had to learn. She knew that in order to survive here, she would have to carry the entire load. Yesterday that fact had frozen her into playing with little boxes. Today it only made her more determined. But, where, exactly, to begin?

Her father had once said to her, when they were looking into the new microscope that he had acquired, "Whenever you have to find out about something, Mandy," he had told the intrigued ten-year-old, "you have to look at it as closely as possible and then take it one step at a time, to find all its parts."

Okay, one step at a time. What were the main parts of the problem? Number one – food. Where to get it and how to fix it. She had never had to do either one, but now she would. Second, the house. It needed to be cleaned and organized. This hut would have to do for now. And she would definitely discard this corset she was wearing. It constricted her movements. She had lost her gloves and bonnet on the train. Now she would shed her corset. Who cared if she looked like a scrubwoman? There was no one here to see or care.

When Amanda got back to the house, she shed her clothes and pulled off the corset, flinging it into the corner. Her plump body sagged a bit here and there, but Amanda felt free. She could also take a deep breath. In doing so, she smelled the pungent sage of the prairie and – herself. How she hated being dirty! Her stepmother had said it was unhealthy to bathe so often, but Amanda still would plunge into a warm bath at least once a week. Bathing facilities. Another item to add to the long list of what she would have to do. But first, her stomach told her, she would have to solve the food dilemma. She looked at her neat stack of things on the table. She would make some bacon and biscuits. First, to cook the bacon. She looked around the room. Where had the former teacher cooked? There was no evidence of a stove, fireplace, or even a fire. What had been done to cook the food?

Amanda was nonplused. That situation would have to be solved later. Right now, she would build a fire outside. To do so in here would mean instant suffocation, of that she was sure. She went outside for firewood. There was an obvious dearth of trees in this particular vicinity. Evidently, this first meal was not going to be a simple process. The trees along the stream to the west – perhaps she could find a fallen branch, or some sticks. The walk to the trees was longer than she thought. Her stomach insistently growled for her to get the job done. The stream was swift and wide, but the water was sweet, Amanda discovered, when she knelt to drink. She should have brought a water jug with her. After some diligent foraging, she managed to find some sticks and returned to make a fire.

She set the sticks in front of the house. How to make a fire? She had never done even that. There was always Aaron, or father, or old Rosie to do it. She was appalled at her own ineptitude and stupidity. She knew there were matches in the supplies she had laid out. She would get them.

It took her ten matches and a lot of frustration, but she finally had a fire going. She had decided against the biscuits, primarily because she hadn't the faintest idea how to make them, much less bake them on an open fire. She retrieved water from the stream in the dirty pan. Then she mixed some grits with the fresh water, and fried some bacon in the other very dirty pan. Melinda had awakened and complained of being hungry, of course. When they finally did eat, the grits were lumpy and undercooked, and the bacon was burned, but in their hunger, they didn't care. They finished it off quickly.

With that problem temporarily solved, Amanda set her mind to what she would have to do to make this a livable habitat. She took the encrusted wash pan down to the stream. Mr. Kinney had neglected to include soap in his supply box, but Amanda always carried a bar of bath soap with her in her suitcase. So at least she had that. She angrily scrubbed at the dirt for a good half hour, barely making a dent in the scum. The cold water from the stream numbed her hands, but she felt a satisfaction when she brought the pan of water up from the stream. It was awkward to carry and she sloshed a considerable amount over the side and onto herself before she got back to the house. When she got to the house, she took one look toward the schoolhouse and dropped the pan she had just been working hard to clean in the dust and mud. Her students had arrived.

In her concentration on the mundane matters of living, she had forgotten entirely her original purpose for being here – teaching the young Indians. When she had applied for the job, it had seemed a good solution to her desperate problems. She had had visions of herself standing in a little red-brick schoolhouse, surrounded by bright eager brown faces and crisp little uniforms. What she was now confronting definitely did not measure up to that vision. Ten dirty little Indians, of various dress and size, were standing, squatting, or sitting outside the sod hut that was her schoolhouse, staring at her with impassive expressions. It was difficult to tell which were the girls and which were the boys. All had long, stringy, greasy black hair. Two little ones wore identical colorless sack dresses, the others dressed in an odd assortment of cotton and leather. Most looked to be about six to ten years old, but there were two that seemed to be somewhat older. And they were all so very dirty. They probably never bathed or washed their clothes. They could have at least cleaned up for their first day here.

Then she looked down at her own dress and chuckled. She was covered with mud and dust. She knew her hair was flying in the wind and her face and hands were streaked with mud. Well, perhaps they were starting out on a more equal footing this way. Melinda was standing by the entrance of the house, staring at the children. Amanda walked up to them.

"Good morning," she said in her most cheerful voice. They all looked down shyly, no one uttering a word. "I'm glad you all could come today." This was directed at the oldest boy, dressed in a breechcloth and an old blue army coat with sergeant stripes still on it. "I hope we get to know each other and like each other." This directed at the oldest girl, dressed in a cotton dress of an indecipherable color. "I'm sure I will like you all." This directed at the youngest child, whether a girl or boy, Amanda was not sure.

No response. Not even a grunt, a shift of the feet, a giggle – nothing but stolid, impassive faces. Now, what to do? Perhaps they couldn't understand what she was saying. It occurred to here that they were an alien people. Perhaps they didn't speak English. Her heart skipped a beat. How, then, was she going to teach them all the things they should know? Dear God. So many problems. And she was the only one who could possible solve them. She felt the old fear starting to creep up on her again. But she also felt something else. Excitement. The kind of excitement she had not felt in years, since, well, since she had raced John-Paul up the hill when she was twelve and he was twenty and her long legs had taken her victory over his short, chubby ones. It was the excitement of the challenge. Only this time, her actual existence depended on her winning.

First things first. She had to get herself and Melinda settled before she could take on the challenge of teaching these savage children. "We won't have any lessons today," she told them. "I must get settled. You can return to your homes."

Of course they didn't move. She really didn't expect them to. But perhaps if she talked to them as though they were already civilized and could speak English, some of what she said would eventually sink in their minds. She would begin the formal train in language later. How she would do it she wasn't sure, but she was confident she could do it.

She spent the morning cleaning out the hovel that was their home. She found that the floor was actually rock. Only the front portion and the entry were made of sod. As she pushed things around and swept with her makeshift broom of prickly sagebrush, she made another strange discovery. Under and behind the stack of boxes and the rickety washstand was an opening, not exceptionally large, but large enough that she could have easily gone through it if she had wanted to. It evidently led to a cave. She found the discovery somewhat disconcerting, if not actually spooky. She resolved someday to explore that part of her abode. When she finished, she was incredibly dirty, but the house was fairly clean. She had managed to affect some kind of minor repairs on what was supposed to be her furniture, with the aid of a large flat rock. Those hours spent in her father's invention shop were paying off in strange ways.

Every time she stepped outside she was very aware of the twenty eyes fastened on her, watching her, probably judging her. Lunchtime came and she found herself ravenously hungry. She tore off some beef jerky that Mr. Kinney had packed and gave some to Melinda, and chewed on the rest of it herself. Miserable stuff, salty and stiff, but in her present state of hunger it was good. Her next order of business was to clean herself and Melinda. A warm tub bath was obviously out of the question. The only alternative was the cold, snow-fed stream. Amanda bustled about, opening her suitcase, getting out fairly clean, if very wrinkled, clothes, for herself and Melinda, and her somewhat smaller, but still useful bar of soap.

When at the stream, she looked around to be sure that was no one watching. The Indians were still at the schoolhouse, squatting on the ground, noiseless as ever. Perhaps they were all deaf-mutes, an inherited peculiarity of the tribe. Amanda had meant only to sponge bathe to get rid of the worst of the offending dirt. But when she realized how incredibly dirty she was, she decided to risk a quick, nude plunge into the icy stream. She waded in to the middle of the stream, it coming only to her waist, but she had to keep her footing carefully because of the swiftness of the current. She made Melinda stay at the bank and wash quickly and then get dressed, drying only briefly with the towel. The cold stimulated her once she had gotten the initial shook over with. She quickly lathered her body, noting with some self-satisfaction that her skin was still marble white and her curves still soft and round in spite of the hardships of the past six weeks. She had had to give up her milk baths when she moved in with her in-laws and had feared that it would eventually make her skin rough and dark.

When she came out of the water, the breeze in the air felt more like February than May. She dried herself and dressed very quickly, becoming very aware of the openness around her. She had never gone nude outdoors in her life. It was a deliciously strange sensation.

When she returned the children were still there, each chewing on some strange sort of food, which looked something like a turnip. She was glad they had had the foresight to bring some lunch at least. She wished they would go home since she would be more ready for them in a week then right now. Why had they come today anyway? Well, they would just have to wait. She must think. She glanced briefly at them, and then crawled inside the hovel, sat down on the three-legged chair, put her hands on the three-legged table and stared hard at the wall. Melinda curled up on the coat and promptly fell asleep. Amanda opened her purse and pulled out her money. She fifty dollars left. Fifty, out of the five hundred she had begged, saved, and stolen. If she had not had to bribe so many civil servants in Washington in order to get here, she would have had more left.

She grimaced as she remembered how she would beg her brother-in-law for a few dollars, telling him it was for some little trinket she had seen in a shop window or some treat for Melinda. She could hear his pontificating as he doled out the money, on how she had gone through her father's money, and now she wanted to spend all his brother's. But he would see to it that it was properly spent. Thank goodness the law had seen fit not to allow women to handle their own money. They had no sense of it at all. And on and on about the ineptitudes of spoiled women. She had endured it. Again and again. The fifty cents and the one and two dollars growing in her drawer, under the rags she used during her time of the month. She knew no one would disturb those, not even pocky Elizabeth. She washed them herself, instead of letting Rosie do it. Usually Rosie did, and Amanda trusted Rosie more than anyone, but she wanted no one, absolutely no one, to know about her plot.

She had a general delivery box at the post office to get

her mail, as she wrote and begged for jobs until this teaching position had come up. John-Paul had mentioned it in one of his letters when he was in Washington. He did not write often, so she treasured every one of his letters. He had been to England and was off to India. "Speaking of India, I've heard our own Indians need another teacher. Poor, pathetic creatures. They just don't have the natural ability to survive in this world of ours." She had grabbed the chance. She applied. And found out what ridiculous chicanery was necessary in order to get it.

She had even condescended to accompany her brother-in-law to Washington. He used the excuse he had to get some legal matters settled in his brother's estate, but she knew what he wanted and why she was to accompany him. But the last laugh would be on him, she swore. He had come to her hotel that night, and raped her, threatening to cut off all her money if she so much as suggested to anyone what had happened. As though there was anyone who would have cared. Then he had sneaked back into his room. She had put herself back together, and after she was sure he was asleep, she had broken into his room. (She discovered she had a hidden talent for picking locks.) She had then stolen all his money, over two hundred dollars, the money that enable her to bribe the civil servants and get the appointment as the new schoolteacher for the savages in some far away land. What an uproar there had been at the hotel when the theft was discovered!

She smiled grimly to herself. Aaron would have saved himself a lot of money if he had stuck to his usual habits and picked up a lady off the streets. He had fumed and ranted over the missing money, telling her when they were along that it had probably been stolen when she had "so wantonly seduced him." She had wanted to kill him then, to see his blood spattered on the walls, and his brains trailing out over the carpet. It was then that she learned to bide her time and bite her tongue. She knew then, it was only a matter of time before she was gone.

She had also robbed Elizabeth, though no so obviously. She had discovered that Elizabeth kept the egg money in the sugar bowl in the pantry. She would make a pretense of wanting to "see what Rosie was cooking" because she was go hungry. Then she would sneak into the pantry and take some money out of the sugar bowl. Poor Rosie bore the brunt of this, because Elizabeth was sure that Rosie was stealing money to buy wine for her drunken husband. "If this were the old days," Elizabeth had screamed at Rosie, "I would take you down to the smokehouse and have you thoroughly whipped.

"Yes'm" was all that Rosie had said.

When Elizabeth and Aaron left on a trip to visits Elizabeth's sister, Amanda had known it was time. She had hurriedly packed Melinda's things and hers, and taken the train west. She had the letter for her job and what was left of her five hundred dollars. When Melinda had asked where they were going, she just said, "Far away from here." It had been enough of an explanation for the child. She never questioned their leaving again. The money had gone fast, and now, six weeks later, she had fifty dollars. She had to spend it wisely, since there was no more source of money, and she would not spend her salary in advance. She wanted to owe no one. She would pay Mr. Kinney for his supplies and then be clear of everyone.

The first thing, then, was to pay Mr. Kinney and get the things she would need to survive here. And on the top of the list was food. If she had learned nothing else these last few days, it was that although there was not a ready source of food here, she would not go hungry. She would plant a garden.

Rosie had had a lovely garden full of those sweet, moist things that Amanda loved so much but had taken for granted on the table. Surely there would be some seed packets at the general store. And she needed something to cook on. An open fire was out of the question in here, and it would also be impossible to always cook outdoors, too. They needed another bed, and a washtub, and some kind of cupboard, or dresser, something to put her clothes in and the dishes. More dishes, also. One pan, one bowl, and one plate did not seem sufficient, even just for the two of them. And soap, definitely. She would make the trip tomorrow.

She was startled to notice how low the sun was in the sky when she went outside. Melinda had awakened and was playing in the dirt, her clean dress covered with fine gray dust.

"Melinda!" Amanda said sharply. "Look at your dirty clothes! Don't play in the dirt like that!"

"I'm sorry, Mommy. I didn't have anything to do."

Amanda swept the child into her arms, hiding the guilt she felt. "Poor baby," she said, "we didn't even get a chance to bring one of your dolls, did we?"

"I'm not a baby, Mommy."

"No, I guess not, sweetheart. Are you hungry?"

"Yes, but can't we have something different. I would like some bread and jam."

Melinda's suggestion sounded delicious, but it was as impossible as if she had said she wanted walrus tongue. Amanda could not face cooking again, so she dipped into the last of the crackers, apples, and beef jerky. The little Indians were chewing on the weed again. They had not strayed too far from the schoolhouse, having spent most of their day staring at Amanda.

"You can return to your homes now," she told them

sweetly. Then she crawled into the hovel, pulled the single blanket over her and fell into a deep sleep with Melinda curled up tightly next to her.

She awoke to pitch darkness. Her feet, number with cold, would scarcely obey her orders to move. She heard a strange whistling sound outside. After tucking the blanket around Melinda, she groped her way to the door and peered outside. A whip of cold snow compelled her to pull her head in quickly. Snow! In May! Something she has seen made her put her head back out. As her eyes became accustomed to the odd twilight of the storm, she discerned shapes huddled by the schoolhouse door. The children! They had not gone home! They were outside in this storm, huddled together. Why didn't they go home? She didn't know why they did not, but she did know she could not leave them out there. They were her responsibility, and it would certainly not look good on her record if all her students froze to death on their first day of classes. She plunged ahead into the storm, never taking her eyes off the huddled forms. The cold wind bit through her thin dress. She felt as naked as she had in the cold stream yesterday.

She yelled above the noise of the wind, "Come with me."

The eldest girl was the only one to look up, but no one moved. Amanda, frustrated, cold and angry, had had enough of their silent inactivity. Grabbing the little one from the center of the huddle, she grabbed the hand of another one and growled, "Come with me now!" and headed back to the house. To her relief they followed her.

The hovel seemed almost warm, after the wind and wet of the outside. Melinda has awakened and somehow lit the lamp, so there was light in the room. They all crowded in together, with Amanda sitting next to Melinda on the cot.

Amanda looked at her charges. What a sorry-looking

group of wet, homeless puppies. That's what they reminded her of. The little collie puppies she had helped raise after the mother had died with their shaggy hair and doleful brown eyes. And the same ineptitude and inability to care for themselves. The puppies had lived, all eight of them, thanks to her getting up in the middle of the night to feed them by hand and cover them. When her stepmother had objected, it was one of the few times her father interfered. Now she had charge of these ten little Indians. She would help them survive.

They were all so wet, and she had no warm clothes to give them. She didn't even have any blankets. Well, maybe she could help the little one. She began to take off the clothes of the little one, but it pulled away and squatted beside the others.

"I want to get you some dry clothes. You can wear some of Melinda's."

She showed the little one the dress of Melinda's and offered it to the child. She knelt down beside it and put her hand out. The little one responded only but putting its eyes down and not moving. Amanda sighed. Perhaps she had done all she could for the moment. She had no warm blankets and no food. She had no warm fire, either. At least she had them out of the wind and snow. If she had checked on them before she fell asleep, if only she had made sure they went home, they would not be wet and cold now.

If only – if, if, if! God, how she hated that word. If only – it seemed to be the story of her life. If only her father had been able to make money, instead of spending what was left from the plantation. If only John-Paul had stayed to help them instead of running off like he did. If only she had not had to marry old Mr. White when she was sixteen, and he was forty-five, five years older than her father, but very rich, and a Yankee who pretended to be a well-born southern gentleman. His cold, very fat body had helped create Melinda.

She had been almost grateful when she had discovered that on her seventeenth birthday she was pregnant. How she knew, she wasn't sure, because no one had really told her what would happen when she became pregnant. But she knew. There was no blood that month. And when she was sure, she made the announcement to Mr. White. "About time," was all he said. But that stopped him from coming to her bed. Stopped the nightly ritual she hated so much, and stopped the insinuations from her in-laws. If only she could have stayed pregnant forever. Those months were easy for her. If only she had not given birth to a daughter. When Mr. White had seen her after her hours of labor and pain, and had seen the child, and learned that instead of a glorious son, he would be burdened with another female, he had said, "Perhaps next time you can manage to give me a son." And then he had disappeared for the night.

If only Mr. White had not died, she would at least still be living in comfort. What a ridiculous way to die – choking to death in a bordello over a piece of under-cooked meat. It would happen in such a way. He couldn't die a noble death, but an ignominious one. At the funeral, when the pastor had said how tragic it was that one so great should be struck in his prime with a bad heart while helping a lady in distress, Amanda had almost choked herself. It had to be her marvelous sister-in-law who thought that one up. If only her in-laws had been the Christians they professed to be. If only the law did not say that women could not manage their own money or property or children. It had to be a man, never mind that he was something of a lunatic. If only – that great phrase had been haunting her all her life.

Well, she didn't have any food, or any blankets. So the

little savages would have to be content to be out of the wind. She decided to take the opportunity to see if she could tell one of them from the other. She studied each one carefully, starting with the oldest (or at least largest) boy. She had already dubbed him "Old Army Coat." He wore the coat open now, and had only a breechcloth to cover himself. She found his casual exposure somewhat disconcerting, but then, what could she expect of savages? He had a thin, aquiline nose, high cheekbones (as they all did) and a shank of very long, stringy, wet, black hair. He was not looking up, so she could not see his eyes, but she was sure they were the same doleful brown.

Next, she analyzed the oldest girl. The dress, now wet, revealed the girl's form and startled Amanda. The girl was pregnant, perhaps four or five months along, or more. Her breasts were full and her legs muscular. Her hair was also long, but had been done into braids, each one intertwined with what was probably a red ribbon. She had a very high forehead, and except for her dress, looked very much like Old Army Coat. Brother and sister? Or just from the same, very inbred, tribe? Amanda looked hard from one to the other, until she began to see the discernable distinctions in the faces. She was sure as she became more familiar with these people that they would cease to look so much alike. After all, she had heard many Yankees say to her that all the black people looked alike, when she could easily tell there were vast differences in her servants. She decided to name the oldest girl student "Little Fawn" because of the soft brown color of her skin reminded Amanda of the deer she has seen when riding through the woods with her father. One second thought, better make it "Little Doe" because this little doe was going to give birth to a little fawn.

Sitting next to Little Doe was a young boy. Amanda was surprised she had not noticed before that he was breathtakingly beautiful. He glanced up at her shyly with his large liquid-brown eyes, framed in long, dark eyelashes and perfectly arched eyebrows. He reminded her of pictures of angels she had seen by a painted. Such a beautiful angel should have an angel's name. She would call him Raphael.

Leaning against Little Doe, sound asleep but sitting up, was the littlest one of the group, the one who had refused the dry clothes. Whether it was a boy or girl, Amanda still couldn't tell. But she would call it the Cherub. At least the child now had a name.

As she went from child to child, Amanda gave each one a name and began to see them as individuals. She felt like Adam in the Garden of Eden, giving each creature a name. And they were like creatures. So quiet, so distant. If they did not speak her language, and she had no idea of theirs, how was she to teach them anything, much less communicate the basic daily things to them? Like going home when she told them to go. She put her face in her hands and sighed.

The wind stopped. Sunlight shone into the door, bouncing off the wall. She got up and looked outside. The snow had drifted against the hut, but because of the direction of the door and wind she could still get outside. The air smelled clean and crisp and the sun warmed the air. Already, some of the drifts were beginning to melt and form little streams down the hills.

She knew Melinda would want something to eat soon, and there was very little left. She had the bacon, or course, and the flour and sugar. But not being sure how to cook anything, that wouldn't do her much good. The spot she had had her fire yesterday was washed away and the firewood she had meticulously gathered was gone. She would have to go to the agent's store. There was no choice in the matter. She had no food and must get some. She had to have things to settle her and Melinda into their home. And since she had no horse or buggy, she would have to walk. It would be quite a hike.

And then there was Melinda. She hated to put the child through it, but she would also have to walk. Amanda gathered up her skirts around her as the wind blew. She did not have time to hesitate. She ducked back into the hovel. The little Indians were still squatting on the floor. They, too, had nothing to eat. Well, if they could find a way to cook it, they could have the bacon. She and Melinda would have to get by on that terrible beef jerky. She wished she had some fresh beef or even chicken. Fried chicken. All she could think about lately was food.

"Melinda, we have a long walk ahead of us. You take this and eat it. I'm sorry there isn't anything more."

The child looked so small and pale. Her hair tumbled about her head in a mass of fine blond knots. Poor baby. Amanda hadn't even combed her hair for her in three days. She always had an aversion to fixing Melinda's hair, perhaps because it reminded her of her fat, dead husband. That wasn't fair. Melinda had no choice in who her father was. Amanda began fussing over the little daughter, straightening her clothes and combing her hair.

"That hurts, Mommy," she whined as Amanda it a particularly bad knot and tried to jerk it through.

"Just a few more, dear," Amanda replied.

She thought about the fact that the Indians would probably stay here while she was gone. She remembered what Mr. Kinney had said about their penchant for thievery. She would have to hide her trunk and clothes.

"Please go outside and wait for me," she said in her most pleasant voice as she took the hand of the little one and pulled her outdoors, the others understanding and following.

Then she returned to the hovel. She pushed the washstand to one side, lit the lamp, and poked her head inside the opening of the cave. After the initial narrow opening, there was a spacious cave, with a high ceiling. It was cool and dry. She decided she would put her clothes in here. She tried to pull the trunk through the opening, but it wouldn't fit. So she took the clothes and other things out of the trunk and laid them neatly inside the cave. Then she returned the washstand to its place. With a shawl for her and her daughter, she grabbed what was left of the bacon and went outside.

"Take this," she said to Little Doe, shoving the bacon into her hand. "If you can figure out a way to get it cooked, you may have it to eat. But you are to touch nothing else here. Do you understand?" Of course, no answer from the girl. "I'll be back this evening. Perhaps it would be best if you returned to your homes and come back tomorrow." She knew they would only stare at her. "Come, Melinda," she said.

And they turned up the trail that she had come down with the sheriff. The storm had washed some of it away, but it was still discernable. The ground was damp, but if they watched where they were walking, it wasn't too muddy. Most of the snow had already melted.

Melinda's short, chubby legs had to move fast to keep up with Amanda's long ones. To a passing traveler, it would have been a strange sight – the dark-haired woman in the full, long skirts and the small, cubby blond child running and stumbling after her, both of them small, insignificant specks in the great plains, dwarfed by the sagebrush and the rocks.

"Mommy, slow down," Melinda cried. Amanda turned around to see her daughter picking herself up out of the mud. She rushed back to help her.

"I'm sorry, my darling. Let me help you. Do you want to rest for a minute?"

Melinda nodded. They found a group of large rocks and sat on them to rest. Amanda put her hand to shade her eyes and looked over the prairie. It was incredibly hard to believe that there had been a snowstorm here last night. It looked more like a light rain, since all the snow had melted. She smelled the sage and flowers and the fresh scent that comes after the air has been cleared by a shower. And it was so vast. And she and her daughter were so small. They had a long way to go.

"Come on, Melinda," she ordered. They began their march anew.

"Mommy, where are we going?"

"To the agent's store."

"Why?"

"To get some food,"

"Why?"

"Because we don't have any."

"Why?"

"Because I didn't get enough when we were there. And we are going to plant a garden. Would you like to help me grow a garden?"

"Yes, I'd like that. Rosie sometimes would let me help her in the garden. Then she would clean me up before Aunt Elizabeth came in." Melinda giggled. "Rosie used to say when I got so dirty that I looked more like her child than yours."

Amanda laughed with Melinda. But the laughter hurt. She had really been more Rosie's child than hers. Amanda could not remember helping her get dressed, or reading together a book or any of those little things that make a mother and child become friends.

"What did you do in Rosie's garden?"

"Oh, she let me plant some seeds and then put dirt over them. I liked picking the strawberries the best, though, because I got to eat some, too."

"That sounds like fun. Well, I don't know if we will have strawberries. We are going to have to plant some things that will keep over the winter."

"Like what, Mommy?"

"Well, let me think."

And she did think trying to remember what it was that they had stored in the vast cellars at the plantation. But that was down south, where the winters were not harsh and bitter, as she had read they were here. If it could snow in May, it could probably freeze in September. "Well, we could have potatoes, and carrots, and beans."

"Ugh," Melinda opined.

Amanda smiled. It sounded good to her in the present state of hunger. They could plant the beans and peas and dry them. Beyond that, she didn't know. Perhaps she might be wise in planting a few onions, corn and squash. Where was she going to get some meat? They surely couldn't live on this terrible beef jerky.

The sun climbed to the top of the sky and was on the stairway down before she and Melinda reached the trading post. She stepped up to the door, only to be stopped by the sounds of voices, men's voices, coming out of the store, voices of anger.

"How long do you think this dame will last out there?" one was asking.

"I don't think very long. If the snow didn't already kill her, maybe one of her students did." Kinney's comments produced a round of laughter.

"Well, having her there is a damned inconvenience. We can't really carry on this cattle operation with an outsider looking in on it. We can always keep the Indians quiet as long as we keep'em cold and hungry, but there might be questions if something happens to her," another voice joined in.

"I think the best way to handle her is to keep her in her place. I think she realizes how far my authority can go around here, if you know what I mean." Again, Kinney's comments produced some snickers.

"I hear she's quite a looker," the third voice said again. Whose?

"Yeah," Kinney said, " Maybe I can get her to replace my little cook I had for a while." And more snickers. "Damn little bitch had to get herself pregnant. Wouldn't let me take care of the problem for her. Hate'em when they get fat like that, so sent her back to her people."

Little Doe, perhaps, thought Amanda. She was angry. She knew what rape was, and if Mr. Kinney had done this thing to Little Doe, then she knew what kind of man he truly was. She hated him. Melinda was pulling at her skirts. She put her hand over the child's mouth and shook her head. Melinda understood and was quiet.

"I think," Kinney was saying, "that I will just keep her at her schoolhouse until she decides to leave. If she survives, that is. I'm sure she won't be able to take much. One of those spoiled grand southern ladies, you know. By the way, there are a few hundred head coming in from the government this weekend. Troopers will probably bring them in. I want to just keep-em in the corrals until the troopers leave. Then we can take them out to the railroad and get top dollar for them. We'll have to leave a few old ones behind to give to the Indians. Got to have a few of the bastards alive or the government won't send us any more cattle."

Again, the camaraderie of snickers. Amanda controlled her white-hot anger.

She chose this moment to let her presence be known. She adjusted her smiled, whispered to Melinda that she was not to say a word to anyone while they were here, and entered like debutant entering the ballroom. Kinney looked up in surprise. Three men surrounded the counter, one chewing tobacco with it dribbling out the side of his mouth. He was small, and very dirty and very ugly. The other was a tall, blond, handsome young man with dazzling white teeth that showed when he flashed his wide smile.

"Why, Mrs. White, how ever did you get here?" Kinney asked.

"Well, I just had to come and see you again," Amanda drawled in her most sugary manner. "I did so enjoy our last visit. But, my, I didn't realize you were so far away! Do you mind if I sit down for a tiny minute?"

The blond gentleman swiftly got her a chair, while the ugly one just stared at her. She fanned herself daintily with her hand. She knew she was dirty and windblown, but perhaps if she looked pathetic enough, her act would work.

"And who are these handsome gentlemen?" she asked coyly.

"Oh, I beg your pardon. I was so startled by your coming here like this. I would like you to meet Mr. Graves. He's the doctor at Harlan." He pointed to the tall, handsome man. "And this is Mr. Jacobin. He's the blacksmith. Gentlemen, this is Mrs. White, the new schoolteacher for our young Indian friends.

"How do you do, gentlemen?"

"It is a pleasure, I assure you, Mrs. White," responded Mr. Graves, of the third voice, taking her hand in his. His hands were soft and white, with long, tapering fingers and his touch was gentle and warm.

"I was just telling these men how I hoped you would be able to manage out here in this wilderness," Kinney's whiney voice was grating on her nerves. But she kept her smile frozen on her face.

"Oh, I do hate to be a bother, but poor little Melinda here is very hungry. I wonder if you have something for her to eat."

"But, of course. I'm afraid it won't be much. I lost my cook, you see. Ungrateful b——-" he started to say, bitch, thought better of it, and instead said "girl. She ran back to her village. No appreciation from these people for your efforts. Terribly uncivilized and unchristian. Here, child, this is the best I can do for you now."

He proffered a somewhat wormy apple to Melinda, who, in her hunger, was not going to be particular. She munched on it.

"I'm afraid I wasn't thinking very far ahead when we left here last time. I would like to get some food from your store. And I thought perhaps some seeds for a garden." Kinney look at her sharply when she said this. Planting a garden mean that she was planning on staying. She couldn't let them know her plans. "The child has very little to do out there and so she could dig in the dirt and plant a garden to keep her busy and amused and out of my hair. She can get one one's nerves. And perhaps I could teach the children some fundamentals in civilization with it."

Kinney seemed ready to accept her explanation.

"I think I can help," he said. "What do you want?"

She had been surveying the store while she had been chattering. She could not arouse his suspicions about her intentions. There was no way that he was going to chase her out. She was done with running and hiding from his kind. She was going to fight. She began picking and choosing seemingly at random, around and around the tiny store, more waltzing than walking.

"Oh, those canned pears do look delicious. I must have those," she would squeal with delight. "Oh, I do love peas with cream sauce and biscuits."

She proceeded in this manner until she thought she had enough provisions to last them for a while. She sensed that Kinney felt some displeasure in giving up some of the rarer delicacies. She had picked out several packets of seeds, including peas (they take time to shell and would keep Melinda entertained) and squash (they are hardy, and the youngsters would at least be able to get them to grow) and beans (they are hardy, too). She was amazed that they were gullible enough to accept such frivolous excuses for her choices and behavior, unless they were playing a game with her. Whatever.

She was disconcerted at the stack of things she would need. She realized that she would have to make this trip her last one for a while, if she was to ease Kinney's suspicions and keep him at arm's length for awhile. But she would very much like to see those cattle that were to come in this weekend. If she remembered right, this was Monday. That would give her a few days to settle in. She would leave a few things for later, to give her a good excuse to return. But she did need the soap now.

"Goodness, what a stock of things," she exclaimed. "How am I even going to get it all out to the house?"

She smiled to herself at their surprise at her reference to her quarters as her house. But not one of them volunteered their assistance to help her. Part of the plan to discourage a long stay, she suspected.

"I know just the thing. That cute little bucket there. That would be just the thing for Melinda to play in the sand with," she drawled, thinking all the while it would make a handy item to carry the water.

She also spied a small pair of those types of pants that all the cowboys wore. She would need something sturdy to wear when she was doing the heavy work. It was certain these dresses would not endure. But how to get them without arousing suspicion. Of course.

"I'll bet I could make a darling little jacket for Melinda out of these," she breathed as she selected them. "Now, how much do I owe you for all this?" Kinney seemed a little overwhelmed by her shopping spree, but not too suspicious or angry, Amanda hoped. Not yet.

"Twenty-five dollars," he state flatly. Amanda was shocked. She hadn't expected the price to be that high. But she didn't want anyone to think that she was anything but a spoiled child on a lark. "Oh my," she said. "I almost forgot. I do owe you for those few little things you were so kind to put out at the house for me."

Kinney cleared his throat slightly. Since he didn't want his cohorts to think he had helped he, he couldn't admit it was more than just a few trivial things.

"Oh, that wasn't anything. The twenty-five ought to cover it," he said.

Although she knew he had charged her ten times what it all was worth, she would not let them know it. Never. She was tired of being the spoils of war. This time she was going to be the warrior. She was going to have to plan her campaign and fight her battles courageously. She smiled sweetly as she rolled out the twenty-five dollars from the fifty. Since they were all ones, she knew there looked to be more there than she actually had. She put as much as she could into the bucket, and the rest in a burlap sack that Kinney begrudged her, and sailed out of the room with Melinda in tow.

The sun was frighteningly low in the sky. She hadn't

remembered if there was a full moon last night or the night before, but, please, God, let there be one tonight. She didn't think she could find her way along the road in the dark, especially since the rain had washed out so much of the trail. The country was so vast, and every place looked the same as the last. She walked briskly for about a mile, knowing Melinda stumbled, and tripped behind her, finally giving up her whining, both of them hungry, dirty, and tired, and Amanda, angry. She decided to follow a new motto: Trust in God, but never a Christian.

The moon rose full and bright in the sky, revealing a strange appearance in the great desert, and in the mountains that seemed to form some huge blue dragon. When the sun went down, it took its heat with it, and the cold of the night stabbed her to the bone. But they would be all right if they kept moving. Her arms ached with her load, and Melinda ceased all whining and crying, realizing its sheer futility. They didn't walk. They dragged. The house did not exist, the warm dark hovel with its blanket and bed.

"Damn!" Amanda exclaimed for the first time in her twenty-two years. "I forgot to buy blankets."

Melinda, encouraged by the break in the silence, looked up at her, dark circles under her eyes and her hair knotted and windblown, and in a very small voice, cried, "Mommy, I'm so tired."

Amanda looked down at the child. If they stopped, they might freeze. But the child could not walk another step, and she could not carry her. Must every moment of life be a major decision? Amanda stopped to think.

"We'll stop for a little while, just a little while, sweetheart. We must get home."

Home. Strange name for a strange place. She found a dry

spot next to a large rock and a clump of sagebrush that shielded them a little from the wind. She sat down and Melinda curled up in her arms. Amanda threw her shawl over the child and put her head on top of the snarled blonde curls.

She awoke with a start at the hand being placed on her shoulder. She had been in the middle of a dream of strawberry shortcake, black servants, and pockmarked Elizabeth. The hand stifled the scream that was forming in her throat. She looked up to see her student, Old Army Coat, staring down at her and she felt so cold. The boy gestured at Melinda. At first, Amanda could not understand who was with her, much less what he wanted. Then she realized he was offering to carry Melinda home for her. Amanda felt tears starting to well up in her eyes, and she averted her head from the boy so he would not see her cry. She would not lose her dignity for anyone. She felt the boy lift the heavy load from her lap. Her shoulders ached so badly she longed just to leave the bucket and sack where they were and walk home to a warm fire and hot chocolate. But there would be no fire. And she had no choice but to carry her burdens if she wanted to survive. She forced her stiff joints to move, pick up the burdens, and blindly followed the brown and blue form in front of her. She wasn't even sure he was leading her to the cave. She had to trust that he would. She smiled to herself in spite of it all. Well, at least she had stuck to her motto. She wasn't putting her trust in a Christian.

He did lead her to the hovel. And there was a fire. And all her students surrounded it, with Little Doe cooking the bacon, the delicious, aromatic bacon, in a skillet, without burning it. Amanda dropped to her knees in front of the fire. Melinda woke up when Old Army Coat set her down by the fire. She looked at him without any trace of fear, just an expression of perplexity.

"Mommy?" she murmured.

"Here I am, sweetheart. We're home," she said.

Little Doe pulled a piece of bacon out of the skillet with a stick, and offered it to Amanda. Amanda smiled at her, then took the stick, blew on the meat until it cooled a little, then fed it to Melinda. Old Army coat took his own slice of bacon out of the skillet, and then Little Doe passed the rest around to the others. Amanda surveyed the small brown faces around the fire, ending with her daughter's very white face and very light locks. And strangely enough, she felt as though she were home.

CHAPTER TWO

The next night Amanda meditated on her plight as she stared at the dancing flames of the fire. She gradually reached some critical decisions while the little ones slept. Strangely, Old Army Coat had been her silent companion in sleeplessness, studying the fire with her. She had deliberated carefully. Her conclusions did not resemble the flighty impulses of the Amanda of long ago. These were practical steps needed to survive.

She resolved not to let Kinney and Company drive her from this place. She enjoyed the isolation and self-reliance she had here. Never would she relinquish these for a spoonful of strawberries and feather bed.

First, they must eat. She knew now that these children would be staying here. Therefore, they would have to earn their keep if they were all to eat. She needed help to plant the garden. Maybe one of them knew something about planting. Also, she must learn to cook. Little Doe had been Kinney's cook, so she could teach Amanda. These children would have to learn to speak English. They would set up the schoolhouse for their home. She would dry the meat and vegetables for the winter and store them in the cave. She would survive.

In spite of her stiffness, hunger, and lack of sleep, she set her plan in motion on the first light of day. A stiff and sore Amanda diligently stored her supplies in the cave. She had decided that she would make her actual living quarters in the cave. Since it was well shielded from the weather, it would not need much heating even in winter, and would also offer some cool relief from summer's heat. Then she would build some sort of stove in the hut for cooking and find someway to vent the smoke outside. Little Doe had built a fire last night from something, but it was not wood. She would find out what it was.

She actually sang softly to herself as she bustled about, turning the cave into a home. The entranceway provided ventilation and the lamp cast a soft glow on the brown and gray walls. After an hour or so she had it organized She stacked the cans and tins of food neatly along the forward wall and piled the clothes neatly along a low ridge on one side. She had found a large nook slightly raised from the floor on the other side where she could put straw or something on the rocks and the blanket for a bed. Right now she laid their winter coats down as a mattress. Now Melinda had a place to sleep.

Melinda! The poor child. Probably hungry again. Amanda scurried out to discover Little Doe cooking again. Someone had managed to catch a rabbit and she was roasting it over the fire. The children chewed on the strange weed.

"Mommy! Taste. It tastes like an onion!" Melinda bounced up to Amanda, who bit gingerly into the weed.

"Yes! It does! It's good. Did you help get it?"

"Oh, yes, Mommy," then she giggled. "But the funny little one sat in a cactus and everybody laughed."

Amanda smiled. She enjoyed seeing Melinda happy. It felt good.

Perhaps now was the time to begin the lessons in communication. Simple words and simple things. She sat beside Little Doe, who did not seem to notice her presence. Amanda touched her gently on the arm. When Little Doe looked at her, she point to the fire.

"Fire," she said slowly. Little Doe looked at her, then the fire. "Fire," Amanda repeated.

"Peta," Little Doe replied.

"Fire," Amanda insisted.

"Peta," Little Doe retorted.

Amanda stared at the fire. Then she looked up at the sky and out to the prairie. All right. She had to be able to communicate on a very basic level. This was not the time to civilize the savage.

She touched Little Doe's arm again, and smiling slightly, pointed to the fire, and said, "Peta."

Little Doe clapped her hands and laughed. Then she patted her head. "Pa," she said.

"Head," Amanda replied, trying one more time.

"Pa," Little Doe repeated.

Amanda patted her own head. "Pa," she said resignedly.

Little Doe pointed to her eyes. "Ishta," she said.

"Ishta," Amanda answered.

Little Doe slumped down and looked at her. Amanda, nonplused, repeated, "Ishta," but Little Doe did not react. Oh, all right, my word now, Amanda thought. "Eyes," she said as she pointed to her own eyes. Immediately Little Doe brightened.

"Ishta," she chortled.

"Ishta," Amanda now understood. It was a game. First me, then you, then together.

Little Doe point to herself and then patted her belly, "Wing yang ihdushake."

Amanda hesitated. At first she thought the girl mean she was hungry. But then it struck her that Little Doe was telling her about the fact the Little Doe was pregnant.

"You're going to have a baby!"

"Wing yang ihdushake," Little Doe repeated.

Amanda tried to repeat the words, but the sounds were strange and difficult for her tongue. The one she had named Raphael, who had been watching the proceedings, burst into laughter and rolled on the ground. Amanda was completely abashed. Even Little Doe was smiling. Amanda was indignant at being laughed at, but the child's ingenuous laughter and beautiful grin destroyed any anger. Amanda grinned back at him and made another attempt. It resulted in another paroxysm of laughter, this time with all three of them joining in. Little Doe repeated it. Amanda imitated it. Finally, she got it right. They continued the game until the rabbit was done and Raphael hunted up the scattered tribe and they settled into the feast.

The next few days Amanda concentrated on putting in the garden, a very frustrating experience. She had no spade, no hoe, and no rake. She crafted a digger from a long stick, but it broke when she tried to dig the hard ground around the cave. She finally compromised and put the garden by the stream where the soil was soft. It would be difficult to watch, but at least it would be close to water. The instructions on the packets were not meant for her situation, but she approximated measurements and hoped. She used her makeshift spade to furrow in the dirt. Then she planted. Row upon backbreaking row. But she determined to over-plant. She was sure to lose something to the rabbits and the birds, as they had back home.

She had changed from her dress to the pants she had bought. She wore a camisole for a blouse, all the while hoping Kinney would not decide to pay a surprise visit.

Her ten little Indians proved absolutely no help with the garden. They refused to dig, plant, cover, or even carry water. Melinda tried to carry water but the bucket proved too heavy for her and she ended up taking a mud bath, much to Raphael's amusement. Amanda had discovered that behind that beautiful face lurked the soul of a rapscallion. The child was an imp, delighting in mischief of all kinds. He put a frog in the bucket when he thought she wasn't looking. He sneaked green wood onto the fire and they all teared for hours from the unexpected smoke. And just when she thought her patience was ended, he'd look up at her with his beautiful smile and all was forgiven.

She discovered the others also had their talents. Little Doe continued to play the word game with her. She was also learning some of the signs they made with their hands. She could ask them to do such things as build a fire or gather the spring onions. At least now they could speak beyond the silence of the first couple of days.

She was also learning to cook. It would have been so easy simply to let Little Doe assume that responsibility completely. But Amanda, determined not ever to be helpless again, stubbornly insisted little Doe teacher. She learned to make biscuits in an open fire, and to cook the rabbits and birds on a spit without burning them.

Thursday evening she explained to Little Doe, through their limited vocabulary, and signs and pictures drawn in the dust that she would be leaving the next day to go to the agent's. She explained the cattle were coming, and she wanted to get one for the school. Most importantly, she wanted to leave Melinda in the care of Little Doe. It was a tortuous decision for her. She had not left the child alone with anyone else since she had left the east. But she could not succeed in her mission if she were to take Melinda. It was too far for her. Little Doe seemed to understand her concern and what she wanted.

She lay awake in the stillness of the cave that night listening to the child's gentle snoring. Her body ached. Muscles she never knew she had cried from the strain of the last few days. Her hands were rough from the water and dirt. She was exhausted. Yet it was not the kind of deathly fatigue that drugged her on her first night in the cave. When she finally slept, no specters from the past haunted her conscience.

"Melinda, Mommy has to leave you here for a while," she said the next morning.

"Why, Mommy?"

"Because I have to see Mr. Kinney and I can't take you with me."

"Why?"

"Because it's too far for you to walk. You stay here with Little Doe."

Melinda studied her mother's face. God, what a serious child she is, Amanda thought.

"Okay, Mommy," Melinda whispered, hugging her and clinging to her.

Amanda kissed her child and hugged her tightly. Then she turned abruptly and raced down the hill, holding her skirts high. She had attempted to put together some of the silly debutant she thought they expected to see. She had apparently lost some weight because she didn't fill out the dress as well as she had when she rode in Sheriff MacGregor's wagon. Without Melinda in tow, she discovered she could walk at a much faster pace.

Somehow she wasn't surprised to see Old Army Coat appear from nowhere and match her long stride. He said nothing. He never said anything, at least that Amanda had heard. As they walked in silence measured by their steps, Amanda allowed the boy to subtly guide her when the trail became faint and she became unsure. Just as they came to the rise to the trading post, Old Army Coat squatted down and studiously planted himself to await her return. She accepted his decision not to go with her to the illustrious Mr. Kinney.

She could hear the cattle before she could see them. A much busier scene greeted Amanda than the last time she had been visiting. Blue-uniformed troopers circled the herd of cattle, more cattle then Amanda had expected. Mr. Kinney stood on the veranda of the post, talking to Jacobin and an Army captain. So engrossed were they in their conversation that they failed to notice Amanda walking swiftly across the prairie. For once she appreciated her long legs and the long stride they could take. She made sure she approached so the first eye she caught one that of the Army captain.

"Why, Mr. Kinney, I don't believe I've met this handsome gentleman," she lilted.

Kinney whirled around, unable to conceal his shock. His oily charm failed to grease his vocal chords, and no sound gushed from his open mouth. Amanda chose to ignore him, zeroing in on the huge Army captain instead. This wasn't a man. It was a mountain that had walked away from the others.

"I'm the new teacher for the Indian children," She delicately extended her hand. "My name is Amanda White." The captain's hand engulfed hers.

"Ma'am," was all he said. He and Sheriff MacGregor could have a wonderful conversation of single syllables.

Kinney recovered. "What a pleasant surprise! Two visits in one week! Is the teaching going well?"

"Of course," Amanda smiled. "The first few days are just to get acquainted, you know."

"Do you have many students?" The Captain asked.

"Oh, enough to keep me busy. Goodness, whatever are all these cows here for?" She directed the question to the Captain.

"For the Indian meat ration for the winter. They'll come and get them Monday," he replied.

Kinney interjected. "Why don't we all adjourn to my dining room for coffee?"

He turned to enter the store, but the Captain's steady gaze stopped him. He followed its direction and once again Kinney was lost for words. His watery eyes simply opened wide, as did his mouth. Over the hill, mounted on their multi-colored ponies, with a steady gait, rode the Indians, warriors once, now the dignified defeated. Following them, with equally dignified pace, but on foot, were the women and children. They flowed down the hill and came to a quiet halt about a hundred yards from the store. One rider continued until he stopped at the front of the store. He raised his hand in greeting and the Captain returned the gesture.

"We have come for our cattle," the man spoke in a very deep voice that seemed to rumble from his chest.

"They are here," the Captain replied.

"We will take them and go," replied the Indian.

Amanda had been watching Kinney during the brief exchange. She had once seen a rat caught in a trap, that knew it was about to die, but was still looking for a way out. Kinney looked very much like that rat.

"Just a minute, here," he stepped forward and pulled himself up, squaring his shoulders. "I am the authority around here and those cattle cannot be released until Monday."

"We are here today," replied the Indian.

"Not until Monday. No siree, not until Monday. That's what the papers from Washington say, and that's when it will be. Now I'm the only one who can release those cattle to you, and I say Monday."

"We will not be able to help you with them, Mr. Kinney," the Captain interceded. "We must return to the fort. It might be wiser to get them off your hands now."

"Captain, I am responsible for what goes on here, and I will not release those cattle until Monday."

Amanda knew that Monday these cattle would be gone. It wasn't any of her business, but Kinney irritated her so, and she might not get any of her own for the school if she didn't do something, Right now, her own survival was linked to the survival of her Indian students. Otherwise, she would have to find somewhere else to go. And she was very tired of running. Her mind churned with ideas of how to interceded in this transaction. Her influence was minimal, and Kinney already has hostile toward her.

"Mr. Kinney," she began sweetly. "Surely Washington has given you power to use your own discretion and judgment. Isn't that why they send such men as yourself out here?"

"Well, yes, I have that power," he answered uncertainly.

"Well, then, why don't you just use that power and change the date. I mean, you are the only administrator out here, really. I'm sure those people back in Washington don't realize what tremendous decisions and difficulties you're faced with out here."

Now it was Kinney's turn to hesitate. Amanda's moves were subtle. She advanced her pawns instead of her knights and bishops to lure Kinney's powerful queen. His own aggression could be turned against him.

"Perhaps a compromise is in order," he replied, shifting his attention from Amanda back to the Indian with the deep voice. "I'll release some of them to your today so you can begin the slaughter, or whatever. Then I'll release the rest of them on Monday. That way the authorities in Washington will be satisfied and you will not have made the trip for nothing."

The Indian studied Kinney a moment, then nodded, and slowly returned to his people. He conferred with some of the other riders, one younger man obviously angry.

While the Indian conferred, Kinney addressed the Captain. "I will show the troopers which ones to cut out for the Indians. Perhaps you can return to the fort sooner and get this chore over with."

"Sergeant," the Captain called. A young man ran up to the Captain and gave a smart salute. "Go with Mr. Kinney to help the troopers cut out some of the cows for the Indians."

Amanda could see her chance slipping away. "Oh, Mr. Kinney. I understand that some of these would be for the children at the school. Perhaps I could prevail upon the captain to have one of his men bring them to the house?" Always sweetly said, hesitantly, as though she were an orphan child asking alms. Surprisingly, the Captain stepped in to support her cause, before Kinney even had a chance to answer.

"Oh, I'm sure it would be no trouble, Ma'am. If you would allow me to be so bold, I will pick out the animals myself." He did have a nice smile, even it was barely discernible. Kinney's queen had been captured, checkmate certain.

"The school is only authorized two animals. However, I personally will chose them," Kinney countered. Amanda had the distinct impression that if Kinney chose, the animals would be two that would not even make it back to the house.

"Oh, dear, I can't have you two gentlemen differing over little old me. Perhaps if the young sergeant chose as he helps get the others?"

"Oh, very well," Kinney agreed, a trace of petulance in his voice.

The Captain gave Amanda that small smile, and tipped his hat. "I'll tell him, then," he said, and walked away.

"If the Indians had any sense, we wouldn't go through this every winter," Kinney whined. He was unhappy at not having won the whole prize.

Amanda knew that the cattle he would choose for the Indians would be the poorest ones. She also knew that those left would not be here Monday. What excuse would Kinney invent? Did he have to even invent one? She was sure that he and his friends were not going to lose the game simply because of a few dirty Indians and a dumb woman. Kinney stomped off with the Captain to supervise the procedures. Amanda stood on the veranda and watched. An odd spectacle, almost unreal. But she had the grim satisfaction of being right. Even to her unpracticed eye, she could tell those animals given to the Indians were of inferior quality. They were terribly thin. There wouldn't be much meat on them. And they certainly were not good breeding stock. Did the Indians have their own breeding herds? If they did, why did they need these cattle? Why, indeed? She hoped whoever went back to the house with her was not as taciturn and the sheriff or the Captain. She would like to have some answers to the riddles of this strange country. The map showed it to be part of the same nation she had come from, but it certainly did seem foreign in many ways.

Kinney had given the Indians about twenty-five head. Considering the size of the whole herd, that wasn't even enough to notice. There were, in total, close to three hundred head. The whole valley was filled with them. Amanda watched as the young sergeant talked briefly to the captain, gave his smart salute, and jumped on his horse. He rode swiftly into the herd and cut out two of the animals, driving them off to the side by the hill. Amanda looked closely. They were obviously two of the better ones. Amanda's smile was genuine when the Captain came up to her.

"Thank you, Captain," she said.

The Captain nodded "My sergeant will help you get the animals back home. You have a horse to ride?"

"Well, no, I – "

"You're welcome to take mine, then. May I suggest that you get them out of this confusion right away."

"Well, I had planned on getting some blankets and more supplies," she protested.

"Mrs. White, please, I cannot wait all day for my sergeant's return. Take them now."

"Very well, then," she said.

She took the reins of the huge animal from the Captain's hand. She had never ridden such a big horse, and she wasn't exactly dressed for riding. These army saddles were awkward, and the horse very wide. She lifted herself into the saddle, getting an unexpected assistance from the Captain's huge hands around her waist. She didn't have any option but to ride in a very awkward straddle, rather than sidesaddle. Why was he in such a hurry? She didn't question him, but was grateful that she would be riding instead of walking back. She trotted up to the sergeant, who wheeled his horse and urged the two cows on. They trotted along for a while until the animals accepted the new direction and then they settled into a comfortable walk. Amanda hoped Old Army Coat would see them and go home without being seen. The young sergeant adjusted his horse's gait so he and Amanda were riding side by side.

"Sergeant Pepper, at your service, Ma'am," he grinned at her, slightly tipping his hat.

"I'm Mrs. White, the Indian's new schoolteacher," she replied, liking the young man's affability already.

"You like teaching those little savages?"

"It's a job. It's all right." She didn't want to reveal her true motives to anyone.

"Last teacher was a man. Think everyone was real surprised when you came along. Guess they expected another man. They were goin' to ship them all off to that religious school, but I guess the government decided not to."

"You knew the other teacher?'

"Sorta. Met him, mostly. Kinda looked mean, ya know. He and old Kinney got along famous, though."

"Why did he quit?"

"Didn't. Got killed. Rattler bit him. Poison killed him."

"Oh," she said. "That's a snake, isn't it?"

"Yes, ma'am! Have you ever seen one?"

"No."

"Mean lookin' devils. Usually give you warning with those rattles on their tails. But if you come upon them too sudden like, they bite you anyways."

"I'll take care not to come upon them 'sudden like' then."

The sergeant laughed, and so did Amanda. She didn't realize how much she missed ordinary conversation. The young man talked very much like those poor trash over the hill that her stepmother told her never to talk to. But the sergeant didn't seem bad.

"Mr. Kinney said that if the Indians had any sense, he wouldn't have to go through this nonsense every year. What did he mean by that?" Amanda asked.

"Injuns won't raise cattle. Won't farm, neither," the sergeant explained.

"Then what do they do?"

"Well, they say they're hunters. Since that's what they do, they don't farm or nothin'. Won't dig up the dirt. Won't raise animals. So when the government sends these cows, instead of breedin' them, they slaughter them all and next year don't have any left."

"That doesn't make much sense."

"No, ma'am, it don't. But you take these two of yours. Could be a different story."

"Why is that?"

"Well, ma'am, as the captain said. That big one's a mighty fine-lookin' bull. Only two bulls in the whole herd, ya know. And that little one. She'll give ya some fine calves, take care of her right."

Amanda looked again at the two animals plodding ahead of her. A bull and a heifer. The Indians did not breed cattle. She would. So that is why the Captain had been in such a hurry.

Kinney would have found a way to raise serious objections if he had seen which ones they took. But he had been busy directing the Indian's cattle, and so did not see. Did he know the herd had only two bulls? Well, no matter. She wasn't going to give them up now. She had found a very unexpected ally in the Captain. He had probably been in the very wars that put her Indians on their reservation. And now here he was conspiring against his own government to help them. Strange man. But an ally was an ally. She looked at the sergeant and mirrored his grin back to him.

"Yes, they are fine-looking animals. You have an excellent eye, sergeant."

As they rode on, the sergeant chatting away, Amanda mulled over her ideas. If she couldn't use these animals for meat this winter, she was going to have to find some other source of meat. The occasional rabbits and birds the boys trapped were fine, but she didn't know how to get hem herself.

She was sure there were fish in the stream. She would teach the youngsters how to fish. She was puzzled that they hadn't done so themselves. Now she also had the dilemma of caring for the cattle. She would have to keep them within her sight for a while since Kinney might realize he had been duped and try to recoup his loss. She didn't want them wandering away, either. Well, the young Indians would learn to be cowboys, whether they liked it or not. She had done them a favor when she interceded with their cattle. They could return the favor by helping to care for hers, at least for a while, until she could think this whole thing through and find a solution.

When they got to the camp, the sergeant looked puzzled.

"Where is the schoolhouse, ma'am?" he asked. Amanda pointed to the two doorways jutting out from the rocky hill. "But that's just a cave!"

Amanda enjoyed the sergeant's disbelief. Apparently he had never been here before. She wondered who had. The sheriff, obviously, since he had know how to find it. And Mr. Kinney, perhaps. And her Indians.

"I'm in a quandary as to where I am going to keep my pets."

"Huh?" he asked, still staring at the hilly doorways.

"I don't have any fences."

"Oh, yeah. Well, maybe you could use some sagebrush and make sort of a corral."

She nodded. "An excellent idea. I might try it."

"In the meantime, I'll tie them up," he said as he jumped off his horse with rope in hand.

He tied the red, brown and white bull to one tree and the cow to the other. He managed to avoid the garden without even seeing it. Amanda did not want anyone snooping around her domain any more than necessary at the moment, and even though the sergeant had been a co-conspirator, he talked too freely and might let the wrong thing slip. Kinney had not come out here and was not likely to, at least until he had settled his business at the trading post. Amanda suspected that he was confident that the hardships would drive her out in very short order. Amanda looked at the cow again. It was pregnant, its belly bulging just like Little Doe's. And thinking of which, where were the children? Melinda?

"Melinda!" she called. The child came running out of the house, her golden locks flying in the wind. Amanda swooped her up and twirled her around.

"Little Doe said we were not to come out until you said so, especially when she saw the army man. They're all in the house," Melinda said to her, hugging her tightly.

"I'm so glad to see you. We have some cows to take care of now. One is going to have a little one. Isn't she beautiful?"

Melinda had seen cows before and wasn't too impressed. But she did like the young sergeant. He flashed her the wide grin, and asked her if she had stolen her beautiful hair from the fairy queen. He reminded Amanda of John-Paul, and suddenly she was anxious to have the trooper out of her domain and to be along again. She shook hands with him and sent him on his way.

***

The next few weeks passed swiftly and in spite of the very hard work, idyllically. Like Robinson Crusoe, Amanda kept track of time by a makeshift calendar. She had figured out what day it was that she arrived, and made a calendar out of the blanks pages of the books she had found in the school. And what treasure of books she had found in the school! Whoever had chosen the books for the young Indians had truly wanted them to learn their new life and culture – complete works of Shakespeare, of Byron, Keats, Shelly, of Thoreau and Bryant, of Robert Louis Stevenson, Cooper, Mark Twain, even Aristotle and books on mathematics and science. Then, much to her amazement and curiosity, the much-forbidden Darwin, but not any Bibles. It looked as though they had confiscated the library of some well-read heretic, and rather than burn the books, sent them to the nearest place to Hell and the demon savages. Unfortunately, there were none of the more practical books like McGuffey's read, or elementary arithmetic.

It had rained gently and the garden was showing some sprouts. The cow was nearer and nearer her time. Amanda was also concerned about Little Doe, who was also growing bigger by the day. The fact that the girl obviously had no husband also concerned Amanda. For a child to grow a savage was bad enough, but to also grow up illegitimate was to damn it before it was even born. Little Doe seemed to accept her plight calmly, although, since their communication was still at a very fundamental level, it was difficult for Amanda to ask more complex questions. Who would take care of Little Doe and the baby? Where were her parents? What did the rest of the tribe think? And why, indeed, were Little Doe and Old Army Coat even sent to the school? They were considerably older than the others, old enough, she suspected, that the government did not require them to attend school anymore. Such questions couldn't be answered now.

She discovered that Melinda could do more than she thought a five-year-old could do. She washed the dishes after the meals and cooked a few rudimentary things. She started the fire from the coals with no trouble and had a knack for keeping the cow and the bull out of trouble, her small self importantly leading the huge docile creates to the water, the Cherub in the scruffy dress her ever-present companion. With the help of Old Army Coat, who would still only grunt at her when she spoke to him, Amanda managed to erect some semblance of an enclosure for the two animals out of the sagebrush and a small natural canyon in one hill behind the houses. While this was not in her direct sight always, it was secluded, and it would be difficult to spot the animals on first arriving in camp. Although there was no water in the canyon, she carried water to the animals, when she chose to leave them in the pen, to an area in the rocks that formed a natural sort of trough.

She had lost a lot of weight, and her rounded, gentle curves were becoming thin firm muscles. Six months ago she would have been appalled to find herself in such condition and would have cried for weeks. Now she felt good. Wearing the pants the cowboys wore, she had a new freedom and found she still knew how to run and climb. She tricked Raphael into helping carry the water by making a game of racing to the steam and back to the canyon. Melinda's constant companion, the Cherub, seemed to be learning some English words, while Melinda picked up her own Indian vocabulary. The two other girls were actually twins, and Amanda called them the Gemini, and left it at that, giving up on trying to distinguish between them.

Since her little friends were so very unwilling to do any farming or gardening, she set them to work gathering things to eat. They delighted in bringing her something off the prairie that looked strange or smelled different. She pretended to be completely puzzled as to what she was to do with it. They would giggle, and then make a great show of tasting it themselves. Then she would try it, and they would wait in breathless anticipation as she ate it. Usually she found it good, probably because she was usually hungry. And so were they. She was extremely stingy with her larder, breaking open a can of something only if there was absolutely nothing to be had. She used her sugar and salt rarely, except to preserve and experiment with the new things the girls brought to her. She did not know how bad winters were here, or what was to happen, but she was determined to be prepared, somehow.

Her willingness to try things did not always have positive results. One time Ruth and Naomi, the two youngest girls, had brought her some kind of root. They had calmly taken a bite of it, and then given it to here. She had tasted it. It was not bitter, but sort of bland. She had smiled and finished it. But they didn't giggle, just watched her wide-eyes. She learned later, the hard way, that it cured illnesses by causing diarrhea. She had been miserable for three days afterward and her weight had dropped even more. But she never mentioned it to anyone, not even Little Doe, although she felt somehow they knew. She should have been angry, but if she had scolded them, they might not continue to bring her the new things. And she had to know. She asked questions and tried to learn all the strange ways about trapping small animals and digging roots.

In time, she learned more and more of the hand language these people used. It was much faster to learn and much clearer as to meaning than some of the spoken language. She felt as though she was teaching a school of the deaf at times, but it worked.

One of her students, though, she rarely spoke to. The next oldest girl, perhaps ten or eleven, was Little Doe's constant companion, and silent to the point of being sullen. She talked little and did not fuss over Melinda like the twins, who were perhaps seven or eight. Amanda named this one The Shadow, finding her absolutely spooky. She would have preferred a positive reaction from all the children, but she was not going to push her luck with this one. She did some work and did not cause any trouble. It was enough.

And the next oldest boy, also about nine or ten, Amanda's heart ached for. He was so thin, he rarely smiled, and he was blind. She called him Paul. He did not play, but would sit by the stream, or with the animals, by the hour, almost motionless. The other children did not taunt him, as other children elsewhere might have. They gave him his food, and gathered him in when night came. But they didn't play much with him or talk much to him. He had been blind from birth, apparently. Little Doe had indicated that when he was inside his mother, she had had the white man's disease, which Amanda suspected, from the description, was either smallpox or measles. The mother had lived through the disease, but the baby was blind at birth. Little Doe said it would have been better if the child had died. Amanda was horrified at the thought.

Then, the first week of June, Amanda arose one morning, started the fire and went to the schoolhouse to awaken the children, surprised that they were not yet up. She peered inside. They were gone! She hurried back out and scanned the horizons for any sign of them. But they had disappeared, as quickly and mysteriously as they had come.

"Melinda, did you hear them leave or anything?"

"No, Mommy."

"I wonder why they left?"

"Oh, Mommy, there's no school in the summertime," Melinda giggled. "I'll go check the cows."

Melinda's chubby little legs carried her up the hill. How that child could stay chubby on the diet they were eating was beyond Amanda's understanding. And the other children. Of course, white schools were out in June, but hers had never gotten started, she thought with a twinge of guilt. The young Indians had been sent to her to learn, and instead, she had used them to teach her. She should go fetch them and bring them back. To learn the things they should learn. Fetch them? From where? She had no idea where the Indian encampment was. She would have to get along without them. She would continue to gather the vegetables and dry them, and catch the fish and salt them. She did not understand why the Indians would not eat fish. It made as much sense as those Jews who would not eat pork. Food was food, as she saw it.

"Mommy, Mommy, something's wrong with the cows," Melinda hollered from atop the ridge.

Amanda raced up the canyon. The cow lay on her side, breathing heavily. The birth of the calf was imminent. Amanda breathed heavily too. She had never witnessed a birth before. With Melinda, she had been in a state of confusion and shock and pain. All she truly remembered of from it was the overwhelming compulsion of her body to push that thing from her, and the final push and the pain. She wasn't sure that was a normal birth. She had heard the crying of the child, but they had whisked it away so quickly she didn't even get a chance to look at it. Was an animal's birth the way? What was normal and what should she do if it wasn't? She shouldn't let Melinda watch this, but she couldn't send her away.

Amanda watched, fascinated, praying that all would go well. She saw the animal's sides heaving and finally the slick, wet calf slid out of the mother. Melinda whooped and clapped her hands in absolute joy. The cow began to lick the calf clean, but her sides continued to heave. Amanda, concerned, circled closer. Then stopped. Another shiny calf slid out. Twins! And although Amanda wasn't sure, she thought they were females. She joined her daughter in glee. Strong new heifers would mean that the herd would grow. And next year she could have even more calves.

The idea of next year sobered her somewhat. She knew the animals had to eat. With winter coming, what would they eat? God, was gathering food all there was to existence? How could she take care of so many details? She felt tired. She had been working so hard. She looked down at her hands, with their torn fingernails. They had browned in the sun, as had her arms and face. Her skin more resembled her young Indian friends, than the young woman of a few months ago. Melinda was tan, after an initial bout with sunburn, but her golden locks had turned almost white.

"Mommy, is that how I was borned?" Melinda asked, watching the cow lick her calves clean.

She's too young to know such things. Amanda thought. But she was too young to know about the things that Aaron had done, too.

"Yes, basically," she replied.

She could tell Melinda's questioning was not finished with by the way she frowned and rock on her heels with her hands behind her back. The serious, studious, philosopher child. It certainly did not go with her looks, with Amanda's dark eyes and her father's light hair. With some trepidation Amanda realized that her daughter would be a beautiful woman. A straight small nose was forming from the baby pudgy one, and her eyes were dark blue, fringed with black, long lashes. Her hair was still baby fine, but getting thick and it would curl when Amanda coaxed it so it cascaded into curls and ringlets. That such a beautiful child could come from the ignominious sweating and pain was another strange phenomena of life.

Melinda watched the calves nurse. "Mommy, what are they doing?"

"Getting milk from their mother."

"Did I get my milk from a cow?"

"Uh, no, not when you were a baby."

"Where did it come from?"

She wanted to be honest with her, but Melinda had had a wet nurse, since Amanda had not been allowed to nurse her. Proper ladies did not nurse their own children, she was told. Then, she had accepted the idea because everyone knew it to be so, and therefore it was truth. Now, she resented those who had taken Melinda. She had not even known her own child. She was the lady of the house. She could sit and embroider, whip a servant, endure the attentions of the master, but not choose whether to care for her only child.

"Mommy?"

"Oh, well, you see, babies get their milk from their mother."

"Where?"

"Uh, from the mother's breasts."

"Oh." A brief silence. "Does it hurt, Mommy?"

Amanda laughed and squeezed Melinda. "No, honey, it doesn't."

This child had definitely inherited her own avid curiosity. Everyone, she could remember, would finally lose their patience with her when she was young, with her continual questioning. Even John-Paul, for all his fun and games, would lose this patience and tell her to go away. But she had found that many of the little things she had learned when a child had come in handy for her now, in this remote wilderness.

"They look like they will do fine, now, sweetheart. Let's leave them alone."

Amanda walked down the hill with Melinda. They stopped to check the bull. The grass was sparse in the enclosure and he was trying to chew on the sagebrush. She would have to take them out more often to graze during the day. She would have to hobble them, but would also have to watch them closer. More work and more problems. She felt another wave of debilitating fatigue wash over her. But only for a moment. Melinda's survival depended on her ability to take care of them. She would not send the child back to where they had been. She would rather they both died of starvation here than submit to the sadism of her "civilized" in-laws. For the last few weeks she had been concerned with only what they would be eating come the winter. But now she would have to expand her plans. She must reason it all through. If she were careless or overlooked something now, there might be dire consequences later.

Once again she sat on the three-legged stool at the three-legged table. But this time she did not rearrange little boxes. She folded her hands and put her chin on them and stared at the light playing on the wall at the door. She wished she could write her thoughts down, but the only paper was in the books and she would not destroy the library she had neatly stacked in her cave.

She would rely on her memory and logic. The only logic she had even had to use was in her studies and with her father, in the lab and playing chess. And putting together the patterns for clothes with her stepmother. Oh, how very irritated her stepmother would get when she forgot a gusset or underpinning. How rigid, cold, and severe her stepmother had been. She suspected her father was afraid of his second wife in some ways. Amanda also suspected that her father had married his second wife, not for love or beauty, (her stepmother was ten years older than her father), but for money, since she had been from a wealthy family. So she had to endure her stepmother's rigid rules over every aspect of her behavior. Get up at a certain hour, dress before breakfast, always say your prayers, always sit up straight, don't chew with your mouth open. On and on and on. Discipline yourself, she would say again and again. With every one of Amanda's questions, she had an answer or a rule.

Amanda raised her eyebrows in surprise at this insight. Her stepmother had been the only one, who, if she did not have a ready rule or answer, would tell her who to ask or where to go for an answer. She never would send her away. Never could she remember her stepmother sending her away. If Amanda asked the same question twice, "I told you that yesterday. Remember what you hear, child," sternly said, but not angrily. And her stepmother, in all her discipline, never raised a hand to her at all, although she could straighten her shoulders and raise here eyebrows in a way that would probably scare Napoleon.

Amanda smiled. She had discovered a newfound respect for her stepmother. Somehow, it was a comfort. And somehow, some of the solutions to her problems had present themselves to her. Let the cattle graze out of the canyon during the day. She could hobble them and send Melinda periodically to check on them. If she had them graze on lowlands, she could see them from atop the hills.

Part of her problems came from the fact that she needed so many little things. It was all well and good to try to make certain things from the materials around her. But a stick was no true substitute for a good spade, she had ruefully discovered. Using her ingenuity was exciting and challenging, but there were so many problems to solve, expediency and practicality had to be her guidelines. She needed a good knife, and also a whetstone to sharpen it. And a good axe. The list was long and she was short on money. Her money should arrive from the government. But with all that she needed, that fifty dollars a month would not go far. And she could see Melinda growing out of all her clothes. She would have to make more. She appreciated now the sack dresses of the little Indians. They could wear them quite awhile before they grew entirely out of them. When they became too short for dresses, they would make good tops and blouses. And with winter coming up, Melinda would need a new coat. Amanda wished she had been assigned a school a little further south.

She would like to go to Kinney's store, and see if her check had come in, and also pick up a couple of items. But she was not sure she wanted to risk either his curiosity, or wrath, at this time. She was still not prepared enough. She wished she could make herself invisible, and spy on Kinney, to test the atmosphere before she arrived as herself. Or if her little friends were here, she could at least send Raphael to see what was going on. She was sure with his ingenuity for mischief he would find a way. And a young Indian lad would be accepted without question at the post. Which gave Amanda an idea.

She pulled the small mirror out of the pile of clothes and looked carefully at herself. She dug through her clothes until she found the old shirt of John-Paul's she had kept as a sentimental souvenir of her dear half-brother. The old baggy thing would now serve her well. As she put it on, she was glad that she was a small-breasted as she was. It had been a source of frustration for her stepmother and they had always tried to improve the situation with cotton stuffing. Now, with her weight down, she was even smaller. And with the shirt on, her breasts, for all practical purposes of casual observation, disappeared. Her hard work had slimmed her plump bottom to a round, but solid mass, and the cowboy pants bagged on her. She combed her hair, and patiently, and with a few false tries, plaited her hair in the fashion of the young Indians. She had not washed it for a while, and since it was very greasy it shone as their hair had shone. She stared at her brown eyes and tanned face in the mirror for a moment. No, this was definitely not the lady Kinney had greeted a month ago. She hoped her masquerade would work. She called Melinda. This was going to be a difficult experience for both of them, but a necessary one if they were to continue to survive here.

"Mommy?" Melinda looked at her in disbelief. Then she giggled. "You look like Moksois!"

"Who?"

"Moksois, the one with the blue coat."

So, he had a name. She had never heard anyone call him any name. If Melinda thought her mother looked that way, she was sure she could fool Kinney. People usually see what they expect, and he definitely would not expect the schoolmarm from back east to look like an Indian boy.

"Listen to me very carefully, honey," she said. "You can't come with me. I'm going to the agent's store. I have to go by myself. I'll not be gone long. Will it frighten you to stay here alone?"

"A little bit," Melinda said in a very small voice.

Amanda did not want Melinda to know how frightened she was, so she made her voice as kind but as firm as she could. "I want you to go into the house, and I want you to stay there. I won't be long. Please stay inside. Play with the little doll we made out of the old sock. Pretend she is sick today and you have to take care of her. There is water in the bucket and plenty of biscuits and turnips. I promise I will be back soon."

"I wish we had butter for our biscuits. I like butter," Melinda whined.

It was the first time Amanda had heard the child complain since they had arrived here. She must be very frightened. Amanda took her inside, gave her a big hug and kiss and held her for a moment during one last debate on her decision. Then she hurriedly left before she could change her mind. She gathered up the rabbit-skins that the Shadow had so carefully tanned. Why had she left them here after such hard work? Amanda didn't know, but she intended to use them as barter at the post. It wouldn't do for an Indian boy to have money, and Amanda could think of nothing else that she could trade. She ran over the hills and soon settled into an easy loping gait. A warm summer breeze blew in her face and the hot dust gently puffed up from the ground where her bare feet hit. She had no moccasins and no shoes that would pass as Indian. But she had been going barefoot more and more and her feet were inured to the hard rocky ground. With all the running with Raphael and the climbing with the water buckets, her legs were strong. She was almost at the post before she had to slow to a walk. The sun had not moved very far in the sky.

As she came over the last hill to the valley of the trading post, her heart beat in her throat and she flushed with the excitement of the deception and her purpose. The hot sun beating through the red flannel shirt had made her sweat, and the wind chilled her as it blew her dry. Kinney was not alone. A horse and buggy, and two horses were tied up outside. Perhaps, though, it might be easier if Kinney were preoccupied with other business. She strode down the hill, the rabbit skins tucked under her arm. She hesitated before going in the door to take a deep breath.

Jacobin leaned against the wall. Graves bent over in serious and quiet conversation with Kinney. And Sheriff MacGregor was talking to the old Indian. Sheriff MacGregor. Of all people to be here. She was certain he would not recognize her. It had been over a month and centuries of hard work since he had last seen here.

"What the hell do you want, kid?" Kinney growled at her

when he caught her presence. Amanda had to suppress a smile. First test passed. She imitated the grunt she had heard so often from Old Army Coat and held out the rabbit skins.

Kinney jerked them from her hands. "Trying to trade for sometin,' huh. Goddamned Indians think I'll trade for anything. This ain't worth a hell of a lot. Ain't got no booze, ya' skinny little bastard."

Amanda spied the hunting knife lying on the shelf that she had seen before. That she had to have. It had a thousand uses for her. She grunted and pointed to the knife.

"Hell, these ain't worth no steel hunting knife," Kinney said, throwing the skins back at her.

Sheriff MacGregor, who had been watching the proceeding, came over the Amanda and took the skins out of her hands. As he did so, he looked squarely into her eyes. Then he turned to Kinney.

"Nice lookin' skins," he said. "Say, Jacobin, didn't your wife want a fur coat to keep her warm last winter?"

"Yup. Damned woman always wantin' something," Jacobin muttered. Then he caught the sheriff's meaning. "Give the kid the knife. I'll take the skins off your hands. Maybe Miz Henry can fix'em up for my dear wife. Might shut her up for one day."

Kinney grabbed the skins, threw them on the counter, and snatched up the knife. He shoved the knife at Amanda, point first. Amanda jumped back a little, and then grabbed the knife from Kinney.

"Now, get the hell outa here, kid," Kinney barked.

Amanda had hoped for a look around and to perhaps overhear some conversation. But apparently she wasn't going to have the opportunity. She did get enough of a look to know that Kinney's larder had been re-stocked since she had last been here. She wondered as to how much of this ever got to the Indians. She also noted the new material and blankets stacked in the corner. Imitating Old Army Coat's swagger, she strutted out the door.

"Git, God damn you," Kinney barked again, this time giving her a boot in the bottom to hurry her on her way.

Amanda decided she had better heed the warning. She scurried outside. When she was sure Kinney was no longer watching her she quietly sneaked back up to the door and listened. No conversation. Graves and Kinney were muttering something but in tones too low to hear. She was straining so hard to listen to the talk she didn't hear the door open and the Sheriff step out.

"Can I give you a ride back to the camp, kid?" he asked, looking squarely into her startled eyes.

She stared at him in total surprise. She jumped off the veranda and ran up the hill. Damn him, why couldn't he leave well enough alone? She kept running hard until her legs ached and her lungs felt like bursting. Then she stopped for a moment, panting, flushed, and angry, gripping the handle of the knife. She slowly began to smile. She had accomplished most of what she had set out to do. She had herself a spy. She jumped and let out a whoop.

The sun had reached its zenith, but she hadn't been gone from Melinda long. The little blond head peeked out of the doorway and looked up the hill. She hesitated for a minute to be sure that this wild Indian was indeed her mother, and then ran to her.

"I did it!" Amanda repeated over and over as she twirled her daughter around and around. "I traded for this," she said, showing Melinda the knife, "and no one even knew who I was."

Melinda was not too impressed with the knife and looked suspiciously at her mother's strange appearance.

"I think Bessie is crying," Melinda said.

"Oh, she's probably hungry," Amanda said, annoyed at Melinda's taking the edge of her small triumph. But she was right. They had to get back to the business at hand. Without bothering to change her clothes she ran up the hill to tend the animals, her toughened bare feet immune to the hot rocks and sharp stones. She hobbled the animals and began to drive them out of the enclosure when she heard Melinda cry out a greeting to someone and she saw her start to run toward a rider coming to them. Amanda froze. Who would come here? Then she recognized the dark, hairy face of the sheriff. He scooped Melinda off the ground, tousled her hair a little and set her on the horse in front of him. He looked down at Amanda, who stared back at him angrily.

"Never know what kind of Indians we have on this here reservation," he said to her with a grin.

She looked up at him defiantly, not quite sure what she could say.

"I would have thought an Eastern gal like you would have traded for some fancy colored stuff for dresses," he said.

"A knife has more uses," Amanda snarled.

"No need to get out of sorts." Then, to Amanda's surprise, he chuckled. "Don't think old Kinney ever did catch on. Wouldn't try it too many times, though. He might get wise."

"Melinda, get down and come here," she snapped at the child who was still sitting gleefully with the Sheriff.

"Oh, Mommy," Melinda began.

"Right now!"

Sheriff MacGregor helped Melinda down from the horse. Then, without any invitation from Amanda, swung down off the horse himself and let the reins fall from the bridle.

"Won't he run off?" she asked.

"Nope. Been trained not to. Comes in handy whenever I'm in a hurry." He pulled a weed and chewed meditatively on it while he examined her cattle.

Amanda held her breath. If sheriff MacGregor took back the news of how well her animals looked to Kinney, Kinney would surely come and try to take them away. She was, after all, supposed to be using them for the Indian children here at the school.

"Fine looking animals there," he said.

"Yes, they are," she replied, not wanting to reveal any more of her thoughts than necessary.

"Calves look healthy."

"They are.

"Might be easier to take care of them if you had a corral down here."

"Might be."

"Wouldn't take much wood. Could use a couple of those old cottonwoods down by the creek."

"I don't have an ax or saw."

"I see."

They stood quietly for a moment, the Sheriff chewing on his weed, Amanda making small circles in the dust with her bare foot.

"I have an ax with me," he said.

"Oh," she said disinterestedly.

"Could help you build one, corral, that is."

"I can't pay you."

Sheriff MacGregor studied her face intently. "Don't want none."

Amanda just shrugged. If she said yes, he might change his mind and want payment, of some kind, later. If she said no, she might be passing up an opportunity to get the corral built. Having the cattle closer to her could make caring for them infinitely easier.

The Sheriff ambled down to a large grove of cottonwoods, his horse trailing obediently behind him. As Amanda cooked herself and Melinda some lunch, she could hear the rhythmical chopping of the wood and then the crackle of a falling tree. She watched the Sheriff guide his horse to drag the timber up to the flat land where he evidently intended to build the corral. He chopped the large limbs off the tree. She busied herself with the garden, and the house, and the cows. The Sheriff had removed his shirt and she found herself watching the ripple of his muscles as he worked.

There were still a few hours of daylight left when she realized how hungry she was. Sheriff MacGregor surely was hungry, too. She would have to offer him dinner, at least.

"I have some fish frying. Would you like some?" she asked casually.

"Yes, thank you, ma'am," he replied.

They ate in silence, Melinda and Amanda each eating one of her hard-caught fish, Sheriff MacGregor eating four.

"Is this the only kind of meat you have?" he asked.

"It is enough," Amanda replied.

More silence. The sun was setting and casting its weird shadows. Then suddenly it was dark. No lingering sunset. The fire was low.

"Melinda, you must go to bed," Amanda told the child.

"I don't want to go in there alone," she whined.

"You were alone this morning,"

"That was different," she pouted, snuggling against the Sheriff.

He didn't seem to mind her presence, and Amanda was

too tired to argue. She let Melinda sit beside the Sheriff until she fell asleep.

"You met your students?" he asked.

"Yes, at least some of them."

"Was Moksois with them"

"Who?"

"Moksois, the young man who wears a beat-up old army coat."

"Oh, him, yes. He certainly is quiet. There are nine others."

Amanda found herself talking at length about the young Indians, what they had done, what she had learned from the, even telling about the nicknames she had given them. He listened without interrupting, except to chuckle occasionally at some of Raphael's more outrageous antics.

"Where is the Indian camp?" she asked.

"About fifteen miles of so west of here. They move round some, when they have to, or can. They have a hard time of it since they aren't on their homeland."

"Do you know what Moksois means?" she asked, intrigued by the name.

He stared into the fire. "It means 'pot-bellied.'"

"But he is so thin!"

"It's a name for a child. Indian boys get their names as men when they have counted their first coup."

"I don't understand," she said, shaking her head.

"In the old Indian ways, they were warriors. Everything they did was for this. They didn't have to kill an enemy, but they had to be brave in battle, get in the thick of things, so to speak, and touch an enemy. That's coup. But since they don't fight now they can't be warriors. So Moksois keeps his child's name, even though he is old enough to be considered a man."

"He's just a boy," she scoffed.

"About seventeen or so, more than old enough," he growled.

"If he's a man, why is he coming to school with the little ones?"

Sheriff MacGregor shrugged. "Maybe because he can protect them. Maybe because he has no real family and isn't considered as a valued honored son, and maybe, to spy on you."

"Spy on me! Why?"

"You're very different from any other agent or teacher they've seen."

"How?"

"Uh, you're a woman, for one thing."

"And all the others have been men?"

Sheriff MacGregor nodded. "Most of them helped Kinney with his cattle business."

"Stealing the Indian's cattle?"

Again the sheriff nodded. "But that's just a slice of the pie. He lets ranchers graze their cattle on good reservation land, for a fee, to him, of course."

"But it's wrong! Why don't you stop him?"

The Sheriff frowned. "I have no authority on the reservation. Kinney is all there is."

"Even over the army?"

He nodded. Amanda stared at the fire in thoughtful anger. No wonder Kinney envisioned himself as such a grand potentate. Absolute power. Over what? A few pathetic Indians and a half-desert land in the outer reaches of hell. But from her experience with her brother-in-law, she knew the more petty the power, the worse the potentate. She would have to walk very cautiously if she were to survive here. It wasn't the land that was her only foe.

Amanda realized how late it was and how hard they had both worked. To ask him to leave simply because of some rule of propriety form another time was silly.

"You're welcome to sleep in the schoolhouse tonight," she said casually, as she banked the fire and covered the coals as Little Doe had shown her in order to preserve a little fire for the morning.

The sheriff watched her do it, smiled a little, and nodded his head. "Thanks, I will. It's a long ride back to town."

Amanda carried Melinda into her cave.

She heard the chopping before she ever got out of bed the next morning. She hurriedly put her clothes one, deciding to forgo her daily dip into the stream. She felt she needed it after that long walk yesterday. Also, it seemed to wake her up and refresh her so, that it had become almost a ritual. She blinked a few times to accustom her eyes to the light. Sheriff MacGregor was proceeding quite well with the fences. She started the fire again, sending Melinda after chips and sticks. Then she got the cattle and set them out to pasture. She found she had to take them further each day. She would have to find something to feed them this winter. Another problem she would have to solve soon. The sheriff had a wagon. Perhaps she could persuade him to help her. But she would have to be careful how she did it, not wanting any commitments or debts.

She saw that he had dug a posthole, and was trying to put the post in it, but it was proving difficult to hold the post and fill the hole. She walked over, saying nothing, and gripped the post. He looked up at her, released the post, and filled the hole, tamping the earth firmly with his booted foot when he was done. Strange that he would carry around an ax and shovel with him on his horse, but then he was strange anyway. Silently, they worked together to finish the corral. The Sheriff would sometimes gesture to her when he wanted something to be done. It reminded her very much of working with her father, except he would talk to he and explain as they went along. But the lack of conversation didn't bother her as much as when they had first ridden in the wagon. As they were setting in the last logs, she slipped and cut her hand, crying out briefly at the pain.

"Are you all right?" Sheriff MacGregor asked with his concern showing in his voice.

Amanda looked at her bleeding hand. Although it was bloody, she didn't think the cut went deep, and they were almost done. "I'm okay," she answered.

They finished the job. Melinda has watched for a while, and then wandered off. Melinda never went far. She did not want to go so far that she would not see some part of the house or her mother. Amanda could always call for her since she would be within hearing range. Melinda had picked up the knack from the Cherub of knowing how to find something to eat and was always chewing on something. It was well into the afternoon when they finished.

"I'll fix something to eat," she said.

"Fish?" he asked.

"Yes, as a matter of fact."

"I think I might find something bigger," he replied.

He took his rifle, mounted his horse, and disappeared. Amanda took advantage of his absence to wash herself and Melinda. She didn't indulge in her usually nude plunge in the stream for fear that the Sheriff might return at an inopportune moment.

And he did return, with some sort of strange-looking deer tied behind the saddle.

"What's that?" she asked.

"Antelope," he informed her. "Do you think if I gutted it, you could manage to cook some of it?"

"Yes!" Amanda had not had good meat in so long, she had forgotten what it tasted like.

"Mrs. White, where is that fancy new knife of yours?" he asked.

She blushed. "In the house. I'll get it." she disappeared into the cave as she called over her shoulder, " I wish you would call me Amanda."

She returned. As he took the knife and began to concentrate on his task, he muttered, "My friends call me Andy." She smiled, and went to build up the fire.

Andrew had the antelope fully dressed out by the time she had cooked the shank he had given her. She had cooked it with some wild vegetables and onions in over the spit and the three of them ate with rabid hunger. She told him how she managed to milk the cow and learn sign language.

"You can dry the rest of the meat and it'll keep, you know," he told her.

She nodded. She should also try to stretch and dry and hide as she had seen the Shadow do, although she was still a little vague about what exactly she should do. They sat briefly by the fire, but were all so exhausted that soon. Amanda banked the fire and took herself and Melinda to bed.

When she got up in the morning, the Sheriff was gone. She felt a little lonely. It had been good to have someone to talk to for a while. She was grateful for his help. She would never have managed to build such a fence alone. They had even managed to hollow out a watering trough. Perhaps, later, with a little ingenuity, she could make a windmill to pump the water to the cattle. She did regret her lack of opportunity to persuade him to help her get some hay for the winter. But apparently he had inadvertently left his spade and hatchet, and she intended to use them. And the antelope. If only she had a gun, she could get some of those. They would last much longer and be much better this winter than the fish. And she could use the hides. The hide. Hers was stretched out in the sun as The Shadow had done, but hers was shrinking and brittle. She remembered the girls had put something on it, but she hadn't noticed just what it was. She would have to experiment.

The cattle, the garden, the house, Melinda, and just existing. Each day was a backbreaking, often frustrating routine. Even the simplest problems because a major obstacle. Bird and insects were getting into the garden. She had managed to get one small crop of peas dried, but the harsh climate eliminated any possibility of planting another. The beans were growing, and she was getting a few of those. She tried to limit their meals, but she found after working so hard each day, she was ravenously hungry. It didn't seem that much of what she was growing and gathering was going into the stockpile for winter. She was always so hungry. The meat from the antelope was rapidly diminishing, in spite of the fact that she supplemented it with fish. Once a jackrabbit had gotten itself entangled in the string she had hanging cans in the garden that scared of the birds. She had slit its throat to kill it, almost gagging when she did it. She managed to get the skin off it, although not in the one smooth piece that the young Indians did. She then had gutted it. Melinda had watched in wide-eyed curiosity all the time. The blood and gore didn't bother the child at all.

"That's not the way Moksois did it," she stated.

"Well, he's not here, and this is the way I do it," Amanda retorted, irritated at her own ineptitude.

Her attempt to milk the cow was also frustrating, although she finally did succeed. The two calves were growing and she felt she would take some of the milk for Melinda, who would benefit from it. But the cow, while docile enough when being led to and from her pastures, was not too receptive to Amanda's attempts to milk her. The first time she had simply knocked Amanda down by leaning into her. The second time she kicked the bucket, fortunately not putting any holes in it. Amanda squatted outside the corral, thinking hard, while Melinda frolicked with the calves. The calves. Perhaps that was the key. She waited until the calves nursed and then joined them in getting milk. She had some difficulty in pulling the teat, not knowing how to do it. Watching Rosie in the old days, and doing it herself now, were not the same. But she did get some, and she and Melinda had sweet, fresh milk with their juicy blackberries that night.

Melinda, her companion and her comfort, grew in mind and body. She helped keep the house straight and clean, sweeping it every morning with the makeshift brush broom. While Amanda shook out the bedclothes to be sure that there were no insects, Melinda washed the dishes at the stream. Amanda sometimes let her start the fire if she were there to watch. On the long evenings, when the sun was still up after dinner, Amanda would read to Melinda, and was teaching her to write. The child learned quickly, but most of the books were so difficult that Melinda certainly couldn't read them. They had no paper or pencils, so the dust around the fire served as their slate. She read the "Adventures of Robinson Crusoe." Melinda loved the story, making comparisons with them. She read "Jane Eyre." Although parts of it Melinda didn't understand, she did know it was a sad story. Amanda asked her if she liked it.

"Kinda. But it was side. I don't like sad stories. Mommy, did you love Daddy?"

AMANDA

Amanda silently meditated for a moment on whether she should tell Melinda the truth. "No, I didn't," she finally answered.

"Then why did you marry him?"

"Because, I had to."

"Why?"

"Your grandfather was very ill and we had no money. Your father wanted a wife, and he had lots of money. So I married him so we could pay for the doctor bills for your grandfather."

Melinda thought on it, rolled it around in here mind, and then asked, "If Daddy had lots of money, why don't we have it now?"

"Because, where we lived before, the law says a woman can't have her own money, or her own property. A man has to have it."

"Uncle Aaron?"

"Yes, he has all our money from your father."

"And he isn't nice."

"You're right," Amanda agreed.

'I would rather be here without the money, wouldn't you, Mommy?"

Amanda smiled and hugged Melinda. "Yes, yes, I truly would."

She heard the coyotes howling, and felt the night wind. The sun was gone. Strange, that in this vast and hostile land, she wasn't afraid, not constantly afraid of the nameless things, as she had been back east. She didn't know why. She just wasn't afraid.

CHAPTER THREE

By her calendar, it was the second of August when she saw the two young Indians riding over the crest of the hill on their scraggly pintos. She knew at once who it was, the old army coat a distinctive insignia. The beautiful Raphael came up slightly behind him, on an equally scruffy pony. She waited for them to come to her, and dismount, holding in her curiosity. Then Old Army Coat drew a deep breath, looked at her, and signed quickly.

"Little Doe is having her child. She has trouble. The old women, they say she will not live. She wishes to see you. Will you come?"

Amanda understood enough to know that this was trouble about Little Doe. She swallowed hard and nodded. Scared and worried, her heart beating fast in her throat, she hurriedly rounded up the cattle, got Melinda and her each a shawl, and called Melinda. She swung up behind Old Army Coat when he offered his arm. Raphael boosted Melinda onto his pony and then jumped up behind her. They took off at a gallop, Amanda holding onto Old Army Coat tightly, barely maintaining her balance. The pony's gait was uneven, but she was amazed at its endurance and its ability to take its two riders for such a distance. She didn't see Melinda and Raphael behind them, but could hear the hoof beats of their horse.

The tepees were set in a circle, cooking smoke and dirty children everywhere. Brown faces studied them curiously.

They stopped abruptly in front of one tepee. An old woman stood outside the door. Old Army Coat slid off the horse and Amanda immediately after him, not waiting for any assistance. She told Raphael to watch Melinda. He nodded. She turned to the old woman, who gestured for her to go inside.

The tepee was dark, and it took a moment to adjust her eyes. Lying on a pallet in the back of the tepee was Little Doe. Amanda's heart sunk as she saw her pallor. Little Doe's eyes were so large they dominated every feature of her head. The acrid smoke from the fire stung Amanda's eyes. She heard the old women renew their chanting outside. On each side of Little Doe sat an old woman, one holding her hand and the other wiping her brow frequently with a damp cloth. Blood covered the blanket under Little Doe, its red incongruously brilliant and almost festive in color. Little Doe managed a weak smile when she saw Amanda. Amanda kneeled beside her friend, not caring if the blood and mud were soaking into her pants. She took Little Doe's hand, not knowing what to say or do. She felt so entirely helpless. Little Doe heaved with the pain of another contraction. The old woman put a stick between her teeth so she could bite down on it and not scream. Sweat broke out all over her. Finally, after an eternity, it subsided.

"The little one, he does not want to come into this place," Little Doe whispered. "He knows it is a bad place for new warriors."

"You must live," Amanda blurted out, trying to control her tears.

"Why?" Little Doe asked. "We are born. We die. But the others. They have much to learn if they are to live in this place."

Her words were interrupted with another spasm of her body. Her whole being strained to give birth to the little one inside her. The old women spoke among themselves, and then began to chant a strange eerie song.

"They say the baby is already dead. They sing a death chant for him. Soon for me. You are different, my friend. You will help my people."

Amanda nodded numbly. No words could help Little Doe. Nothing she could do would help to lengthen her sixteen years to more lifetime.

Little Doe groaned. More blood spurted from between her thighs. Her body convulsed, shuddered, and she whispered, "Ungta," and slowly her whole being relaxed as her breath escaped from her body. Then she was no more.

Amanda didn't realize that her friend was dead at first. The old women howled their haunting wail, first one, then the other picking it up. Amanda could only sit with the damp, limp head held in her lap and stare at the pale, drawn face. She felt a total emptiness inside her and at last she felt the tears start down her face. Little Doe, so young, so full of wonder for life. She had expressed no hatred for the man who had impregnated her. She never complained about the hard work she had done. Yet, now she no longer lived.

Amanda felt the old woman gently lift the head off her lap and help Amanda to her feet and lead her outside. Old Army Coat was still waiting, along with Raphael and Melinda.

"What happened, Mommy?" Melinda whispered.

Amanda held the child close to her, caressing her head. "Little Doe is dead," she said simply.

"Is her baby dead?"

"Yes."

"Why did she die, Mommy?"

"I don't know, honey, I don't know."

Amanda began crying again. Melinda looked up at her

mother. She had never seen such tears from her mother. She started crying, too. Old Army Coat touched Amanda's sleeve. She looked into his eyes. No anger there, just sorrow. She had never seen him anything but sullen and angry. Somehow the sorrow made him look older.

"Our elders wish to speak with you," he stated.

When she nodded briefly, he led the way across the circle to a large tepee. Amanda was not even aware of her surroundings. She held tightly to Melinda's hand, as though the child's existence were her only link with reality.

This tent was much larger than the one she had just been in. The fire was in the middle of the floor, the smoked curled up out of the hole in the roof, but some smoke still strayed to other parts of the room. Four elderly gentlemen sat cross-legged on the floor, not talking, staring at the fire. One gestured for her to sit down. Each faced a different direction. She sat down, at the place indicated, facing the doorway of the tent. One man spoke briefly with Old Army Coat. He squatted down beside Amanda. She could pick up only a few words, since he spoke so fast. She realized how pitifully few words of this very complicated language she really did speak. She heard the words "children" several times. The speech lasted about five minutes, with no one interrupting. How was she to understand what he said?

When the old man finished, to her surprise, Old Army Coat began to speak to Amanda in English.

"Grizzly-Face says that you are different from the other white teachers in the white schools that we have had. He says that you understand some of our people. He says that you are a friend of our people. He says that since you are not afraid to learn our ways, we should not be afraid to learn yours. He will send our children back to you so that you may teach them to good ways of the white man."

"All the children?" Amanda asked, remembering that she had seen more children than had been originally sent to her.

Old Army Coat translated to the old man. They briefly discussed it among themselves.

"He says that all the children should learn," Old Army Coat replied.

Amanda thought she had her hands full just trying to keep herself and Melinda alive. And she would not have Little Doe to help her this time, she thought with a dull ache in her chest. She could not take care of all the children. But she had to help them. Little Doe had asked her to help her people. After the help she had given Amanda, Amanda could do no less than to give them what meager knowledge she had.

"Tell him that I agree that all the children should learn. But it is difficult to teach many children at one time. It would be better if I could at first teach a few, the ones that came to me first. Then these children could help me teach the others."

Old Army Coat translated. The old man nodded throughout the speech. He as obviously pleased by the compromise. He spoke to the others and they, too, nodded. He then again spoke to Amanda and Old Army Coat translated.

"I will take you home today. The others will return to you tomorrow, after we bury Little Doe," he said.

"May I be at the funeral?" Amanda asked.

Again the translating process occurred, and then Old Army Coat replied, "Yes. You may wait with her until we are ready."

Old Army Coat arose and gestured to Amanda. She took Melinda's hand and followed him back to the tent where Little Doe lay. They had cleaned away the bloody straw and blanket, and laid her out on a bier made of plaited weeds. She wore a new dress. Her hands folded over her chest held the bright red flowers that Little Doe had liked so much. She once had made a garland crown of them for Melinda, the bright red dancing against the golden head. Melinda had cried when the flowers had wilted and had to be thrown away. Amanda had explained to her that the seeds of the flowers would make more grow next year, but Melinda had still cried over the loss of the beautiful crown.

Little Doe's belly was still extended with the unborn, and now dead, child within her. The old women wailed and chanted and sang as they combed the tangled black hair and braided it again. Little Doe looked so quiet, so asleep. It was not possible she was truly dead. Amanda shivered. The August air was warm and the small fire added to the heat, but she could not stop shivering as she listened to the wailing of the women and the steady dull beat of the drums. Eight young women came in and lifted the bier up, carrying it outside. Amanda followed. Old Army Coat came to her side, and Melinda was on the other as they walked behind the procession of women and medicine men. They set the bier upon a platform, chanting and wailing.

Things that had been Little Doe's were brought to the foot of the bier. The oldest of the women handed something to each of the young women. Then she approached Amanda, holding out to her a lovely robe of rabbit skins and some beaded moccasins. Amanda was not sure what she was to do, but Old Army Coat muttered under his breath, "Take them." She took them from the old woman and bowed her head slightly. Then to Melinda she gave a funny-looking cornhusk doll. Melinda took it and cradled it in her arms.

Amanda looked up at the bier. Horrified, she realized that they were not going to bury Little Doe, but leave her out to the crows and buzzards. She wanted to cry out and stop them, but a strong hand on her arm stopped her.

"It is our way," Old Army Coat said quietly but firmly.

Amanda nodded and shivered. They waited for the death chant to stop. They all left quietly while the wind blew at the robes covering Little Doe.

The return home blurred in her mind. She remembered that Old Army Coat had told her that the elders would send the children the next day. She was aware that he had taken her home at a slow walk, with the moon rising on the land and shadows of the hills and rocks forming demons and playthings. The coyotes howled, but they seemed as far away as the moon they spoke to. She didn't know how long it had taken. Melinda had fallen asleep on the horse, and it was all Raphael could do to hold her on the horse and himself, too. When they arrived, Old Army Coat had carried Melinda in. Amanda didn't even care that he knew about their hidden cave behind the hut. She wrapped Melinda in the warm fur that had been Little Doe's and then curled up in a blanket beside her. She was dimly aware that Old Army Coat and Raphael had curled up with their blankets on the floor of the cave beside the entryway.

The faint light from the morning sun reflected off the walls of the hut and into the cave. Amanda awoke, feeling more tired than she had in many days. Her mind struggled to discover what day and time it was, but it didn't want to respond to her probing. Finally, she let herself remember yesterday. She shivered again in spite of the blanket around her. The sorrow of yesterday, and then her dream last night. She couldn't stop shivering. She had dreamed of her father's funeral. The deathbed apology had been her first true realization of her father's imperfection. At the funeral, her sister-in-law wept and moaned loudly, seeking the sympathy of those around her, ravenous as a vulture, and Aaron hovered in the background. And, of course, because it was a time of sorrow and crisis rather than a time of joy and fun, John-Paul was nowhere in sight. The neighbors had been sympathetic, of course, but shocked that Amanda could shed no tears at the beautiful funeral that was held, and the glorious eulogy. And a very expensive coffin. Father, buried in a box more expensive than anything that he could have afforded in the last ten years of his life.

Then Amanda had dreamed that her father had been walking beside her at his funeral, so they were playing some sort of game, that the death was not real, that they were only pretending. She had dreamed that she was riding her father's spotted gelding, riding in the morning mist, looking for him, hearing him call, and knowing they were just playing a game. But this game frightened her and she didn't want to play hide and seek anymore. But her father would not come home. That is when she woke up, her mind groggy and disjointed.

Melinda still slept in the white fur. She had watched the entire proceedings, not saying a word. Amanda suspected that the questions would come later, after she had thought for a while. Her little daughter did not seem to cry much, nor did she evidence much sensitivity to others. But she seemed to grasp the reality of situations and accept them. Amanda reflected grimly that it would be much better for Melinda if she were to see death and know it existed, before she had to deal with the absolute loneliness and fear it could create.

Amanda did feel lonely. Little Doe was the only person she had met in her life who had like her immediately for herself, not as a pretty porcelain figure to be admired, nor a pet to be toyed with, nor a rival to be dealt with, but just her. They had had something in common, although Amanda couldn't define it. And, dear God, she had been so young, so very, very young. Why? Why had she died trying to bear the child of a man who thought nothing of her except in the same terms as those of a good horse gone lame. Why? God must be a man, Amanda though. No woman would make another woman go through that kind of hell.

Where were the boys? She remembered they had brought them in last night. She knew the cattle needed tending, the garden needed the beans to be picked, the breakfast should be made, and a hundred other little things. But her sorrow and frustration enervated her. Why bother? Because the children were coming today. The children were coming today. Little Doe had said she wished them to learn. Little Doe had taught her. Now it was Amanda's turn to repay her debt. She shook her legs loose of the blanket and gently roused Melinda.

"Let's go wash and get breakfast. You start the fire while I take care of the cows. Maybe I can get some milk today. Our little friends are coming back today."

"Okay," mumbled the sleepy little voice from under the furry cover. She would be fully awake soon.

Amanda gathered the soap and ragged towel and headed toward the steam. She didn't immerse herself anymore. The stream was dried up quite a bit now, and she didn't want to stir in into mud. She stripped down and quickly washed herself with the still cold water. Funny it could be so cold, even in August. It must come from the mountains. As she pulled the pants on she noted how dirty they were. She would have to wash them again tonight. She would have to face Kinney again and get more supplies if she was to see herself and her students through the winter. She quickly buttoned the old shirt. She washed it every other day, alternating it with her camisole, hoping that no one would come to visit and see her dressed so. She was startled when she looked up to see Old Army Coat leaning against a tree across the stream. He didn't seem to be looking at her. Amanda was miffed. How long had he been there? She didn't see him when she came down. That boy could irritate her terribly.

She didn't have much time to think about it. She heard the chatter of the children. The Cherub came running to her and threw his grubby arms around her and buried his dusty, wet face into her stomach.

"Little Doe, dead," he sobbed. She held him tightly, sharing his sorrow, and yet feeling a sort of joy. They could all speak some English after all. If they could speak it, they could learn to read it, and if they could read it, she could teach them all the things they could learn from those marvelous books. She soothed the little boy, letting his sobs subside.

"We all loved her," Amanda said quietly. "But we can't stop living either. She would not have wanted that."

She let him finish his crying, seeing the Gemini's tears, while they held one of Paul's hands. He, too, was crying, but silently. But the Shadow did not cry. She stood apart, and squinted at Amanda.

"My sister would not have died if the white man had left her alone. But she was pretty and he wanted her," she snarled.

Amanda looked at her for a long time. The Shadow and Little Doe, sisters? Such a contrast. But no wonder the Shadow was bitter. Amanda could think of no words of comfort, no explanations for what had happened.

"You're right," was all she could say.

She hesitated. There was much work to be done. They had not had breakfast and the cows needed caring. But these small charges of hers also needed caring. She felt as if she had just shouldered a twenty-pound load. She straightened her back, gently pushed the Cherub away from her and wiped his tears on her shirtsleeve.

"Come with me," she said.

She sent Naomi and Ruth and Melinda to gather the beans and peas and whatever the garden was yielding. She had lost some beans to the insects and weather and birds, but nothing major had invaded her garden, luckily. She milked the cow and began to hobble the bull when she noticed Raphael out of the corner of her eye, watching her every move. She knew that the young Indian men were reluctant to become cowherds. However, Raphael was young, eager, and very curious. Perhaps she could take advantage of these traits to enlist his help. She handed the hobble to Raphael.

"Would you like to try?" she asked.

He hesitated only a moment. Together, they drove the animals out of the pen and to the pasture. Amanda took the bucket of fresh milk up to the cave, and saw that the Gemini had started a fire, and were cooking some kind of meat. Amanda decided to finish the meal with some of the greens from the garden and some milk. If she gave some to each one of them, there would be at least a little for everyone. But she did not have enough dishes so they would have to eat out of a common bowl. The group gathered around the fire, each picking off a piece of the meat. But when Amanda offered the greens to them, they shook their heads. She became impatient. They would not eat fish. Okay. But they would eat some of the things she did if she were to be responsible for them.

"I tried some of your food. Now it is only fair that you try some of mine," she said.

They all looked at her. The Shadow stared at her. Old Army Coat looked down at the ground. Silence. Impasse. Amanda reached into the bowl, and took the turnips, and onion, and green beans. She put some on Melinda's plate and put some in her bowl, and slowly, with exquisite dignity, began to eat. Then the slow hand of the Shadow reached into the bowl, and put a small amount of the mixture into her mouth. The other, one by reluctant one, including Old Army Coat, began to try her mixture. But when she tried the same thing with the milk, she found that only the Cherub and Ruth and Naomi would try it. The others would not. Finally, one of the Gemini, in a soft voice, her English broken and difficult, said, "The food, it is only for babies."

This time the young Indians had brought their things with them. They had their own blankets and some of their own utensils. Old Army Coat had a hunting knife, and other things for everyday living. She found them remarkably self-sufficient for being so young. And she found that they helped each other. Even dear Paul, whom they helped, was expected to do what he could. He could bank the fire, she found, without burning his hands. Apparently he got close enough to the heat to know where the coals were, but not so close as to burn himself. He could skin the rabbits that they others brought back, letting his left hand guide the hand that held the knife. And he was the storyteller of the group. She knew enough of the language to know what some of them were about, but would miss much of what they found humorous or sad in the stories. Once, after the others had gone to bed and Paul was fixing the coals, she detained him by putting her hand on his shoulder. She found it easier to touch Paul then some of the others, perhaps because of his lack of sight.

"Can you tell the stories in English?" she asked him.

"My tongue, not good with your English," he replied.

"And my tongue is not good with yours. Perhaps I can try telling some of my stories in your language and you can tell yours in my language, at least as best we can. Then we can both learn. It might help us learn each other's language, too."

Paul stood silent for a moment. He mulled his thoughts

over the same way Melinda did, letting them roll round in his head and investigate every road before letting them out on their own. Then he asked, "The others, they will listen, too?"

"Yes, it will be our learning time, after the night meal is eaten," she said, thinking that it was the only time she ever seemed to manage to get them all together. It was more like a disorganized family than a well-run school.

Paul nodded. He started on his way to the hut where the children stay. Amanda reached out to guide him, and then checked herself. There was such dignity in the frail young boy that she did not want to infringe on him. The darkness might be frightening to her, but he had been born into it. How old was he? Ten? Twelve? He seemed at time to be closer to eighty, with his quiet dignified manner. She watched the boy disappear into the schoolhouse and then turned to her own cave.

The plan worked. She discovered that the children, even The Shadow and Old Army Coat, loved stories. Oddly enough, she found herself turning more and more to the bible for tales to tell them. Perhaps they might help explain the white man to them. Besides, there were some terrific stories in that book. When she told them about David and Goliath, Raphael and the Cherub asked her to tell it again and again. They appreciated such a young warriors, and said that even though he did not actually touch his enemy, it counted. But when they said that Old Army Coat stormed away, not to be seen again until the following morning.

She did not teach them to actually read right away. The stories were helping with the language, and she had no materials to help them write. She would have to make a trip to Kinney's to pick up her pay for the summer. It should amount to at least $90.00. Perhaps she could get paper and pen and write something herself for them to read. She had taught them a few words, and although it didn't make much sense to them, she had insisted they learn the alphabet. She taught them the sounds of the letters like a game, like the game Little Doe had played with her.

However, she found that the one thing they caught onto very quickly, particularly Old Army Coat and The Shadow, was arithmetic. Once they understood the symbols and the system, they quickly learned to add and subtract and Old Army Coat even learned the way to multiply and divide. Amanda was elated when she saw he could do it. But when he saw her glee, he grunted and erased all the figures in the dust with his foot, and squatted silently by the fire. But she knew he was doing them on his own. She had seen the evidence. Sometimes he would work them in the dust as he stared at the cattle, or out on the horizon, and would forget to scratch them out. She had never been particularly astute at mathematics (Her stepmother had said a girl didn't need it, her father was careless about his own figuring, and her husband had said it was unladylike to be able to cipher well.) But she remembered there was a book on mathematics in the "cave library" and she searched it out, and between all her other chores, began to study it.

Having the children here gave her more purpose, but they made living more difficult because of their demands on her. Again they helped gather the things to eat, and to dry them. The boys would get a rabbit or bird to eat occasionally. But the rations were slim and she worried about the winter. She was still frustrated over her inability to get them to eat fish, but since Paul had told the legend of why they didn't eat fish, it sounded more like a religious reason to her, so she let it be. She could never quite understand it. The Catholics back home would not eat meat on certain days but would eat fish. She decided she would eat either one, because she never intended to go hungry.

AMANDA

Her need to return to the trading post became more urgent as time went on. Her daughter was growing. Her shoes had long ago given up, and the child went barefoot like her Indian friends. Melinda had displayed more facility in picking up the language than her mother had, and sometimes would have to translate words for her. The coat she had last year would not make it through the winter. And her pants were wearing thin. But to purchase another pair would make Kinney very suspicious. She had things going her way here. Kinney had not bothered her, which Amanda found strange, indeed. Why didn't the agent come out to see what was going on? As far as he knew, she could be dead. Perhaps that is just what he hoped. Well, she would have to disappoint him. But in order to get the things she needed, she decided to go to Harlan. It would be at least a two-day trip, especially walking. She debated whether she should take Melinda. She wrestled with the problem overnight and again the next day. She looked at her tanned and raggedy daughter and smoothed her golden hair. She loved this little person, not only because she was her daughter and mothers were supposed to love their daughters, but because this little person was good and brave and she liked to be with her. Her love for her now was so much more than it was before they came here. But she would have to leave her here. Because it was a long trip, and because if anything happened to her, she would rather her daughter grew up with her Indian friends, despite the hardships, then to be returned to her aunt and uncle, despite that luxury.

That night she explained what her plans were. They were silent for a moment. Then Old Army Coat, in one of his rare forays into the conversation, spoke, "I will take you there on my horse."

"Your horse? It won't go that far!" she exclaimed.

"Yes, it will!" he retorted.

"But someone must be here to care for the little ones," she reminded him.

The Shadow spoke, "I am here. We will wait."

"But you're only a child yourself," Amanda objected.

The Shadow stood up, wrapping her blanket around herself. "I have seen fourteen summers. I am here. I will care for the others."

So it was settled for her. The next morning she donned one of her relics from her other life. Old Army Coat was waiting for her on the pony he had taken her to Little Doe with. He frowned at her dress.

"I know it is difficult to ride in, but if I go wearing anything else, they will think I have become an Indian. And I can't have them thinking that."

He looked patiently ahead as she climbed onto the pony. It would be easier on her body to ride, but she wasn't so sure her dignity was going to be able to stand it. So leaving the others behind again, she and Old Army Coat started out on their journey.

Old Army Coat. Why couldn't she think of him as Moksois? She still though of the others with her original nicknames, but when she spoke to them, she called them by their Indian names. Some of them were long and rather difficult, and it had provided Raphael no end of merriment as she struggled to get each one right, especially his, which she found out meant Little Otter. Since otters were playful creatures, she thought the name more than apropos. But when she learned the meaning of Moksois, she could not call him that. As a matter of fact, they never called each other by any name whatsoever. The other Indian children called her Amanda when they spoke to her, although they had their nickname for her also. She found out from Cherub, via Melinda, that they called her the Strange One because she was so different from other white people they had known.

But Old Army Coat never called her by any name, nor did she call him by any name. Considering some of the experience they had been through, it seemed an odd fact. Amanda's curiosity about his name overwhelmed her, and although she knew she might be treading in dangerous waters, she decided to take the plunge and ask him anyway. They were alone. No one would hear. And she had a firm grip around his waist, to keep her from falling off the horse, but it would also keep him from running away.

"Will you get a different name when you grow up?" she asked, as innocently as possible.

Old Army Coat stopped the horse abruptly. He sat absolutely still. His back was ramrod straight and his head stiffly upright. They sat together like that for an eternity. Then he spoke, quietly, an intensity in his voice she had never heard before.

"No, I don't think so."

"Why not? I thought when Indian boys grow up they are given another name."

"It is not that simple."

"I don't understand."

Again silence. Then he asked. "Is it necessary you understand?"

More quiet. Each question and answer spaced with such silence, accompanied only by the distant singing of the meadowlark and the cry of the hawk.

"I need to understand."

He readjusted his shoulders. She kept her arms around his waist and her head leaned onto his back, even though the horse was no longer moving.

"We are given our names after we have had our dream and then fought an enemy or had a great hunt. We must do this before we are given our names as men." He stopped, but Amanda did not comment. She sat still and listened to the meadowlark. His voice was tight, as was every muscle in his body.

"Our people do not fight now. I cannot fight the enemy. Our people, we do not go on great hunts. Our men cannot be brave. I will never get another name." He spurred the horse gently and they continued their trip the post.

Before they came over the rise, he stopped the horse. "I will wait here," he said.

She slid off the horse, looked up into his brown, serious eyes, and picked up her skirts to walk the rest of the way. She wanted to give him a good name that was silent and strong like he was. It would be something between them. She would give it to him because she was his teacher. They respected teachers. She would call him Jason.

This time Kinney was alone in his trading post, at his makeshift, messy desk, poring over some papers. He did not hear her come in, so she knocked on the counter. He whirled around in astonishment, and then quickly covered it up with the eternal smile.

"Well, well, well, this is a surprise. And how is everything going at the school?"

"Just fine."

"Where is the little one?"

"I left her with the oldest Indian girl. She seemed capable of caring for her, at least a little while. Has my money come in from the government yet?"

"Oh, my dear, don't be in such a hurry. Let's sit for a cup of coffee. It isn't often I get the company of a lovely lady, you know."

"I would really like to, Mr. Kinney, but I am somewhat uneasy about leaving the child with the girl."

"Oh, really, Mrs. White, I find they make marvelous maids. Why, I even managed to find myself another girl to, uh, cook for me."

Amanda could barely manage to conceal her rage. Another girl, probably to suffer the same fate as Little Doe. Amanda would like to have broken him apart right there. But she knew she was powerless here. Still, the frustration was bitter.

"Did the money come in?"

"Well, you know. Government red tape and all," Kinney began to say. Amanda became suspicious. Had he taken the money? She would kill him.

"Did it come in?" she did not conceal the irritation in her voice this time.

"No need to get mad, now. Yes, it came in for May and June. But these things take time, you know. And, you know, you don't get paid for the other summer months because there is no school." He went on and on as he scratched through the pile of junk on his desk. Finally, he found the drafts.

"Can't cash them for you here, though, you know. But you could sign them over to me, and I could get the money the next time I go to Harlan," he offered.

Like hell, Amanda thought. "Oh I couldn't put you through all that trouble."

"Well, maybe you could take it out in trade with things I have at the store."

He never gives up, does he, Amanda thought. She had never known anyone so consistently and absolutely greedy in her life.

"No, thank you. It's just so different, getting my own little money, that I think I'll just keep it for awhile and think about all the things I want," she cooed. "But I really must go."

She clutched the drafts in her hand, and set out. It was difficult to keep from running. Once she got over the hill, and saw Jason, she ran to him. She wasn't sure whether to laugh or cry. She was disappointed at not receiving the full amount she though she was due. But she was also ecstatic at having the money, and at having surprised old Kinney. She tried to tell Jason, in between gasps for air, but he simply looked at her, perplexed.

"Don't you see," she explained. "He truly did not expect to see me last this long in this country. He was sure the weather or my students would drive me out."

"If they did not think you could do this thing, then why were you sent?" he asked.

"Politics! And bribery. I had to bribe some of the officials in Washington in order to get the job."

"Then you cannot teach these things?"

"Of course I can. It's just that no one really thought I could," she tried patiently to explain it to him.

"It does not seem a good way to do things. We usually have the people who can do the thing best, do it," he stated.

She found his simplicity irritating. They rode for a while in silence. But she couldn't contain her enthusiasm and started telling him all the things she planned to get with her hard-earned money. First, new clothes for her and Melinda. Melinda needed a new coat.

"The robe of Little Doe will keep her warm," he interjected.

"Yes, it will," she agreed. More silence for a while.

"Why did your people just send the ten of you at first?" she asked.

"We are not needed," he explained.

"I don't understand."

She again felt he was groping for the words. "We, the ones who came, do not belong to anyone in the tribe. We do not have to remain to care for parents. We have not had our dreams and are not men. So we are not needed."

She had walked on eggs again and broken a few. This thing of the dream and the enemy. It seemed all so silly.

Jason stopped abruptly. "I can go no more."

"Why not?"

"This is the end of the reservation. Without Kinney saying so we are not allowed to go further. There could be trouble if I go."

"Then you wait here, and I'll take the pony."

"It is my horse," he said. She frowned at him. "It is an Indian horse, and there would be questions why you had it," he continued.

She sighed. Always a logical argument, at least logical from his viewpoint as a simple savage.

"How far is it to Harlan?"

"Two, three miles, perhaps. Stay with the dry riverbed. It leads to the town," he pointed.

She hiked her skirts up out of the dust, and began to walk. When she was out of his sight, she let her shoulders droop a little and stopped to rest on a boulder. The perversity and stubbornness of her little charges sometimes overwhelmed her, and this boy who they called "Pot Belly" was the worst. "Pot Belly," indeed! She could count each of his ribs when she had her arms around his waist as they rode. She drew her breath in sharply at the thought, jumped down from the rock, and raced for a good half mile before she stopped.

Harlan looked large and civilized to her since her long absence from such settlements. She would liked to have stopped at the stage depot for something to eat, but she wanted to be careful with her money. The few people on the street stared at her. She knew she was dusty from her walk, but that couldn't be the reason, because there were certainly those who were dirtier than she. Probably because she was a stranger.

This general store looked like a palace, compared to Kinney's. So much to choose from. She had to keep her mind practical, and always geared to her survival for the next year. She knew if she could make it to next summer. Next summer. It seemed eons away. She had memorized the list of things she needed. Needles, thread and material for coats and blouses, some of the rugged pants, salt, sugar, coffee. Again, she cursed under her breath for her lack of horse and buggy. She would acquire one soon, somehow. Walking, in this country, was like a baby crawling in a mansion. It took too long and there were places and situations that she could not handle without a horse. But she would have to make it the two miles back to Jason. She simply would have to make it.

The gray lady behind the counter seemed as dusty as everything else in the store. She made no move to offer any assistance or extend any courtesy. She just watched Amanda.

Finally, Amanda asked, "These are government drafts. Will you accept them in place of cash?"

The women took one of the drafts and turned it over and over in her hand.

"Don't know. Hafta ask my husband." She disappeared behind the dusty curtain that served as a door. To Amanda's surprise, it was the handsome Mr. Graves that emerged.

"Well, Mrs. White, what a pleasant surprise. Of course, we will accept the drafts, if you will sign them over to us. Found you needed a few more comforts in this harsh country of ours, did you?"

He was solicitous and flirtatious. Amanda reminded

herself that he was one of Kinney's cohorts, in spite of his good looks and charm.

"Oh, yes. My little daughter is growing so fast," she smiled her best coy smile. "Well, since you will accept the draft, I'll find the things that I need."

"Just a moment. Jennifer, dear, this is the new teacher of our little Indians. You do remember I told you about her."

Mrs. Graves simply nodded and retreated behind her counter.

"If I can be of any assistance, please just ask," Mr. Graves offered, disappearing behind the curtain.

"Thank you for your generosity," she replied, hoping she would never have to use it.

She began to get her things. First, the material. She hoped she could get by on a few things and let her brave little companion wear mostly the blue pants and rough shirts. They were practical, inexpensive and sturdy. She saw Mrs. Graves raise her eyebrows a little when she picked out the pants and shirts.

"Do you think the little Indian boys would wear these if I got them?" she asked sweetly. "It does seem one way I could make Christians of them is to make them dress decently, don't you think?"

"You a Christian woman?" Mrs. Graves sneered.

"I try to be," Amanda answered cautiously not sure if the sneer were at the thought of her being a Christian or just the idea of Christians.

"Then why you out with those heathens by yourself, with no men-folk?" Mrs. Graves demanded.

Amanda did not think it was necessary for this gray woman with the harsh voice to know her life history. But she realized that if she were aloof, she might bring more trouble down on herself then she wanted. She held back the first answer that came to mind, and put her head down humbly, as she fingered the cloth of the pants.

"I am a widow, Mrs. Graves. I had to take care of my daughter and myself somehow. And it seemed I would also be doing the Lord's work by helping these heathens on the right path," she mouthed, reciting some of the litany she remembered from her sister-in-law's spoutings.

It seemed to be what Mrs. Graves wanted to hear. She humphed, and then asked, "What else do ya' think you'll be needin?"

"Perhaps some flour and a little coffee," she said.

Mrs. Graves got the few things she asked for.

"How old is your little one?" she asked.

"She's five."

"And you left her there all alone?" Mrs. Graves was horrified.

"Oh, no, there's an Indian girl who is very responsible. I trust her to care for Melinda. It is such a long trip for one so small."

"Wouldn't trust my kid with nobody," she said.

"Oh, you have children?" Amanda asked.

"Had two."

"Had?"

"Fever took'em last year. Twin boys. Just up and died when the fever took'em. They was three." Mrs. Graves lapsed back into her gray silence. She took two large empty flour sacks and with precise efficiency, stacked the supplies in them. "That'll be thirty dollars," she said.

One whole month's pay? Was it customary to cheat the customers with such high prices, or were things really that dear here? She signed over the money to Mrs. Graves.

"I have another draft here. Could you cash it, too?"

Mrs. Graves nodded and took the draft and gave her the cash. Amanda hoisted the load onto each arm and left. There was no way to keep her skirts out of the dust now. Again, she felt the eyes on her as she left the town. Some children chased her as she left, jeering at her, "Indian lover! Squaw!" She closed her ears and lengthened her stride. The town of Harlan did not seem so civilized to her after all.

She jumped when Jason stepped out from behind the rocks and quickly unburdened her. He tied the sacks across the pony's back and lifted her up onto its back. Then leading it, he set out at a trot, leading them back to the reservation. She, too, felt the urgency to get to the safety of its boundaries, not only for his sake, but hers. It was only when they were well within the boundaries and far from Harlan that they stopped. The sun was close to setting.

"The horse is tired. It would not be wise to ride after dark. We stay here," he said.

"But it is cold!" she objected.

"It is not so cold. We can sleep on the ground," he contradicted.

" I cannot stay out in the middle of nowhere with you. It wouldn't be, well, proper."

He looked at her. "You rode many miles on my horse."

"Well, yes."

"I have helped you?"

He gestured to the bags.

"Yes, but..." she sighed. They could not go any further. The horse was exhausted and so was she.

"Aren't you going to build a fire, or something?" she asked him. "Isn't there something we can eat?"

All those things she had, and they still had nothing really to eat.

"It is too late to hunt. Beside, I have no rifle or bow and arrow."

"Then how did you get all those rabbits and birds when we were home?"

He stared at her, saying nothing.

"I suppose," she jeered, "that you said some magic chant and they fell at your feet." Still no answer. "Or you stole them from some of the younger ones who could get them!"

He stood up angrily. "I had my bow and my traps. I left them at the school," he retorted. Then he turned away from her to stare at the setting sun.

"Well, at least you could light a fire. I am so hungry. I have not eaten since this morning."

"Women get fire chips. That is a woman's job."

"No, it isn't. Men chop the wood."

They glared at each other, both cold and hungry.

"If you could possibly get something for us to eat," she ventured, " I will get something to burn for warmth."

He nodded. "Just don't go too far," he said. "You do not know this place and would get lost."

She nodded agreement.

In half an hour they were sitting around a small fire, chewing on wild onions and other roots. Not the most filling things, but they kept away the spasms of hunger. The fire was not large, but, if they were careful with the fuel, it would last awhile and keep them warm. And the horse could rest. She watched Jason as he tended the horses, relieving it of its burden of sacks and tying it where there was some grass and bushes. He had shed his coat and she noticed that he did not have the profusion of hair on his chest that her husband and father and the sheriff had. He was terribly thin, but still muscular.

Fatigue won over her well-drilled propriety. She let herself slip into another confusing, deep sleep, punctuated with confused dreams of Little Doe's funeral and her father's, with Kinney's face floating along with her husband's, father's and Aaron's. Her father was burying her, not in the manner of the old ways, but on a high aerie, like Little Doe. She wanted to cry out to him, but no sound came. She saw Melinda sobbing and reaching out to her, running to her. She wanted to call to her but no one was listening. There was too much noise from the death chants. She struggled to get to Melinda.

Jason was shaking her, firmly gripping her shoulders, telling her to wake up. She leaned into his chest, forcing herself to wake up from the horror of her dream. The sky was beginning to light. They had been here too long.

"We have to go," she said, getting up so quickly she got dizzy momentarily.

"We eat," he said.

"No, it can't be that far," she argued.

He shook his head. "We eat. I killed a snake. See? It cooks already."

"Snake!"

"It is good eating," he affirmed.

"You will eat snake?" she asked incredulously. He nodded. "But you won't eat fish?" He nodded.

"I don't eat snake," she stated. He shrugged, tearing a piece of meat off the spit. The aroma made her stomach growl even more. She would eat snake.

Again, she mounted the pony while Jason walked ahead of them. The closer they came to the house, the longer it seemed to take them. They avoided the trading post. As they rode into the camp, it seemed strangely quiet. None of the children were running about. Where were the cattle? They had not strayed off, hopefully. Amanda leaped off the horse, shouting for Melinda and running to the cave. No yellow head responded. She tore into the hut. The three-legged stool and the three-legged table had been smashed. She hurled aside the small cabinet hiding the entrance to the cave and dived into it. When her eyes adjusted to the dim light, she saw no small forms. She scurried out of the cave and toward the school in time to meet Jason.

"The cattle are gone. The children are not in the school," he said.

"Where are they? What happened?" Amanda asked hysterically.

"We will go to our camp. Winona, she took them there if there was danger." He grabbed the sacks and put them in the hovel. Then he vaulted onto the tired pony, and helped her onto it. They galloped to the Indian camp.

The horse was near dead when they came into the camp. Jason pulled to a stop in front of one tepee, and threw the flap back. There, huddled next to the Gemini, was Melinda. The Shadow sat opposite, looking up only at Jason. Quickly, they exchanged words, talking so fast Amanda could not understand any of it. All she comprehended at the moment was the Melinda was alive and safe. She hugged her daughter close, crying and petting her.

Finally Melinda wiggled to get free as she complained, "Mommy, I can't breathe."

"What happened? Why are you here? Are you hurt?" Amanda asked.

"Last night some men came. We could hear them outside. They took the calves, mommy. That's not fair. Those are mine!" Melinda was highly indignant.

"They didn't hurt you, did they? How did you get here?"

"They couldn't find us. Winona made us all go into the

cave, and she shut it with the cabinet and then we turned out the light and it was dark and Winona said not to even sneeze. When they were gone, we sneaked out and came here," she explained to her mother.

"Who was it? Who could do such a thing?"

"One was called Jacobin," said Winona, The Shadow.

Amanda sighed, holding her daughter tightly. She had not won anything from Kinney. He had his little game. His greed had won. They had her bull, her cow, and her calves. It would do no good to claim them. They would be long gone, into some rancher's herd, or even slaughtered, by now. All her care and hard work. All gone. She had lost. She felt the tears in her eyes. But then she saw Jason watching her and she blinked back the tears. There was no time now for them. Her mind started to whirl. If she was to get them back at all, she had to do it now.

First, she had to find out if the cattle were still alive. Then she would get them back.

"Do you know where they took the cattle?" she asked Winona.

"The trading post," she answered.

"Then we must, I must, return to get them

Again, she would have to leave. Melinda. No, she would take the child. Her visit would seem more plausible. If only she could have a witness to the transaction! If it were just she and Kinney, he would refuse, deny, or somehow wield his petty power. But if it was in front of others, he could not refuse. Not his cohorts, certainly. And not the Indians. The Sheriff? Too hard to find and she still was not sure of his support. The Captain! Yes, or course.

"Is there anyway Captain Greenwood could be at the trading post in the morning? With a little luck, I may be my cattle back."

"This is important to have him there?" It was Raphael.

"Yes."

"I can get him."

"It would mean you would have to leave the reservation without permission from Kinney. You could get in very big trouble."

Raphael grinned. "I am always in very big trouble. He will be there tomorrow morning."

She turned to Winona. "Thank you." Winona looked down.

"We will walk back. Our horse is very tired," she said to Jason.

She smiled down at Melinda. She could win, could live her way. But she would never again think it would be so basic. This was not a chess game with John-Paul. This meant her life and that of her daughter and friends.

As she stepped out of the tepee, one of the older men in the tribe came up to her, leading a small, brown and white spotted mare. He offered the reins to her, saying something about a warrior. Amanda looked at Winona. "What did he say?"

Winona smiled slightly, surprising Amanda. "He said that the woman warrior must have a horse to help her fight her battles."

"He is giving me the horse?"

Winona nodded, still smiling slightly. Amanda's newly acquired suspicious nature made her hesitate. She remembered something Little Doe had said about a man buying his wife with so many ponies.

"I thought men only gave away horses when they were wife-shopping," she stated, trying not to sound as suspicious as she felt.

When Winona translated, those around them laughed. The man laughed and shook his head. When he recovered from his laughter, he said something else.

Winona translated. "He gives you the horse as one warrior to another, not as man to woman."

Amanda was still puzzled, but not to look a gift horse in the mouth, so to speak, she accepted the reins of the pony, commenting, "If this is an exchange between equals, I owe him something, don't I?"

"It is our way," Winona answered.

"But I have nothing."

She felt the small gold band around her finger, her last vestige of her former life. It would not fit the wide hand of the warrior in front of her, but it was valuable, and pretty, and could be worn as a necklace or sewn on his shirt for decoration. At least it was a gift. She took the ring from her finger and offered it to the man. He said something to Winona.

"He says he thought it was only when a woman married a man that she offered him her ring," she said to Amanda.

This time it was Amanda's turn to laugh. "Tell him it is merely a decoration, to use as he likes. I don't give it to him as a woman gives a man something, but as warriors share the rewards of a fight."

Again the translation. The warrior cocked his head, nodded once, and took the ring. Amanda put Melinda onto the horse, and vaulted onto it, in spite of her long, bedraggled skirts. No warrior of any dignity would have to be helped onto a horse. She trotted out of the camp with dignity.

The next morning, just as the sun burst over the hill, she and Melinda set out. She washed herself, put on a clean dress, and dressed Melinda in her bonnet and blue dress. She took the sturdy pony as far as she could without being seen.

Then she tied it to large sagebrush. No one could see it with its brown and white spots among the brown and white of the rocks and trees. Then she and Melinda walked to the top of the rise where she hid partially behind a rock. She didn't think she could be seen from the post unless some one was deliberately scanning the horizon for her. Then she waited. She had brought some turnips and salted fish for Melinda to chew on to help her keep quiet, and then let her play down the hill near the pony. She waited until she saw the huge blue figure appear in the distance. Her cattle were confined to the corral at the far end of the post. She called to Melinda and together they walked to the post. Amanda wanted to reach the post ahead of the Captain. Melinda had to race to keep up with her mother's long strides. She leaped up the steps, straightened her bonnet, and began the attack.

Kinney was not around she rapped loudly on the counter with her knuckles. No response. The Captain was getting closer.

"Mr. Kinney, oh, Mr. Kinney," she say out, testing the door to the back rooms. They were unlocked. She poked her head in. "Yoo hoo, Mr. Kinney?"

Kinney stumbled out of the bedroom, fumbling with his shirt and pants. Obviously, he was stirring things up with the cook, Amanda thought disdainfully. But true to form, he regained his composure and his odd smile.

"Why, Mrs. White, what a surprise!" he said.

"Oh, Mr. Kinney, I'm so happy to see you've found them," she said loudly, hearing the heavy footsteps of the captain on the stairs. "I was so afraid those stupid things had just wandered off. I did so hope someone would find them for me."

"What are you talking about?" Kinney evidently had not heard the footsteps.

"Why, my poor little cows. Don't you know, those silly things would just wander off like that. My Melinda and I did so enjoy the fresh milk," she said sweetly, sensing more than seeing the huge military man behind her.

"Them cows ain't yours," Kinney snarled. "They have no brand and since I found them, they're mine. That's the law of the range."

"Excuse me," interrupted the Captain, pushing the door open all the way and escorting Amanda into the dining room by her arm, "but those are certainly the two that you gave to Mrs. White for the school."

Kinney recoiled. Captain Greenwood was a different sort of adversary. "She was to use them to provide meat for the school, not to establish her own private herd!" He retorted.

"Oh, but Mr. Kinney, you told me how much difficulty you were having civilizing these savages. I thought if I could provide the children with the right sort of example and train them in the proper care of the animals, they would begin to learn and become more civilized," she said ingratiatingly, always so ingratiatingly. She knew he didn't trust her, but as long as she didn't give him a wedge, he couldn't split her determination.

"It does make some sense, Kinney. If we could get these Indians to raise their own herds, we wouldn't have to mess with all this nonsense and then the government wouldn't have to feed them," Greenwood reaffirmed her good intentions.

The three stood there in their little game. If the cattle stopped coming, Kinney would lose a valuable source of revenue. If he admitted to his game, he might lose everything. He retreated.

"Well, if you're sure they're yours, of course, they will be returned."

"I'll help you take them back," the Captain offered.

"Oh, that won't be necessary. I'm sure we can find some help here," Kinney said. "You are a very busy man, Captain Greenwood."

"Nevertheless, Mrs. White appears to need some lessons in how to care for livestock. Perhaps I could give her some advice," Captain Greenwood was adamant.

Amanda smiled sweetly at him and gracefully made her exit, marveling at Melinda's ability to remain quiet. Most children her age could not have resisted the temptation to tell of their adventure. But one warning from Amanda had been enough.

"I'm afraid it would be more practical for you to walk and me take the horse, in order to keep the cattle in line, Mrs. White," Captain Greenwood apologized.

"I understand," Amanda answered, knowing she would have to reveal her new asset to the Captain. But he had come to her assistance. What had Raphael told him? She was almost afraid to find out.

The Captain dutifully released the gate and drove the cattle out. Amanda and Melinda raced ahead, reaching the pony just as the Captain came over the hill with the four plodding animals. They had been on greener pastures at Kinney's and seemed to have grown fatter. The Captain expressed surprise at the acquisition of the horse.

"It's an Indian pony. Did you borrow it?" he asked.

"No, it was given to me," she said.

"Indians are not in the habit of giving good horses away, Mrs. White."

"She is nice, isn't she?"

"Yes, but I wouldn't ride her too much."

"I know. She's in foal. I wonder if the warrior knew that when he gave her to me?"

"I'm sure he did. Pardon my curiosity, but how did this all come about?"

"He gave it to me when I went to the camp after Kinney stole the cattle."

"Kinney stole the cattle?" the Captain seemed surprised.

"Of course he did," Amanda laughed. "Once he had discovered that the snakes and the wind and the Indians had not done me in, and what the full value of these animals was, he had to try."

"Then they didn't just wander away."

"Captain, I am inept at some things, but not stupid." She went into details of the way she had been keeping them, her gratitude to the sheriff for the corral, and the worries she had for the winter for the fodder for them.

"I'm just going to have to find a way to get some hay for them for the winter," she sighed.

The Captain looked at her with a quizzical frown, and then chuckled. It seemed an incongruous sound. He was so serious, like Winona.

"I see I did not underestimate you. I saw more spirit in you then Kinney did. I had hoped that perhaps you would be able to teach these young Indians our ways. It will be the only way they can survive on this reservation. There is simply not enough game for them to make it in the old ways."

"I suppose, but," she said meditatively, "I can't see where all their ways are bad, from what I know of them."

Again, the Captain gave her the quizzical frown.

"I'd like to know more about them. I mean, I have the students telling me things, but they can't always explain them, at least so I can understand them. They seem so different, like why do they not bury their dead?"

"You saw that? Who died?"

"Little Doe. At least that's what I called her. She died in childbirth, trying to give birth to Kinney's child."

The Captain nodded. "I knew her. A very kind young woman. Too kind, I'm afraid. When Kinney asked for her sister to cook for him, she went instead."

"Her sister? Winona? She went instead of Winona.

"Yes"

Now Amanda understood The Shadow's anger even better.

"If you were allowed to watch her funeral, they must consider you something special." He smiled a little. "And I think I am beginning to see why."

They came over the rise. "Where is your house?" he asked.

Amanda pointed to the entranceway in the hillside. "And that's the school," she said pointing to the other hovel.

"You live there? When my sergeant told me, I thought he was just using his wild imagination. How can you live there?"

"It's not so bad," she commented, dismounting from the pony.

Her students were nowhere to be seen, but that is what she had expected. Now that she had her cattle back, she was in high spirits again and couldn't resist teasing the Captain, seeing his surprise at her house.

"Would you like to come in for a cup of coffee?" she asked.

The Captain, still on his horse, did not hide his amazement as he surveyed her domain. Recovering himself, he replied, "No, thank you, Mrs. White. I must return to the post before nightfall." He turned his horse to go, then pulled up again. "If you should need my assistance, again, send the boy."

AMANDA

Amanda wanted to ask him what Raphael had said that convinced him to come. But then she decided it might be better to ask Raphael.

The students did return, led by Winona. Raphael grinned at Amanda conspiratorially, never offering any explanation of what he said that prompted the captain to hurry to her aide.

The biggest problem facing Amanda now was providing for her animals for the winter. She had managed to lay in some supplies for herself and her students, and the trip to Harlan had netted many of the little tools and things that made it much easier for her to work. She dried peas, beans and other roots, and buried the squash, potatoes and carrots in the back of the cave where it was cool. She salted and dried the fish. The students and Melinda gathered berries, which she boiled with sugar and put in the few jars that she had. Raphael and Jason had managed to get birds and rabbits with some regularity, which kept them in meat, but did not provide enough to put away.

"One good buffalo would have given us plenty in the old days," Raphael had complained.

"You were not around in the old days, small one," Jason jeered at him.

Enraged, Raphael had charged after him. "I know the old ways. My grandfather has told me." He was half-crying, half-screaming, kicking and hitting at Jason, who wrestled the younger one to the ground and pinned him there.

"Telling of them, and living them are two different things," Jason reminded him.

"You're just angry because you will never get a name of a warrior," Raphael spat at him.

"Neither will you, you dog," Jason growled as he released the boy.

Winona watched as both of them stormed away from the evening fire. "We cannot even marry in the old ways."

"Why not?" Amanda asked, surprised.

The elimination of a warrior cult she could understand. It prevented the Indians from making war again. But marriages? That seemed silly.

"The missionaries said our ways were heathen. It used to be we would dance at the weddings and sing our songs. We cannot do this anymore. A man was allowed to have as many wives as he could care for. This meant that no woman's tepee would go without meat. But now, we cannot do this, and many women have no sisters to help them. We cannot even dance the spring dance to welcome the thunder," she chewed these words bitterly.

Amanda was puzzled. "These dances were for your religion?"

Winona looked hard at her for a moment, and then seemed to decide she would let this white person know some of their ways. "Yes, some of them. Others, we just do because were happy to be with the others, just to do because it is good."

"I see. Something like the dances we used to have when the weather was bad and everyone was bored."

They were silent. The fire glowed warmly in front of them as it burned down to the coals. Melinda had crawled into bed long ago, as had most of the others. Amanda could see Jason silhouetted against the sky as he sat on the hill, his back to them, his face to the east, and the vast prairie.

"Is there no way a boy can become a man in your tribe without killing another man?"

"Not really. He must fast, have his dream, and touch the enemy," Winona answered. "Many of our warriors drink the firewater in order to forget they can no longer be men."

"But killing does not make a man a man!" Amanda protested.

"Our men are warriors and they are hunters. But now they cannot be either one, so they drink." Winona replied in the stony voice she used to put back up the barrier surrounding her. Amanda had heard the voice often enough to know what it signified. She asked no more questions.

She became involved in thinking about the absolute necessity of getting some feed for the animals. She hoped her last money would buy some. But where from? And how to get it here? She would just have to gather as much as she could. She decided she would store it in the small canyons where she had kept the animals. They would have to return there when the bad weather came, because there was no real shelter in the pens against the winds.

So a new routine began. Every morning she would set out in a different direction. Using the hatchet and knife, she would cut down bushes, grasses, anything that looked like it would feed the cattle, tie it in a bundle, and have the pony drag it or carry it. At first, she had both Jason and Raphael accompany her for fear of being lost, and to help her. But soon she developed a sense of direction and could tell the landmarks that would lead her back dome. She discovered that when Raphael went alone with her, he would gather the things and help her. When they were alone, Jason would help her tie the stuff onto the pony and lead the animal home. But if both Jason and Raphael went, neither would help. She then took only one at a time. Melinda accompanied her at first, but tired of the routine and hard work. Instead she chose instead to watch the cattle, and then have her freedom to run with the other children.

***

One morning Amanda awoke very early, before the sun was even up. She decided to go out alone. She heard Melinda's light breathing next to her. She was sure she could get back before the children were even awake. She felt an overwhelming desire to be completely alone, away from the weight of all her responsibilities here. She needed some time to think and be by herself. She put the harness over the pony's head, and quietly slipped away. But the time the sun first over the horizon, she was a good half-mile from the house. She slipped onto the horse, and rode straight east, farther than she had even gone before.

The air was crisp, and cool, like it had been the first morning she was here. And it smelled different. Autumn air. She saw a large clump of bushes and trees. She would probably find something there. She reined the horse and began her methodical, difficult gathering. Then she heard a strange, gurgling sound. She slowly crept toward it. Perhaps it was just a small pond. But as she came closer, her nose told her before her eyes that this was no ordinary pond. Mineral water! Warm mineral springs, bubbling out of a small tower. The centuries had built it up around the spring. Cautiously she inched toward the spring. She remembered the old women that came to visit her stepmother would tell of all the wonderful things mineral water could do for a person. She also remembered them telling her of a man who had been getting some of the water, and had broken open the crust and been swallowed by the earth. But her curiosity overcame her fear and she carefully inched to the edge and peered over. It bubbled and gurgled lazily, the bubbles barely showing on the top, only to pop slowly and then the thick water slid down the side, forming a small pool around the tower until it was absorbed into the ground. Gingerly she cupped her hand into it as it came down the side.

It was quite warm, probably boiling-hot down deeper. She tasted it. Although it wasn't bitter, it didn't taste particularly good either. But if it could do all the marvelous things it was supposed to do, she would have to return with her bucket and take some back with her and have Melinda drink it also.

"Well, Mrs. White, you do pop up in unexpected places," a male voice chuckled.

Amanda whirled around. The gorgeous Mr. Graves stood leaning against a tree, running his long fingers through his shiny blond locks as he grinned at her. She realized with annoyance that she was in her pants and shirt, and out of her "lady" disguise.

"And even speechless!" Graves chuckles again. "Where is your little girl?"

"At home," Amanda replied, without thinking.

"Oh, then, you're all alone. That's dangerous, for a woman to be alone in this country." Then he sneered. "But not for a squaw."

Before the full import of what he had said penetrated to Amanda, Graves grabbed her wrist, and pulled her tightly to him, kissing her roughly and fully on the mouth. She felt his tight grip around her waist and his other hand massaging her breast and pinching her nipple. Memories of her brother-in-law and husband flashed through her mind. Same problem. But this was not the same Amanda. She brought her knee up swiftly, catching Graves hard in the groin.

He flung her back toward the spring.

"Bitch!" he screamed, holding himself between his legs and sinking to his knees.

She regained her balance, but not her composure. She seethed with a blind, hot fury, the kind of which she had never felt before. All reason was gone. She saw before her the hated husband and brother-in-law. Her hand clenched the hatchet she had been using to cut the bushes. Graves crouched and glared at her. Then he lunged toward her, growling. She raised the hatchet with both hands, ran to meet him, and struck it into his skull. Blood and brains scattered as the body fell to the ground.

Amanda stood for a moment over her victim, trembling, her fury receding as the horror of her deed began to seep into her mind. She stared at her victim and fell to her knees next to him, and shaking with a deep, internal cold, vomited until her stomach offered no more sacrifice. She didn't know how long she had been sitting and rocking and staring into space, until she realized it was raining, a very cold, dark, rain. It had washed away some of the blood and vomit, but the body still lay there with its cloven head.

"I must bury him," she said to herself.

But how? She had no spade, no digging stick. She couldn't even burn him in this rain. But she remembered from the old women that the mineral springs had their beds, not like lakes and rivers, where men could see them, but deep in the bowels of the earth, where only the devil knew what lay there. And that is where she must send the once beautiful Mr. Graves. She grabbed him by the heels, with his ruined head bumping against the rocks and collecting mud, and dragged him to the tower. Then she heaved his body slowly over the tower, and sent it sliding, sinking slowly into the spring, the mineral waters splashing over it, and blending with the rain.

The effort drained her strength, and she sat by the spring to regain it. The rain had soaked her thoroughly, but in doing so had cleansed her of the spattered blood and vomit. She heard the neigh of a horse, Graves' horse. She would have to free it. She was tempted to keep it but she couldn't risk the explanation. Then she saw the gleam of the rifle butt. That she would take. That would get her the meat for the winter. She had propitiated the warrior gods of her Indian friends, and now they would reward her with a more powerful weapon. She shuddered. How could she think this way?

But she did take the rifle and its case off the saddle. And the bullets and the money from the saddlebags. She didn't count the money, just took it all from the saddlebags, not even thinking about where it might have come from. But the bullets and the rifle she wanted. Then she wrapped the reins around the horn of the saddle and turned the horse loose and sent it on its way. She pulled herself onto her own wet little pony, and gave her her head, hoping she could find her way back in this storm. The lightning flashed above, making the land briefly appear like an ocean, and then, with the crashing thunder it became the dark again.

The pony found the house. She was exhausted. She felt someone put their arms around her and pull her off the horse into the house. Four hands stripped off her wet clothes and wrapped her in some warm blankets. She felt them drying her hair, and the last thing she remembered seeing was the flicker of the lamp on Jason's face before she fell asleep.

***

"You feel better?" Jason questioned her when he saw her eyes open.

"Yes," she answered, trying to get her bearings. Her mind was cloudy, and her body ached. "Melinda?"

"Out with the others. Winona is with them. We hid the rifle and other things under the clothes." He pointed to the other side of the cave.

Neither spoke. She knew he had questions about what

had happened. She wanted to tell someone. She had to. The guilt was too strong, the horror too great. So many times she had wanted to tell someone when she had experience fear or sorrow. But always it had been a pat on the head, and "It's okay, sweetheart, let daddy take care of it. Don't worry your pretty little head about it." But it wasn't the worry, or even the doing. It was the sharing she needed. Jason sat on the floor next to her, cross-legged, staring at her with his very brown eyes with their golden flecks, and frowned.

Finally, he spoke. "The rifle belongs to the one called Graves. I have seen him use it. It is not a common one here."

"I, he," she wasn't sure where to start. "He's dead. I killed him." Her flat tone of voice seemed incongruous to the meaning of the words.

"It was necessary?" Jason inquired, smoothing her hair back.

In anguish, she rolled over and buried her head in his hand and arm. "I don't know. I could have run, or simply fought him off. I had already hurt him. I felt so angry, so angry."

Then she remembered the blood, the rain, and she began to sob, quietly. She was not only crying because of the horror, but because of the death and the stupidity of it all. Because she was different. Maybe it was the tears she couldn't cry when her husband died, and when she left her other life.

She felt Jason's arms around her and his body next to hers. He was warm and his caresses gentle. She was nude beneath the blankets and he wore only his loincloth. She felt the hard demand his body was making. But he did not yield to the demand. Instead, he continued to gently caress her hair and shoulders while she cried. And when she was finished, they lay together. He kissed her eyes closed when she looked up at him, then slipped out of the blanket.

"You're hungry. I'll tell Winona you're awake," he said, clearing his throat, and he disappeared.

Melinda flew in. "Mommy, what happened? You weren't here when we got up and the pony was gone and then you came in last night in the rain. I was scared you left me. Oh, Mommy, don't every go away like that again." And she threw her arms around her mother.

"I'm sorry, darling. I left to get some more brush and hay and must have lost my way. The pony found the way back, though." She hugged her daughter tightly, partly to comfort her, but also to get herself back to reality.

The youngsters had managed to get some things done, but not without some quarreling. But still, the cattle were fed, and watered, and the pony had been taken care of, but only when Raphael condescended to let the Cherub and Paul help him. She hugged each one of them, except Raphael, who had managed to find a little spider to put down her neck. She had retrieved it, and chased after him until she wrestled him to the ground and put the spider down his neck. Then they were secure in the knowledge that things were the same between them.

When all the children were in bed that night, after another tale by Paul and Amanda, Winona, Jason and Amanda sat by the dying fire.

"Can you use it?" Winona demanded.

Amanda shook her head.

"Then what use is it?" she asked.

Amanda looked at Jason. "Do you know how to use it?"

Jason studied the fire. "We are not allowed to have rifles on the reservation. We are not even allowed bows and arrows."

"That's not what I asked. I asked if you could use it."

"I have such knowledge," he replied, looking her in the eye briefly.

"Fine, then I can hunt."

Both Winona and Jason looked at her and then at each other. Amanda was hoping they would understand the finer points of the proposal without having to explain. But evidently they did not.

"We need meat, especially enough for the winter, and especially if I am to have you all in my charge. With the rifle, we can hunt bigger game. I believe Paul said the deer come out of the mountains when it beings to get cold up there. As I see it, we have no choice but for me to hunt with the rifle."

"You said you cannot shoot it," Winona countered.

"Jason will teach me."

"Such shooting takes time to learn. And many bullets. We have neither," Jason countered.

"Then, when we find the deer, you will shoot the gun."

"I can't have a gun. The agent says."

Amanda interrupted. "No, the agent said you could not own a gun. He said you could not hunt for yourself. But he said nothing about you being, uh, let's say, gun bearer? For me. When I hunt. If I decide you will shoot the deer for me, it is still I who will be hunting. Therefore, you are not hunting. I am."

Jason shook his head and looked down. She knew he would love to hunt, to gain some portion of dignity in the eyes of his tribe and himself. But he doubted her logic. But Winona was smiling slightly at her, her head tilted to one side.

"We need good meat," Winona stated. "I can dress and the hides and the meat, uh, for you, of course."

"Of course," said Amanda.

The difficulties of instigating the plan were more than Amanda had envisioned. She thought they would simply walk out on the prairie, shoot the deer, bring it home, and that would be that. First, she had to convince Melinda to let her leave her sight again. This was no small task. Since the scare the she had had recently, she had become Amanda's shadow. At first, Amanda was gentle with her and tried sweet-talking.

"I'll bring you back some nice flowers," she said.

"I don't want any flowers. I want to be with you," Melinda retorted.

"Then you can play with the others, and have some extra milk."

"I don't want any milk. I don't want you to go."

Amanda grabbed the child by the shoulders, knelt down and looked intently at her. " I must go with Jason. We must get some meat to eat for the winter or we may all starve. I must go."

Melinda bit her lower lip. "You will come back?

"Yes, I will."

"Okay." Melinda hugged Amanda around the neck. "I love you, mommy."

"I love you too, Melinda." She kissed her forehead and went to meet Jason.

The first few times they went out, Jason was very irritated with her. She made too much noise, he complained. She even walked with noise.

"Well, I'm sorry I don't walk three feet above the ground, like you do," she huffed.

He sighed. "Take care where you put your feet. Don't step on the loose rock. It slides and makes noises." He showed her how to walk quietly, what to watch for to know that the deer or elk had been this way. Sometimes, when they rested, he would tell her quietly of legends of wolves and eagles, or great warriors and the wise elders. He would tell her how they must be part of where they walked.

"When we kill the deer, we must release it spirit and apologize to it for taking its home. Then we must show it was necessary by using every piece of it," he explained.

"Why?" she asked.

He sighed at her simplicity. "Because it is not right to kill something without the need."

"But the buffalo hunters only took the skins, didn't they?"

"They were white," he huffed as he got up to continue the search.

The wind talked in the pines above them and they became one with the trees and the wind. Their moccasins told no tales of their presence. He motioned to her to stop and crouch down. He pointed. Down the hill, where she could barely discern them, were three deer. Slowly, quietly, they crept closer. Jason raised the rifle. Two quick shots and the buck and one doe fell to the ground. The other doe jumped stiff-legged away.

Jason jumped up and whooped. It echoed off the rocks.

"Do you remember where we left the horses?" he asked her.

She nodded. She ran back to get them, elated as he was over their success. By the time she had returned, he had already slit their throats and had them hanging from a tree, letting the blood drip to the ground.

"The blood will replenishing the ground for feed to grow for the young ones next year," he said.

"Oh, I see," she answered.

He tied the two deer onto the horses and they walked back to their camp. They didn't speak. Their success was their bond.

All the children whooped and hollered when they saw them coming. They began to sing and dance exuberantly around the two. Amanda laughed, swinging Melinda high into the air.

Winona grabbed the Gemini. "We are not allowed to dance," she told them sternly.

"Oh, they aren't dancing. They're, well, celebrating the return of their teacher," Amanda said gaily, squeezing the twins and looking at Winona. With that, everyone set into another round of whooping and hollering.

"If the agent saw them dancing, with Jason holding a gun in his hand, we would all be in much trouble," Winona said quietly.

"Oh, God, Winona, I know. I know. But they have to have some joy in their lives. But you're right. We must be sure he never sees us this way," Amanda said.

And while the Gemini cooked a huge roast slowly over the coals, Winona and Jason cleaned one of the deer hides while Amanda watched. Then Amanda insisted on helping with the second one.

"I must know how," she explained.

When the meat was hung, Winona showed her how the stretch the hide to dry and told her the secret of keeping them soft. Amanda almost gagged when she saw the children chewing on the intestines of the animals, but they seemed to relish them. When Winona ground the hooves into powder, she explained that it would make a healing poultice for sores. Then she hollowed out some of the bones, eating the marrow in them. At first Amanda couldn't even watch her, but again, her curiosity got the better of her, and she tasted the marrow. It wasn't too bad, if you could forget what it was. Winona explained to her what tools could be made from the bones and antlers.

As they sat eating the juicy meat from the deer, Amanda

thought how she owed these ten little Indians a great deal. True, she had taught them their counting and adding and some reading. But she had learned more from them. They could have left her to die when she ran out of food or when she came in wet and delirious from her ride. She would have to repay them somehow. She knew they believed a great deal in their tribe. And they cared for the people there. Perhaps, in a small way, that was they way to repay them. She looked at the hanging meat. It would be enough to keep them all winter. But she still had the rifle, and they might be able to get some more.

"The cattle your people were given were very poor ones," she began, addressing herself to Jason.

He nodded, still chewing the meat.

"You have relatives in the village? " She gestured to all of them. They all nodded. Of course, it seemed to her, when they tried to explain the relationships, everyone was related somehow to almost everyone else.

"Then perhaps you would like to visit them?" No one moved, or nodded.

"You do not want us here any more?" Winona ventured.

"Oh, yes, I want you here. But I thought you might want to show them what you have learned so far. You know, your counting and adding and the letters. And perhaps, you would want to take a small gift, perhaps some of the meat we have."

"My mother's sister enjoys new stories. Perhaps I will go back for a visit to tell her these stories. I would take her the venison heart, since she likes it so well," Winona said offhandedly.

"I'll salt some of it for the winter. Perhaps the hindquarters of the doe. When you all return, Jason and I will go hunting again." She smiled slightly and stood up. "I am very tired. I think I will sleep. Would someone care for the fire before you all go to bed?"

The next morning they were all gone. And so was all the meat, except for the hindquarters of the doe. It seemed like so little after so much had been there last night, and Amanda felt a momentary twinge of panic when she though of the coming winter. She pulled the shawl around her. It was nice to have a brief respite without the children here. A sort of quiet had descended.

"Mommy, Mommy, somebody's coming," Melinda said as she ran and danced ahead of the rider. The Sheriff. Amanda's heart sank. In spite of the ice in her feet, she smiled at the approaching figure and walked to him. The wind had picked up and was whipping her hair around her face.

"Well, good morning, Andrew. What brings you out here?"

"Business, I'm afraid, ma'am," he said, as he dismounted.

"Oh?"

"Could we get out of this wind?" he asked.

"Oh, yes, I'm sorry. Excuse my poor manners. I'm just not accustomed to having visitors." She led the way to the hovel with trepidation. Did Jason put the rifle back in the cave, or did he take it with him, or had he left it propped up in the corner of the hovel? If the Sheriff saw it, he would have many questions that would difficult to answer. With relief, she saw the rifle was gone.

"I'm afraid I can't even offer you a place to sit," she smiled at him weakly. As their eyes adjusted to the semi-darkness, she kept hers riveted to his face while he inspected the hovel as he spoke.

"Mr. Graves has mysteriously disappeared. I suspect something bad has happened to him."

"Mr. Graves? The gentleman I met at Mr. Kinney's that owns the store in Harlan?" she inquired.

"How do you know he ran the store?"

"Oh, I, uh, went to Harlan once to get some things."

"I see. What did you get at the store?"

Amanda was very aware that her little hovel was very bare. "Oh, a few odds and ends. Some cloth to sew some clothes for Melinda, mostly."

Sheriff MacGregor brushed some dust from the hat in his hand. "Did Mr. Graves pass by here, by any chance?"

"By here? Oh no."

"If you do see him, you will let me know?"

"Of course, Sheriff MacGregor, although I can't imagine what he would want here."

The Sheriff smiled slightly at this comment, which confused Amanda. She wished he would leave, but he didn't budge.

"It's Andrew. Remember? Are you all right out here, ma'am?" he asked unexpectedly.

"We're fine," was all Amanda could reply. She would not let him know more than necessary.

"If that's your venison hanging out there in the wind, better bring it in. Wolves might get it," he said as he ducked out the door and put his hat one. "Good day, ma'am." He tipped his hat and was gone, after a wink in Melinda's direction.

"I like him, Mommy," Melinda observed as she and Amanda carried the meat inside.

Amanda angrily applied the salt to the meat, carelessly getting it into an open cut and swearing at the pain. How could she tell the child that the man was really an enemy, that if he knew exactly what went on, he might hang her from the nearest tree?

"I know, honey," she said. "Let's care for the cows."

They braved the wind together to get the cows down to the stream. The trees had lost their green, and had turned a dull brown and gray. There was none of the brilliant colors of fall that Amanda remembered from the trees back East. The cows were reluctant to venture out into the wind to graze, but Amanda did not want them to stray too close to their winter food. She would have to watch them while they grazed.

"Why don't you go get that little book we were reading and we can read it while we watch the cows," she instructed Melinda.

So they read the poetry of Emily Dickinson, the recluse from society, but not from life. Amanda had memorized many of the short verses, both for the beauty of the language and for their meaning. Many had taken on new hues of meaning with this new life of hers. Melinda struggled through the words that she knew, and Amanda helped her with the new ones. The cattle had not had their fill, but Amanda was tired of the wind and she felt very dusty.

They returned to the cave, and Amanda lit the small lamp. It cast shadows on the walls. The hard floors were not her four-poster bed, but she felt more secure and warm on them. She would make a bed from the skins of the deer, just as Melinda's rabbit fur enshrouded her. They were both hungry, but Amanda did not want to light a fire in this wind. She was going to have to learn how to light a fire in the front hovel, in order to cook this winter.

She looked at the empty cans lying in a pile. This was the time. She would have to hook them together, somehow, to form a chimney and stove. She used the knife as her tool, to curl up the edges and snip them and to fit one inside the other. Then she took others to make sort of a tent. Then she put this on the end of the chimney to form a hood over the fire. There was little danger of the fire spreading, since the floor was rock. She chose an area around the corner from the door so the unexpected gusts of wind would not fan the fire wildly. Then she wound the chimney out and up the door. It would still be smoky in the hovel, but that would be minimal if she kept the cooking fires low. She was sure that if they stayed in the back, and kept the entrance covered, and dressed warmly, they would not freeze in the cave. She listened to the wind howl around the hovel. It had a numinous quality about it, as though the devils had come up from the warm springs. She shuddered, the memory imposing itself upon her. She shook her head to free it.

"Melinda, bring me some chips," Melinda ducked out briefly, and then ducked back in.

Amanda took the coals from the old fire and placed them on the new one, seeing the spark ignite the dry kindling. The fire worked and the smoke was minimal. Amanda put two small pieces of meat on the rocks by the fire to cook and backed away from her fire, letting her mind drift while her little daughter slept curled on her lap.

CHAPTER FOUR

She heard a noise outside the entrance, and then Jason appeared in the doorway.

"I have returned. The others will follow tomorrow," he stated.

"Come in," she said, suddenly not wanting to be alone anymore.

She and Melinda pulled their meat from the fire. She offered part of hers to Jason. He took it without comment. I wonder if Indians ever say thank you, she thought.

"I'm tired, Mommy."

"Okay, sweetheart. Go on to bed. I'll be in as soon as I tend to the fire." She saw Melinda hesitate for a minute. "I'll be in," she reassured her.

Melinda had been so easy to care for now, except for this obsessive fear that her mother was going to leave her. Amanda found it annoying at times. She realized that she was all the child had, but sometimes, even when the Indian children were here, Melinda would break off from play and find her mother to make sure she was still around.

"I'll go to the school," Jason said.

"No, it's all right if you stay here. It's a miserable walk in this snow," Amanda suggested.

He just shrugged. His rudeness annoyed her. A lot of things seemed to annoy her lately. Perhaps it was the fear of the coming winter.

Melinda had lit the lamp. She seemed to have an unerring instinct for finding the thing, so Amanda let her carry the small stick from the fire each night to light it. Then the child had curled up in her white rabbit's fur and slept. With the fresh air, hard work and play, and big supper, Melinda would sleep soundly until the morning. She no longer had nightmares as she had when they first came here. Jason pulled his blanket around him, and sat on the floor close to Amanda, enigmatically quiet.

"My grandmother liked the taste of the meat. She said it was very good," he commented finally.

"I'm glad she liked it. Did you tell her that you got it?" she asked.

"I explained how I was making myself useful," he said, unable to suppress a grin.

"And you were as proud as a peacock," she teased.

He jumped to his feet, "Why do you make fun of me?"

"I wasn't making fun of you," she replied in astonishment. My God, he was touchy.

"One deer does not make a hunter. So it was not truly mine to give," he muttered angrily.

"But you did get it," Amanda protested.

"I am still Moksois," he said miserably, pressing his head against one cold wall of the cave.

"A name doesn't make a person," Amanda argued.

"It tells what you are."

"And if your name would tell what you are, what would your name be?"

"Matcikineu, Terrible Eagle," Jason replied, standing straight and firm. Then he abruptly turned to leave the cave. "I should not have told you this. A man does not talk of such things with a woman."

Gambling on her acceptance by the tribe and his respect for her, she pointed out, "But I am your teacher, and you talk and learn with your teacher." She hoped that would stop him, help him, and keep him with her.

He stopped and looked at her, and smiled, and then chuckled, "I would end up with a woman warrior to be my teacher. And my teacher has already given me a name. What is it you call me? Jason?"

"Do you want to know the legend of that name?"

"It has a story?"

She smiled and nodded and gestured for him to sit across from her. When he had settled cross-legged and attentive, she told him of the legend of Jason and the Golden Fleece, and the battles he had fought and the monsters he vanquished and the maidens he won. When she was done, Jason smiled at her.

"It is a better name than Moksosis," he said.

He lay on his side, his head propped up in his hand. The lamplight flickered on his brown face. She had thought of him as a boy when she came. But he wasn't. Nor was he fully a man. She leaned up and smothered the flame in the lamp, rolling in her blanket and staring into the darkness. She sensed his nearness, wondered why it bothered her. She didn't fear him as she did Kinney, or even the Sheriff. Nor did she trust him completely. Yet he had never given her any reason to distrust him. Quite the opposite. He had helped her, and they seemed to share an understanding with each other, the feeling of being lost, unfulfilled, whatever it was that still gave her fits of melancholy and despair. She felt free, freer than she had ever been, in spite of, or perhaps because of, the responsibility for herself, her daughter, and these ten little Indians. It sounded like a childs's finger play. Ten little Indians standing in a row. One died in childbirth, and then there were nine. She shivered. Her thoughts were slipping into that melancholic path again.

She slept fitfully, seeing the split skull, seeing the face as half her brother-in-law's, half her husband's. Had she truly killed Graves, not because of what he tried to do, but because of the gender he belonged to? Did she sacrifice him for someone else's sins? She had dreams of Little Doe's funeral. And then again she was on the high bier. She awoke with a start, as Melinda of her dreams had joined her on the bier. In spite of the cold of the cave, she was sweating and crying. Jason's hand was on her shoulder and face, pushing her hair back, talking to her.

"It's a dream, one like you had before?" he asked when he became aware she was awake and more in control of herself.

"Yes, yes, many times, too many times," she sighed.

"Our old people say that when you dream a dream many times, it's a picture of the future."

"Oh God, no this can't be. If it is, there's no point in living."

"Perhaps it tells you something else."

She told him the dream, halting to catch her breath frequently, as though she had been running.

"It's not a good dream," his only reaction had been.

She was comforted by his presence until the fear had passed. Then she felt the restless distrust and pushed his hand away from her face, sat up and lit the lamp.

"Is it daytime yet?" she asked.

"Soon, I think, my teacher," he replied.

Irrationally irritated, she snapped at him, "I have a name, also!"

"Yes, Amanda. Perhaps I should give you an Indian name," he said logically.

"And if I were an Indian?"

"Well, if you were with my people, I would call you Black She-bear."

She knew he was teasing her, but rose to the bait anyway.

"A black bear! Why, they are clumsy, ugly things."

"They have courage, even though they do have bad tempers. One is never sure of what they might do. But they protect their young. And they eat any kind of food they find."

She didn't know whether to be complimented or insulted. She retreated into her only surety. "They are ugly."

"I suppose that depends on who is looking at them," he laughed. "To another bear, they are quite beautiful."

"Well, I know where I stand with you. You said you were an eagle, who most assuredly, is not particularly attracted to a bear. And I am not black!"

"You are not all white as the new snow, as you were when you lived with the white man."

"How would you know what I looked like?"

"Because those parts of you that have not seen the sun are still very white, but your hair is black and your skin is almost as brown as mine on your hands, arms and face."

"How do you know how white I am?"

"Remember? Winona and I could not leave you in those wet, cold clothes when you came back in the storm," he chuckled.

She was horrified, furious, and embarrassed. "How dare you!" she screamed and flew at him in a rage, trying to beat on him with her fists.

But he deftly pinned her hands at her side and her legs with his and wrestled her to an ineffectual rage on the floor.

"Shh, now you'll wake the child," he laughed.

"But I'll kill you," she growled.

"I am not as stupid as that man Graves. I know what an angry woman warrior can do. Why does this upset you?"

She could only shake her head. She ceased her fighting, but he didn't release her.

"We couldn't leave you in the wet clothes. Then you would be sick, and we would lose you," he said very quietly.

"Does it matter, that you might lose me?" she whispered.

"Yes, to me it matters," he whispered back.

She moved so she could face him. He released her hands. He lay slightly on top of her, his legs still pinning hers down. She traced an aimless mosaic on his face with her fingers, studying each feature carefully. Some strange thing was moving, churning inside her. Why? She studied his brown eyes, seeing the small flecks of black and gold do a dance on their own. He was no longer smiling at her. His hand caressesed her neck and shoulders, moving down to slowly release each button from its prison on her shirt, until she felt her breasts rubbing gently against his hard chest as he leaned to kiss her forehead. She lifted her shoulders and arms so he could pull the shirt off her, and as she did, she saw him smile a little.

Then he kissed her, her mouth, her eyes, her throat, each breast, gently but firmly. Her body trembled. A small part of her mind told her to stop him, to run, but her body reveled in the exquisite sensations he was producing. As he pulled at her pants, she lifted her hips to help him. He continued his exploration of her body with his mouth and tongue, and his hands seemed to have a life of their own. But as he reached her knees and feet, she panicked for fear of losing him. She sat up and pulled his face to hers and wrapped her hands in his masses of long, black hair. Its strange luxuriant softness whetted her appetite, and what was a vague pleasure before, now became an aggressive need. He dropped his loincloth from his hard body. His need matched hers and his insistent hardness slipped between her legs. They matched each other, paced each other until she exploded, knowing nothing but their locked bodies and their glorious turbulence.

Moments later she laid back, warm, content, still holding him. His face was buried in her shoulder and hair. Slowly, the coldness of the cave crept back into her. He pulled his blanket over both of them. She remembered Melinda and looked in a panic toward her child.

"She sleeps. She is a bear, like her mother, and hibernates when she sleeps," he teased.

His allusion no longer made her angry. She didn't know why. Nor did she care. She knew a contentment she had never known before. He held her and gently caressed her. She wanted to stay like this forever.

He kissed her lightly on the lips, rolled out of the blanket, swiftly putting on his loincloth and moccasins.

"Where are you going?" she asked.

"I go to the stream to bathe."

"It's awfully cold."

"It doesn't seem to bother you when you want to bathe."

"How would you know?"

Again he laughed, kneeled quickly and kissed the top of her head. "I have watched you."

"You're just a damned Peeping Tom," she sputtered, sitting up and ignoring her present nudity.

He let his eyes wander over her. She blushed, but didn't make any effort to cover herself.

"If that means I enjoy watching a beautiful, naked woman, I guess I am," he replied.

"Why didn't you attack me, then?"

He looked puzzled. "Did I attack you now?"

"Well, no, but...well, it was different, now," her voice was very soft and hesitant.

"If I attack a woman, I seek revenge on her husband or her people, not to show her love," he explained.

"Oh, I see."

"Isn't that the way of your people?"

She shook her head. "No, I don't think so. Not what I know."

He started to ask her a question, but she silenced him with her hand on his lips, "Never mind. It doesn't matter now."

He leaped up and was gone. She, too, wanted to bathe, but decided to wait until he was done and gone. She was reluctant to give up the warm glow she felt. Finally she put her clothes back on and started the fire for breakfast.

***

The children returned and they settled again into the routine, but with more urgency. The cold winds were more frequent, the rains colder, and almost all the leaves were off the trees. She examined her storage of food and fodder, and could only hope she had enough to make the winter. They ate nothing from storage, only what they could gather or kill. Finally, if there were nothing else that day, then she would agree to dip into their reserves. Unfortunately, those times were becoming more and more frequent. They would not have much left at this rate. The meat was almost gone. She regretted her generosity of earlier times, but could not go back. It was done. They would have to get more meat, which meant she would have to go out with Jason.

They had not made love since that one morning. But the few times they were briefly alone, they would touch each other, on the hand, the face, it didn't matter. She was often aware of his presence when she bathed in the stream. He would watch her, and not disturb her ablutions. At first he made her uneasy, but then she accepted his presence as a tacit compliment. At times she felt the churning inside her again, and then the constant company of the children became an annoyance. The cave was colder now, with the winter winds, and she no longer pined to be absolutely alone.

After the first big snowstorm the urgency of getting more meat was final. There was no gathering of food that day, so Amanda cooked the last of the deer. She and Jason now had no choice. They had to risk using the rifle again and find something. She had a meeting with Winona and Jason that night. They no longer gathered outside, but in her small hut around her makeshift stove.

"I will go alone," Jason declared.

"No!" Amanda insisted.

"It is your place to care for the children, here," he stated.

"I am going with you. I will do no good here."

She glared at him. Dear God, but he was so stubborn, sometimes. This warrior's pride was an anachronism interfering with their very existence.

"If Kinney should happen to find you alone with that rifle, he would have you thrown in prison. Then we would all starve. At least if I am with you, I can claim it as mine, and avoid unnecessary trouble."

"You would have to explain where you got it," he retorted.

"At least he will take time for an explanation then!"

Winona interjected, "I will care for the children."

Amanda and Jason glared at each other, and then he nodded. "We leave early in the morning, before the sun," he stated flatly, as he got up to make his way to the school hut. They had discovered the school hut also led to a cave, which made it much warmer for the children to sleep in. Sometimes it would have been easier for the children to stay in hers, but she had to have her time of privacy.

She awakened Melinda to tell her of the plans. She knew her little one would be very frightened if she did not know where her mother was when she got up the next morning.

She thought she had just closed her eyes when she felt Jason shaking her awake. She had not undressed for bed but before she left she put on another shirt and her coat. The once beautiful thing had been divested of all decorations and was strictly utilitarian now. But it kept her warm and the late November winds were cold. It had snowed already twice this month. The snow hadn't stayed long, but it presaged worse thing to come. This snow was deeper. Winona had made some moccasins out of the skin of the doe for her, showing her how to use the bone needle and leather. As they trudged through the snow, Amanda was grateful for Winona's skill. No snow seeped in, and the warm fur on the inside kept her feet warm.

Amanda spotted the dark shapes against the white snow first, grabbing Jason's arm and pointing. He stopped and crouched down, frowning, evidently annoyed at not having seen him first. The wind shifted directions, coming in from the north instead of west. They would have to circle far around them first.

Then Jason shot. He got the big buck. Now they could eat! But it wouldn't fall. It staggered around while the others bounded away. Then it began running awkwardly. Cursing under his breath, Jason shot again. This time Amanda could see the blood spurt out of the head, and the big animal slowly crumpled to the ground, but still fighting for its life. Jason ran to the animal and deftly slit its throat. He drained the blood, kneeling on the ground, and sang his chant to the spirit of the deer. Amanda was impatient. It seemed stupid to waste the precious daylight hours to sing to a song to a dead deer, when they should be getting it home. She hurried to get the horses.

When she returned, Jason was still performing his rituals. When Amanda tried to touch the deer, he stopped her with a firm grip on her hand. She squatted by the horse, waiting and stewing. When he had finished, he tied the animal to the horse. The wind howled furiously around them and the snow blew in their faces, stinging their skin.

"It's a long way back. We'll find shelter and wait out the storm," he said.

She looked at the dark sky and felt the bite of the wind and nodded her agreement. He led them to an overhang in the cliffs. Although it was cold, it was out of the wind for both of them and the horses. He took the deer off the horse and buried it in the snow close to them, while she searched for something to make a fire with although she didn't know why because she had no matches and no hot coals. She managed to find a few twigs and cow chips.

Then she watched in fascination as he withdrew two small rocks from his pouch on his belt. He struck them together again and again, until she saw a spark and a small stream of smoke. He gently blew on the smoke until it became a fire. They huddled together by the fire under their coats. She enjoyed his hard body next to hers. She had never thought she would enjoy the sensation of a man's body next to hers, but with him, she did. It was such a contrast to her husband's fat, cruel body. Jason's was hard, but gentle, an incongruity she didn't even try to analyze. She didn't protest when his hand slid under her shirt to touch her breast while his teeth nibbled gently on her ear.

"You taste good," he whispered.

This time she laughed, pulled him closer, scratched his back gently and loosened his belt. This time there was no doubt in her mind what it was she wanted when her insides churned warmly. She didn't notice the cold or the hard ground, just the beautiful floating sensation, then an explosion and another and another. They lay still then for some time, still locked together. The gentle rhythm of his breathing told her he was sleeping lightly. She held him close until she saw the fire was beginning to fade. Then she gently extricated herself from him, covered him, and tended the fire. The storm raged fiercely around them, but they had chosen their shelter well, and the wind did not reach them here. The ponies whinnied nervously, but they too, were protected. She stared at the fire and put her hands close to warm them.

What if I get pregnant? She asked herself. She chilled at the thought. The responsibility of Melinda was hard enough, but to have a little half-breed bastard, what would she do? She looked at Jason and felt the stirring within her. He wasn't particularly beautiful, as Raphael was, but he was handsome, and something in their spirits understood each other. She didn't know what she would do if she got pregnant, but she knew she couldn't turn Jason away because of the fear. The need was too strong. She added a few more chips to the fire and lay down beside him. She knew she should try to sleep, but her mind was working too hard and she was still restless. She wanted to wake him and make love again. What would he do? What would he think of her?

She traced his cheek with her finger, twined her fingers in his hair, and kissed him. Her hands wandered over his body, releasing the organ she had imprisoned in order to build the fire up again. When she touched him there, he responded. He was hard and his eyes opened.

"Didn't I make you happy before?" he asked sleepily.

"Too happy," she blushed.

He laughed his teasing laugh and they made love and this time it was she who slept and he who tended the fire.

***

Winona had fed the children some roots and vegetables. All were happy to see them home again, Melinda hanging onto her mother, chattering like a blue jay. Raphael and the Cherub had tended the cattle without too much quarreling.

She found with the winter settling in, they had more time to talk and learn. She was amazed at the rapidity with which Raphael would learn things. His mind was quick and frequently he was two steps ahead of her, anticipating her questions, finding the answers before they were asked. He thoroughly enjoyed reading aloud to the other children, and his vocabulary had increased so that it was seldom necessary for Amanda to prompt him with some of the easier books. It was Jason who was quick with mathematics, and he was rapidly getting to the point that she felt she could no longer teach him. Among her other treasures from the heathen donor, she had found an old, dilapidated chessboard. She taught the older ones to play and soon had to make up a schedule to eliminate the fighting that occurred when more than two wanted it at the same time. The Gemini would play each other, and it would invariably end in a draw. They seemed to link minds and know the other's strategy move for move. Even Paul learned to play, keeping his hand on the board, touching each piece to locate it in his mind before he made his next move. Jason and Amanda would play and it became a pitched battle, each determined not to let the other win.

And they did dramas and plays. Ruth and Naomi could sing, so they began the same trade-off that she had done with Little Doe and the languages, and Paul and the stories. She would learn one of their chants or songs, and they would learn one of her songs and frequently interject an impromptu dance. When they read "Hamlet," an argument ensued as to whether Hamlet did the right thing. It seemed that they thought he should have killed his stepfather after the first prompting from the ghost. She found their belief in spirits and dreams so very absolute and undoubting.

She and Jason went out twice more on hunts, once being very successful and bringing home two elk, the next time bringing home nothing. Each time they found some place, somehow, to make love. And each time, when they came back, she found it emptier to crawl under her blankets alone.

The reality of Kinney and the Sheriff and Graves slipped to the back of her mind, occupying the same kind of dusty room that her existence in Atlanta and Philadelphia had. City lights and Indian agents seemed distant and unreal.

She should have known the idyll could not last. Paul developed a cough. At first she thought it was only a slight cold, so she kept him with her in the cave instead of having him go through the cold snow to the school. But that night, while she and Winona watched, he became feverish, and his breathing labored. They bathed his hot little body in cold water to cool it down, but it would immediately heat again. Winona explained the sweat lodge that they sometimes used at the village for such sickness.

"But if it is the one sickness, and not the other, it will kill him," she warned.

"Does he have any parents?" she asked.

"No," Winona said, "none of us have any true parents alive. Other care for us."

So, she truly had orphans, the ones who were as displaced and lost as she. She had already lost one of them. And now she might lose another. Her heart ached. She looked at Paul's unseeing eyes and drawn face.

"We have to try something," she whispered desperately. Jason helped make the sweat lodge outside the cave and the others gathered the stones and fuel.

"He can't just lie in there alone," Amanda cried.

"I will go in," Jason offered.

"No, I will go. You are my children, and I will go," she said.

She sat inside the sweat lodge for an eternity and a day. Paul's thin chest heaved and he coughed and spit; she, too, sweated. She stripped off her clothes and sat with the child in the dark, hot steam. He whined and she soothed him with an Indian lullaby. He moaned and she gently held his hand, stroking his forehead. Then the breathing became lighter, and he didn't cough as much, and although he sweated, it was not with the feverish fits that he had had. He fluttered open his eye. She spoke to him and he answered her. Then he was well. She put back on her damp clothes, put her head out and asked for a blanket, and then carried him swiftly into the cave. She let Winona dry him while she dried herself and changed her clothes.

***

It was Christmas. She had no presents for anyone. She told them the story of the Christ child, looking at their trusting, upturned, rapt little faces.

"What would you like for Christmas?" she asked the Cherub.

He thought. "To return to my people for a while."

She was startled. If they were orphans, how could they go to a home they didn't have.

"But you have no parents there," she protested.

"But we have our people," Paul explained. "There is someone there who cares for us. I have a brother of my mother. He keeps the stories of our people. He is teaching me these stories so that they will not be lost."

"We have an old grandfather. We care for him, and he cares for us," said one of the Gemini.

"I, too, have a mother's brother who calls me daughter," Winona murmured.

Each one told of who they had to return to, to tell the tale of their adventures.

"I should return to my old grandmother," Jason said, "to be sure she has enough for the winter." Then he whispered to her, "But I will return soon."

Again she sent meat with them when they left. She felt the still loneliness of the snow and cold when they left. The icicles gleamed like long diamonds from the roof of the hut outside. It was a clear, cold day and she watched until her eyes blurred with the snow and she could see them no more. Then she curled up in the bunny suit with Melinda and cried. Melinda cried a little too, but Amanda cried longer. She would miss the children. And she would miss Jason.

"They will come back, Mommy," Melinda tried to reassure her.

The fodder she had for the cattle was seeing them through, barely. There wasn't a lot left, but if she rationed it to them, she would be able to get them through alive. The snow kept them in water, so she was spared the ordeal of having to carry it to them. The rocks protected them well, and while the cow had ceased to give milk because of the low feeding of rations, at least they were alive. The mare and her colt were managing to survive the same way.

She took the time she now had to sew some needed new clothes for she and her daughter. She showed Melinda how to use the needle, but their hands were cold and it was difficult to sew for any length of time because their fingers would go numb. They couldn't use the lamp too much because she feared they would run out of oil for it. They spent time in front of the cooking fire, sewing and reading until it died down, and then they would take care of the cattle and get their water and return to the cave.

She felt dirty. She had not bathed in weeks. And their clothes badly needed washing. Finally a January thaw came. It felt like spring. She gathered all their clothes in a bundle and took them to the spring. She found a place where the ice was thin and broke through it, and washed the clothes and then she and her daughter took a very cold and very quick splash bath. She dried herself and Melinda very quickly with the blanket and drew on some old clothes. They raced back to the hut and cuddled under the cover of the fur and blankets while the clothes dried slowly in the cave.

With a burst of energy, Amanda cleaned the cave with her makeshift broom, sweeping dust and debris outside. She hung the blankets out in the south wind.

It was well she had taken advantage of the two-day thaw. The winds hit that night with increased intensity. Even her protected fire sometimes flared because of an odd gust of capricious wind.

"Amanda." She listened again. She was sure she had heard someone say her name. "Amanda!" There it was again. Was it the wind? Or had she been alone too long? "Amanda, help me!"

No doubt about it this time. She wrapped her coat around her and braved the wind and snow. Laying face down in the snow was the form of a man. She ran and pulled it up. Jason! He moaned as she lifted him and he passed out in her arms. He was incredibly heavy with his full weight against her and the wind blowing hard against them. She dragged him into the hut and then into the cave. She laid him out on the skins and stripped him of his frozen clothes. Melinda watched, enthralled and worried.

"Mommy, is he okay?"

"I don't know. Get me your robe."

Melinda brought the warm fur. Amanda inspected his body for some sign of injury, but could find no cuts or blood. There were bruises around his ribs, but that was all she could see. She put the robe over him. He was so cold and still. If only she could start a fire in here to warm him.

"Melinda, get under the blankets on the other side of him. We must keep him warm," she said.

The two of them crawled under the piles of blankets and fur next to the young man. Still he did not move. Finally, they both slept too.

Melinda awoke first. "I'm hungry, Mommy."

"So am I. Why don't you see what you can find?"

The child pattered around, went to bank the coals in the hut and brought a twig to light the lamp. She crawled around and she found some dried vegetables and salted fish and brought them to Amanda. Together they quietly ate their cold breakfast, Amanda intently watching Jason.

"Do you love him, Mommy?"

"What a strange question!" Amanda retorted sharply.

The child retreated into herself, bowing her head. She always did that when Amanda was sharp with her for no apparent reason. Amanda cuddled the child close to her.

"I'm sorry, honey," she said. "I didn't mean to get angry.

People do that sometimes when they are worried. Yes, I love him. I love all the children. I don't want them hurt."

"How can you love them and me too?"

"I do love you. You are very special to me, because you are who you are. You care about them too, don't you?"

"I guess so. I just don't want you to go away from me"

"I'm not going away from you. I came out here with you so we could be together and no one can take us away from each other."

"I wonder what happened to him," Melinda mused.

"It seems like he was hurt, but I can't see where."

"You act different to him than you do to the others," Melinda observed.

"Different? How?"

"I don't know. Just different. Maybe because he's biggest."

"Probably. Probably."

They huddled together and kept their vigil. Melinda melted some snow in the bucket for water and Amanda put a small slice of meat over the coals to cook slowly. She fervently wished for some hot tea, coffee, or even milk. Something warm. She was so tired of being cold. Warm tea might help Jason. She was so totally helpless. All she could do was wait for him to get better, or die. The waiting was harder than the working she had to do to survive. As long as she could work to do something, she could believe things would get better. But not knowing, just waiting, waiting, waiting.

They waited two days. Finally he opened his eyes a little and begged her for some water. She lifted his head slightly and gave him some. Then he fell back into his deep sleep. The second time he awoke he said he was hungry, and he ate. The third time he woke fully. While he ate, she found out what had happened.

"My horse tripped. When he went down, I wasn't fast enough and he fell on me. He hit his head or broke his neck when we went down the mountain. He was dead at the bottom. I had to free myself from under him. My inside hurt, but I just kept walking until I got here. I don't remember after that."

"You passed out after you had called out for me. Why did you come back?" she asked. "Will the others come back?"

He shook his head to the last question. "The snow is deep and the winds are cold. They will not come now until the spring swells the streams."

"Then why did you come?"

He licked his lips and gulped more water. Slowly he sat up. "My grandmother died. There is no one else there I must care for."

"So you came here?"

"You didn't want me to come back?"

"No... I mean, yes, I wanted you to come back." She blushed a little. She was admitting her need for him. She didn't want to talk about it, so she changed the subject. "How old are you, Jason?"

"I have seventeen summers," he replied, a little defensively.

"Seventeen! I somehow thought you were older," she sat down beside him, he leaned his head on her breast.

"How old are you?" he asked.

She smiled. They had made love and rescued each other from the clutches of death, but they truly knew very little about each other.

"I'm twenty-two. I feel a hundred."

"Mommy?" Melinda ventured sleepily.

"Come and sit with me, honey," she answered.

"Bring the book and we will read a while. Then we will have to care for the animals."

"Can I stay here with Jason while you go?" she asked.

"I suppose. That might be a good idea," Amanda answered.

Jason smiled at Melinda. "Come, little one. I will teach you a song about a brave she-bear."

So, while her daughter watched over her lover, she tended to the animals, got a bucket of water and what fuel she could find. The days were getting longer and although it was still February, she could feel a quickening in the air. The mountains were shrouded in clouds and the snow still blanketed the ground, but it was not hard and crisp, but mushy and dirty.

He recovered quickly. Within a week, he was helping her with tending the animals. He had an understanding of them, talked to the cow gently in his native language, the strange intonations sounding like some Oriental song. She still could not speak the tongue fluently, but could manage at least a minimum of conversation. When he spoke of his tribe, and the things that were close to him, he would use his native tongue, and she would sometimes have to guess at the words.

Words did not come easily to either one of them. The glib coquette of six years ago had been supplanted with a hardier, silent woman.

A woman who needed a man. Her need for Jason drove her more than her hunger for food. She was glad that Melinda was a deep, sound sleeper. He never demanded from her, never forced her. But tease he did. He could play a rhapsody on her body like a musician on a violin. He refused to carry the water or gather the firewood, averring with a religious ferocity that was "woman's work." She threw the water at him in spite of the freezing temperatures, vowing that he would have it then only when she saw fit to give it to him. He ripped the wet clothes from himself, chased her and caught her, rubbing her face with snow, accusing her of having the temper of the she-bear. They fought angrily at first, then lovingly, Amanda finally pushing him away because Melinda was watching them.

Melinda accepted his presence. She did not love him as she did the Cherub, nor warm to him as she had done the Sheriff. But they showed a mutual respect for each other, and when she went to get the water, Jason would help her. He played chess with her when Amanda was cooking, and when mother and daughter were engaged in teaching and learning or in deep conversation, he never interrupted them. Their food supplies were getting low and all were getting lean on the sparse rations, but none, not even the once chubby Melinda, complained.

"The others will return soon," Jason said one March morning. The spring thaw had already begun, and sometimes it rained instead of snowing.

Amanda's heart skipped a few beats. She wanted her students to return. But with their return, Jason must leave her blanket. She couldn't explain their relationship to the students. She couldn't deal with that yet. She said nothing.

Spring burst on them in the next two days. The flowers peeked through what was left of the snow. The warm rains replaced the snow, and the wind was often from the south. The edible roots were delicate and fresh. She and Melinda set out one morning to gather some roots, and maybe even a few flowers.

Melinda was dancing up and down the deep gully where they were gathering the early wild onions. In spite of its granite walls and seemingly stony floor, the dry bed was covered with small blue flowers and the onions were plentiful.

"Mommy, look at this one!" she laughed, waving a light blue flower in her mother's face.

"Oh, it's just the color of your eyes," Amanda said, squeezing her.

Melinda's hair had grown, and it lay down her back and flew behind her as she ran back up the gully. Amanda had tied the front up in a ragged blue ribbon. Melinda was growing so tall. She would be tall like her mother, not short like her father. She was losing the chubbiness of her babyhood, and she had lost her front baby tooth, which gave an impish look to her when she smiled.

Amanda heard a deep rumble, looked up, just in time to scream at Melinda. But it was too late. The huge wall of water thundered and rolled at them like an angry mountain. It rolled and thundered. Amanda saw the small girl's body swept up and thrown to the top of the crest, barely hearing Melinda's screams before the wall crashed down on her, crushing her as cruelly to the bottom as it had lifted Melinda.

In a wild panic Amanda thrashed in the water, fighting its weight and its power, gripping for anything in the pathway, desperate to reach the top for some air, for her precious daughter, for life. The water beat at her with its thousand cold, mighty hands. Blindly, she gasped at the air, she looked wildly around for Melinda. She saw Melinda nowhere. She released her grip and tried to swim with the current.

As fast as it had arisen, it abated, and she was no longer swimming with a raging current. It became a river, and then a stream. She fell, battered, and bruised, her clothes torn and muddy, against the stony walls of the gully. The flash flood had stripped the façade of dirt and only the stone remained.

Melinda, Melinda. Melinda. Where are you, my Melinda. She staggered drunkenly along the bed, finally climbing above it to see better. She strained to see a sign of her daughter, anywhere – along the water's edge, in the bed, on the top of the ridge. She kept running and stumbling.

"Where is she?" she screamed to the sky.

Then she saw it, a crumpled blue and yellow muddy rag wrapped atop a boulder near the edge of the gully. She slid, tumbled, tripped down the side, cutting her arms and legs on the rocks. Slowly she reached out to it. It was muddy, and bloody, the tiny blonde head askew on the body.

"She can't be comfortable lying like that," Amanda said.

She tried to lay the tiny body down, but the limbs and head flopped around. It was like carrying a rag doll who needed sewing. One of the opals had been gouged out of its socket, and a large gash on the cheek oozed scarlet in contract to the white of the rest of the face. No breath came from the small form. No movement. No laughter at the pretty blue flowers.

Amanda screamed at the sky, holding the small limp body. She thought no rational thoughts, prayed to no God. She screamed the primeval sound of the grieving mother for its murdered young. She beat her fists and head against the stony floor of the gully until they too, began to bleed. She sobbed and screamed and railed at the universe – until she slumped over the dead body of her child, in her unconsciousness as inert as the dead.

When she came to, it was night and it was raining.

"I must get Melinda out of the night air. She will catch cold," she thought.

She picked her way up the side and walked in the cold, soaking rain with the child, singing the lullaby she had learned from her friends. The rain stopped and the moon glowed full and clear, outlining this strange beast stumbling across the prairie.

Jason met them about two miles from the house. He

stopped short when he saw them, and then ran to Amanda, looking down at the child, and then at Amanda. She had stopped her singing to look at him.

"We must get her warm. She'll catch her death of cold from this rain."

He offered to carry the burden, but Amanda smiled and shook her head.

"I've carried her this far, I can go the rest of the way."

Jason watched her and followed a few steps behind, his head hanging. She continued her lullaby until she reached the cave. She set the little body down on the lovely white rabbit's fur, the damp red blood spotting an erratic pattern on its purity.

"Bye, baby bunting, Daddy's gone a hunting, to get a tiny rabbit's skin, to wrap the baby bunting in," she sang over and over and over as she squatted by the fire and began to prepare them something to eat, rocking on her heels and singing.

Jason squatted near the far wall and watched her intently, making no move to stop her. She prepared the dinner and went to her small one to feed her.

"Melinda, honey, you have to wake up and eat now," she coaxed.

But the pale face and blue lips would not move. Her eyes were closed. Amanda frowned. They had been open, at least one had. Why was she closing her eyes? She couldn't remember Melinda ever having refused food. Why wouldn't she eat?

"Very well, if you won't eat, neither will I," Amanda said, putting the food aside and kneeling down beside the form.

The lamp was lit. Melinda always managed to get the lamp lit. She sat by the form and rocked, singing lullabies and nursery rhymes.

***

"We must bury her," Winona said to her gently. Winona? When did she come back? Bury who?

"Little Doe will be buried by her people," Amanda explained.

"No. Melinda. We must free Melinda's spirit," Winona said patiently.

Free Melinda's spirit. But Melinda was always a free spirit. Winona lifted the little body up gently wrapping it in the white fur.

"No, no, no, no," Amanda screamed, grabbing at her. "She has to eat her dinner. Put her down."

Jason pulled her away from Winona. " Do you want to bury her like the missionaries bury their dead, or do you want to free her spirit like the Indian?" Jason asked.

Bury Melinda? Under piles of dirt and rock? But then she couldn't run free. She would get her clothes all dirty. Amanda shook her head.

"Don't put her in the ground," she said.

Jason carried Melinda out, holding her tightly to his chest. Amanda rocked, staring into space, seeing but not seeing the faces of her students watching her. Raphael wasn't there. But he never seemed to be where he was supposed to be.

"Come," Winona finally said, helping Amanda to her feet. They had Melinda lying atop a tall thing. She was lying on the beautiful rabbit skins that Little Doe had bequeathed to her.

They were singing and chanting a song—her students. Why would they be singing? They only did that at night, around the campfire. Jason put his hand in Amanda's. She looked at him, puzzled. What was she to do? He keened a song of death. She watched in a detached stupor at the wind whipping at the white fur and the blonde hair.

Then she knew. Melinda was dead. Falling to the ground

she sobbed, her body convulsing, her face buried in the ground. She looked up as Raphael and Jason took the makeshift ladder from the high bier. She heard the hawk scream and saw the crows circling overhead. The vista before her shimmered in the sun. She saw Melinda step down from the high loft with a blue flower in her hand and then slowly shimmer away. Everything she saw lacked reality. She watched until the sun went down. She stood, numb to the cold and indifferent to those around her. The moon came up and bathed them in its bright cool light, but she stood her vigil. Winona and Jason stood with her.

When the sun came up, Jason scooped up dirt into both hand. As he faced the rising sun, he said many words that Amanda could not make herself understand, except that he spoke of the joy of a child and the freedom of her spirit. The wind took the dirt and scattered it across the prairie with Melinda's spirit.

Amanda staggered back to the cave with the help of her two friends. She sat on her blanket and stared at the cold gray walls.

***

"You shame the memory of your child," Jason barked at her, two weeks later. She looked up at him.

"She is dead," she said flatly.

"She is dead. But while she lived, she loved the land and the people. She worked and laughed and lived," he growled at her.

"Don't I have a right to mourn her? Don't the others feel the loss? You only feel sorry for yourself. You do not even think of her," he yelled.

"How dare you say that? I loved her. I think of nothing else!" She screamed at him.

"You sit in this dark cave while the animals starve, the children do not learn and fear to go home. What do you do? You feel sorry for yourself. Melinda was teaching the littlest one to sing. Will you leave this undone? Or will you finish it for her? She shared her robe with them when it was cold. Will you share with them, too? Or will you rot in this cave and feel sorry for yourself?"

She was furious. How could he be so callous, so cruel? Had he no understanding, no feelings? She threw the bucket at him, which he deftly ducked.

"Melinda would be ashamed to have such a coward for a mother. She had courage!" He spat at her, fanning her fury.

She wasn't content to just throw something at him. She swung her fists at him, which he simply backed away from.

She sank to her knees. She felt so weak. She picked up the cornhusk doll that had been Little Doe's that Melinda played with. Melinda had carried it everywhere she went. Now it would go on no more expeditions. She looked at the blue calico dress she had just made for Melinda. It, too, would not see her life. One by one she gathered the things that were Melinda's, remembering each thing, the things they did together, and the giggles and smiles. She also remembered how her small daughter had been treated at her other home, back East. She had saved Melinda from that, and brought her to a new land—where she couldn't save her. But she had been happy here. Amanda's sigh shook her to the depths of her soul. Her arms were full of Melinda's things. It took awhile to adjust to the bright light of the day, but eventually she saw her students looking at her. She spoke to Winona.

"I wish to give these things to the children of your people. There are many warm clothes and moccasins and boots here. The coat also." She looked at the doll. "This, too, needs a new home."

AMANDA

Winona nodded, and took the things. Jason helped her onto the pony and she rode slowly away. Amanda slowly went to check the cattle. With the heifers and cow all pregnant, the size of the herd would increase this year. Melinda would have more cream. Amanda shook her head. No, Melinda would never again eat the sweet cream of this earth. She would have to get used to that. But it would take time, a lot of time.

When she returned from grazing the cows, the children had disappeared. She looked up when she heard a horse and knew why. The Sheriff was paying another visit. He stood watering his horse by the stream

"Kinney wanted to know if you were still alive," Sheriff MacGregor opened.

"Then why didn't he come himself?" Amanda asked.

"He doesn't ride much. His hip, ya know," he explained.

She waited for him to continue.

"Uh, I'm glad to see you made it through the winter okay," he said uneasily. This was not the same gay young woman he had brought out here a year ago. He was confronted with a different woman, and Amanda could see his uneasiness. She stood with her hands on her hips, not even attempting to brush the dirt from her pants or shirt. She adjusted her hat to shield her eyes from the sun.

"Where's your little girl?" he asked.

"She's dead," Amanda stated, the words reverberating in her head.

"Dead! How?" the Sheriff asked.

"We got caught in a flash flood. She was killed."

He swallowed hard. "I'm, I'm sorry," he whispered. He turned his back to her and stood still for a very long time. Finally he turned back to her, his face ashen, and asked, "Where did you bury her?"

Amanda pointed to the high hill and then swept her hand in a circle, indicating the vast prairie they were standing on.

MacGregor frowned. "You buried her Injun style?" He was incredulous.

Amanda nodded. Again he turned his back to her, looking out, over the land. "She sure was a pretty little thing. Awful brave for her age," he finally whispered.

Amanda's eyes began to fill with tears. She didn't want to talk about Melinda yet. It still hurt too much. The acceptance of that reality would be long in coming. She wanted to change the direction of the conversation.

"Since you are Kinney's messenger, perhaps he would be so kind as to send my money with you," she stated.

He turned to her sharply. "I am not his messenger. I was worried that you might not have made it through the winter."

"Not concerned enough to visit me, though."

"Your Indian friends seemed to be doing the job of helping you quite well," he snapped.

"How would you know?"

"I did come by. But you seemed content with them. I left you alone."

"Well," she said, "You've fulfilled your duty. Now you can leave."

"I'll rest my horse a minute, if you don't mind."

They both watched the horse finish its drink. He tied it to one of the cottonwood saplings and sat down on a rock by the stream. The sound of the gurgling water disturbed Amanda. It reminded her of the flood. And she started hurting again.

"They might not have a school here soon, ya know," MacGregor said.

"What do you mean?"

"The government wants to try a new plan to civilize these

Injuns. Instead of giving the land to the whole tribe, they decided to give each family so much land to raise crops on."

Amanda remembered Raphael and Jason's aversion to working with the soil. They would starve if they had only to be farmers.

"But they are not farmers," she protested.

"Not ranchers, either from the way I've seen them handle their cattle."

"But the reservation is so large. And the tribe had always worked as a group."

"Yea, well, maybe if they break up the tribe, they'll learn to live right."

"How big are the farms?"

"About 160 acres."

Amanda did some quick calculations in her head. Knowing about the size of the tribe, and remembering how large the agent had said the reservation was, she knew that would leave thousands of acres free.

"What will happen with the rest of the land?"

"They'll auction it off to settlers," he told her.

"And what part of the reservation will the Indians have?"

"The east part."

"But that is just like a desert!"

Just as she thought. That part had very little grazing land and little rain. All it had was sagebrush and wind. Since the buffalo were gone, even the hunting was very poor there. And if they left, the school would close down, and if the school were closed down, she would have no home. She would have to leave this place, this place where Melinda was, where she had been buried, and where her spirit had been set free to roam. No, she would not leave this place.

"Will the settlers have to buy the land?"

"Well, actually, I think they are selling it to the highest bidder in an auction."

"An auction? When? Where?"

"About a month from now. June fifteenth, or so, I think. At the post office, in Harlan, since that's the only federal place around for a spell except the Fort," he told her.

Her mind reeled. She couldn't leave here. This was her home. It was the only true home she knew and she had to keep it, or die trying. No more running, she had promised Melinda. She would not break her promise. She was angry, and frustrated. How? How to get the land?

The first thing she needed was money, and lots of it. Where to get it? She could not borrow from anyone. She would be getting her pay soon, but that would certainly not buy much, and if she knew the land-grabbers, just as the carpetbaggers back east, they would have the money. She couldn't earn enough in time and she had nowhere to borrow it. That left only one alternative.

"Is there a bank in Harlan?" she asked off-handedly.

"Yes. Why?"

"Oh, uh, I have an inheritance. I have kept it with me, but I think perhaps it would be better off in a bank. I will have to consider going there one of these days. Perhaps when they have the auction," she said as she smiled.

He released his horse and swung into the saddle, tipped his hat, and rode off. She barely noticed. She had one month to save this place. She couldn't change the government's ideas about the Indians. She didn't have the time, money or power. But if she could buy part of it, they would have their hunting rights on her land. And most importantly, she would preserve the freedom of Melinda's spirit. She could not give up their home.

She had to find out about the auction, and the money in the bank. She also had to see the details of the bank building. She would go to the reservation agent and then to the town. First, she would have to get her clothes in shape. They were probably out of style, but they had to look "civilized". She could not reveal her true self to them, to put them on guard. Her tan from last year had faded, and she would have to make sure it stayed that way. She looked at her hands. She would have to get them in better shape so it would not seem that she worked so hard. Perhaps, she would make some gloves.

She enlisted Winona's aid in the repair of the clothes. She badgered Raphael and the Cherub into caring for the cattle, and Jason into caring for her horses. The Gemini did the cooking, and Ruth and Naomi kept the caves and huts clean. They were convinced she was still crazy from the loss of Melinda. Perhaps they were right. But if she were going to go crazy, she would do it where she was at home, not at the mercy of some kind relative.

***

A few days later, she set off for the agent's.

He was standing on the porch with Jacobin. He smiled broadly at her when she came up, extending his hand. She extended her own small, white hand. "Well, Mr. Kinney, I do hope you had a warm winter," she smiled.

"I'm so glad to see you survived our weather. It does get nasty out here," he said. "I suppose you've heard about poor Mr. Graves. Disappeared last fall and never has been found."

"Oh, I'm so sorry to hear that," she said.

"I see you left your little one with the Injuns again," he observed.

She said nothing. She had no need to let this ugly man into her very private grief.

"I would like the money due me from the government," she said.

"Oh, do stop for some coffee. It isn't often I have the company of a beautiful woman," Kinney smiled and Jacobin smirked.

"Oh, very well," she agreed. She had much information she had to get from this man, without his understanding why she needed it. He seemed to get loquacious whenever he drank his coffee. Probably, Amanda suspected, because it was made more with whiskey than coffee.

A young Indian girl brought the coffee, keeping her head down. Amanda did not recognize her, except that she knew her to be very young, twelve or thirteen at the most. Damm him!

Fortunately, Kinney began opening up and so did Jacobin. Amanda proved an appreciative audience. The auction was to be held June fifteenth. Interestingly enough, payment was to be made immediately, with cash to be kept in the local bank. This was in order to make the transaction final at that time, without any delay for proof of credit, or identification. The quicker to move the Indians, Jacobin observed. Kinney had mentioned that he would still be the agent, but would have to move his quarters further east. He regretted this only in that he would have to build a new house. He already had the plans made and was putting in the foundation. Of course, the government would pay for the inconvenience.

"Do they have a good solid bank in Harlan?" she asked innocently.

"Yep, one of the best," he said. "Good and safe. Why?" he asked.

"Oh, well, you see, I have an inheritance I really should keep in a safer place than I have it now."

"Then why are you so anxious to get your money from the government if you have money of your own?"

AMANDA

"One must be prudent about spending their inheritance, Mr. Kinney," Amanda explained. "Once it is gone, it can never be regained.

He smiled. "Speaking of it," he said. He went to his cash box and brought her three drafts from the government. Now they were six months behind in their payments. But there was the letter there stating that as of June fifteenth, her services would no longer be needed, and unfortunately, since they had no more openings at this time for reservation teachers, her employment would be terminated.

Amanda looked at the letter in Kinney's presence, but made no comment, in spite of his intense, curious stare. She merely shook hands with him, and slowly, with the mincing sway she used to use walking across the ballroom floor, walked up the hill. Once out of his sight, she lifted her skirts up, raced to her pony, flung herself on it, and raced to Harlan. Jason again accompanied her as far as he dared.

She deposited two of her checks in the bank and cashed the third. She took in every detail. She talked casually with the teller and with the owner. Their curiosity about the Southern lady who had come to teach the Indians kept them talking until she satisfied herself with information about the auction procedures. They had immense pride in the role the bank was playing in it. It seemed there would most likely be three large businessmen from the East who would bid on the land. They planned on putting their money in the bank the night before, in order for it to be more difficult for any robbers. The Sheriff and some soldiers from the fort were to guard it all night, with the auction taking place at eight the next morning.

Amanda went to the general store. She purchased what she needed. Jennifer Graves did not speak to her, just quietly filled her order. Amanda felt guilty when she spoke to the woman; she was so gray and so quiet.

"I, uh, understand your husband, uh, has disappeared. I'm sorry to hear it," she had to say that much.

"Thank you for your sympathy, Mrs. White," the gray lady said.

"It must be very difficult, being so alone," Amanda added.

"We're alone most of our lives, I think," Mrs. Graves added.

She handed Amanda her strange order. "Sorry to hear you'll be leaving these parts," Mrs. Graves said.

Amanda nodded. The two women looked briefly at each other, each carrying her sorrows inside her. Amanda grabbed the packages and left.

Again, Jason was waiting beside the road. They took off down the road, not saying anything. When they reached the edge of the reservation, they slowed to a walk to rest their horses. They came to the stream, and Jason dismounted to let his horse rest and drink. He lifted Amanda from her horse, but didn't release her when he set her down. He kissed her hard, holding her tightly. She tore away from him.

"Why do you push me away?" he asked angrily.

"After what has happened, I am supposed to be eager for such pleasure?" she snapped.

He hung his head, and kicked at the dust with his bare foot. "I need you, Amanda," he whispered, admitting the thing which she was afraid to admit to herself. "I need you," he repeated. They were silent.

"You know the tribe has to move," she whispered.

He nodded.

"I will have to go with them," he stated.

"And they want me to leave, too," she whispered. She turned quickly to him, burying her face in his chest. He kissed the top of her head and his hair entangled with hers, tickling her shoulders under her shirt. Her skin tingled. She stood very still, while his hands caressed her. He lifted her chin so she had to look at him. "Will you push me away again?"

"No," she whispered, kissing his lips lightly. He released her, tied the horses, and led her to a shady patch of grass. They made love, slowly, sadly, sweetly, the sorrow mixed with the joy.

It was night when they returned to the house. When Jason started to the school, she took his hand and led him into her house. They lay with each other, each thinking their own thoughts, and sharing their fears.

She sent the others back to the tribe a week before June fifteenth, reluctantly releasing them, fearing that she would never see them again. It was a painful parting, with no one allowing themselves the luxury of tears. Jason stayed with her. She didn't tell him of her plans. She only asked that he stay with her as long as he could. It was what they both wanted. She told him on June fifteenth she would go to the auction, and that she would leave the night before. He protested, but she quieted him, telling him she had to do it, had to know what was going on. He assented, knowing he had no way to argue with her anymore. She knew that he, too, would soon have to do certain things.

She had had one advantage when she was at the bank. In order to get her cash, and deposit the drafts, the owner had been forced to open the safe. In his pride in his modern establishment, he had shown Amanda the safe, and she watched intently as he opened the safe. She had used her facile memory to fix the combination firmly in her mind. And now her years of spending time in her father's laboratory would pay off.

She carried her "civilized" clothes wrapped neatly

together. She wore her work clothes. It was night. Jason had followed her as far as the edge of the reservation. Amanda made sure he promised to stay there with the horses until she returned. It was not an easy promise to elicit, but she had to get it, knowing he would not break it if he made it. She crept toward the town, watching it from atop the hill as though she were stalking a deer. The town was afire with celebrations and excitement, except for the bank, which was set off from the rest of the town and was dark. Two soldiers paced up and down in the front and back of the bank, meeting twice, once on each side, to affirm each other's existence. At the other end of the town, the firecrackers, whooping, and hollering were deafening. The bar was filled to overflowing, and Miss Mae's local house was busy as a beehive.

Amanda unwrapped the chemicals. The gas would not kill. But it produced the false sleep that surgeons and dentists found a boon to their profession. She counted the paces and the timing of the soldiers as she inched closer, always in the shadow, grateful for her dark hair. She pulled the collar up on her coat. The soldiers met, and she slid under the boardwalk.

She opened the chemicals and let their vapor seep through the cracks in the not-so-solid floor of the bank as she held her face away and buried in her sleeve. She counted the minutes. Long ago for her little dog, it had taken three minutes; for these big men, it would take longer. She heard them gently thud to the floor. When the soldiers held their brief meeting at the side, oblivious to the drama in the building, she quickly pulled up the window and climbed inside, crouching low, her hand on her knife.

The Sheriff and his two soldier assistants were passed out on the floor. The cloth over Amanda's face would protect her only so long. Grabbing the lamp, she quickly worked the combination on the safe. She was so intent on her purpose she didn't have the time or the thought to be afraid. She shoveled the money into her bag, and closed the door of the safe. She didn't know how much she had, nor did she much care. She had what the other buyers would not have. She waited until the soldiers met at their blind spot, vaulted out the window, shut it, and dived beneath the boardwalk. She waited breathlessly, watching the feet of the soldier as he passed close to her. When he met the other one, she raced to the shadows, and crept as silently away as she had come, taking the care Jason had taught her to avoid the loose rocks. Her heart beat wildly.

Breathlessly, she reached the cache where she had left her other clothes. She changed quickly, buried the work clothes in the rocky cache, and smashed the big glass jars of chemicals and worked the broken glass into the soil. Then she counted the money, setting it neatly into the satchel. It was close to fifty thousand dollars. She wasn't impressed by the amount, only with the fact that she might be able to save her home this way. She had no compunction about the robbery. It was her only present method of survival. And she would survive.

The wind blew hard and she huddled against the rocks for protection. A small cry in the night startled her out of her half-sleep. Melinda used to cry in the night like that, when they first came her. But eventually Melinda had slept deep and untroubled. Amanda sighed shakily. She would not let some strange person buy the land, her land, and disturb the spirit of her daughter. No one was going to take away what was hers ever again, she vowed bitterly. Where was the right of Aaron to steal what was hers, to abuse both her and her little one? She hated him. Kinney, she merely despised, for his greed and cowardice. He didn't even admit to what he was. She detested them all. But she now had the one thing that all of them seemed to understand – money. She knew she had the upper hand this time. She had them checkmated.

The sun burst on her with incredible brilliance. The spring morning was gay and bright. She brushed the dust off her skirt, and bathed her face and hands in the stream and gulped some water. She had brought dried fish and vegetables with her, which she ate quickly. It might prove to be a long day, one in which she should be prepared for anything. She squared her shoulders, lifted the heavy satchel, and walked swiftly to the town, rehearsing her lines to the melodrama which she had written in her mind a hundred times in the last few weeks. With some luck and care, the other actors would understand their cues, even though this would be the first and only time they would play in this drama.

Captain Greenwood greeted her first, even tipping his hat in spite of his rush to the confusion surrounding the bank. Amanda let herself be drawn with the crowd to the bank, where Captain Greenwood, and several other men, and Sheriff MacGregor were all talking, gesturing at once. A very fat, very proper-looking man stood in the midst of them with his hands folded and occasionally would shake his head, which would send one of the strange men into paroxysms of angry gesticulating. Amanda gripped the satchel tightly to her chest and inched her way to the edge of the crowd to hear the conversation.

"I'm sorry, gentlemen," the portly one orated, "but the government order says I am to auction this land at precisely eight a.m. That is five minutes from now. It also says that I must see the cash in hand, that I am not to accept merchandise, stocks, bonds, drafts, or any such sundry items in place of cash. I cannot be responsible for the security of your cash. Once it is transferred to me, I will have the whole United States cavalry to help me get it to the federal bank in Denver."

AMANDA

"But, my God, man!" one of the strangers exploded. "How are we to get money? We had the plans all drawn up. It was all settled!"

"This is a public auction. Nothing has been settled," the government man said, "Now, if you'll excuse me, this is to be done properly, in the democratic way of this great country."

Amanda smiled to herself. Act one was complete. She had counted on the dictatorship of the bureaucrats to start her drama. She caught a glimpse of Sheriff MacGregor's face – perplexed and down cast having failed at his duty. Her passing curiosity about his qualifications was dismissed as the portly man mounted the podium erected beside the post office.

He read from a long, pompous document, stating why the land had been suddenly made available, because of the wisdom of the President and Congress in civilizing their Indian brothers. He explained that the plots would be sold in five hundred acre blocks, that cash was needed for the purchase, and that all sales were final.

Amanda discovered Sheriff MacGregor standing at her side. Her stomach knotted and she hoped her fear and anticipation did not show in her face. All her practice at coquetry would serve her now. She tried to look the curious innocent.

"Do you think land is a sound investment, Sheriff?" she asked him sweetly.

"A very sound and profitable investment, if I may say so, ma'am," Captain Greenwood interjected.

"Then I would be wise in putting my inheritance in something like land?" she asked.

Greenwood nodded solemnly.

"Especially if it is a large inheritance?" she ventured, hoping she wasn't overacting in her self-written drama.

"Do you have such an inheritance?" The red-haired woman standing by the Captain, inquired sweetly.

"Mrs. White, my wife, Mrs. Greenwood. Liza, this is Mrs. White, the Indian's schoolteacher," he introduced them.

"Oh, yes, I've heard so much about you. When that little Indian boy came rushing to the fort last year in the dead of night, I thought for certain the whole tribe had risen up against you."

Amanda smiled her acknowledgment of the woman, but her attention had returned to the auction block. She saw the huge map, marked with many little red dots. After some concentration, she managed to figure out which parts were where. She recognized the section marked where the schoolhouse and her home were, and where the hot springs were. The man took a long drink of water after his speech, while the crowd cheered. Then he raised his hand for silence. Captain Greenwood and the Sheriff excused themselves saying they had business to attend to, which left the two women standing together. Mrs. Greenwood began chattering about all the excitement, but when she realized Amanda wasn't paying any attention, she stopped talking.

They began the auction in the upper quadrant of the old reservation. The bidding was low, since it was known that the country there was very mountainous and did not lend itself well to raising cattle, or crops. But it would lead into the land she wanted. She calculated her money, and because she knew it would go low, she bid.

Everyone registered a mild shock that she would have such effrontery, as she was part of the Indian settlement, and therefore, really had no right in town business. But, it was, after all, a free country, so they didn't interfere.

Block by block, acre and acres, Amanda bought,

calculating how much of the money she had left after each sale. She saw her name being sprawled on section after section. This strange turn of events obviously disturbed many of the town's leading businessmen. They had counted on many new people and industry moving into the country. If all of it went to this small woman, the territory should be in serious trouble. But they had the same problem as the men from back east. They had entrusted their money to the bank.

When it was all over, Amanda had the bulk of the land, including the precious site at the school, and those lands abutting the new boundaries of the new reservation. There were many mutters and grumbles. But she had anticipated that. She heard someone even go so far as to suggest that she and her Indian friends probably robbed the bank. The good Sheriff took umbrage at the remark, and a nasty scene could have ensued, but Amanda sympathized with the poor man's frustrations at losing all his savings, and suggested the government man count her money, all of it, not only that which was due him for the sale of the lands, in order to affirm that the amounts were different. And besides, "her poor little head had so much trouble with figures, she wasn't even sure of how much she had bought."

"You have just bought, little lady, some of the finest cattle-grazing land in the whole Wyoming territory," one of the gentlemen in black boomed at her. "J.D. Thomas is the name, ma'am. My card. If you should decide to invest in cattle for your land, I can get you some of the best in the world."

"Why, thank you. I will remember you," she smiled.

She was sure she had enough left to invest in a decent-sized herd. The addition of Graves' money and her own small paychecks made the amount in her bag even more than what had been in the bank. There were oohs and aahs, and suddenly the strange, Indian-loving schoolteacher with the dusty clothes, was somebody in the town. Several of the women, who, the first time she had come to town, had managed to avoid talking to her, now extended cordial invitations to their homes. She smiled politely and turned them down. However, when Sheriff MacGregor offered her dinner at the local establishment, she accepted, noticing the wags of heads behind their backs.

"Sheriff MacGregor," she started, stabbing her steak with the fork.

"It's Andrew, remember?" he said.

"Andrew, I need some advice. Evidently, the bank is not too secure a place to keep money." He blushed when she said this and hung his head.

"Oh, I'm sorry, I didn't mean it as a reflection on you. After all, there were many men guarding the place. They must have been very clever people, the robbers," she said.

"I should've been more on my guard. I figured there would be some kind of ruckus. It was all done so quiet like. What was it you wanted to ask?" he asked, pushing his food around his plate.

"What do you think I should do with the rest of my money? I have no idea of how to run a ranch, or buy cattle, or horses, or any of those things. Do you know anything about it?"

"I used to work on a ranch when I was young. The man that raised me had a ranch," he replied and then drained his coffee cup in one long gulp.

"Could I ask you for some advice, then?"

"Sure. First thing I'd do with that money, is do just what you started to do, and invest it in something like land. It isn't as easy to steal land and cattle as it is just plain money."

"I see your logic," she commented. "Is this Mr. Thomas a reliable cattle dealer?"

"Seems to be, from reports," Andrew assured her.

"Would I have to give him some money to get me those cattle?"

"I suppose he would have to have some kind of advance in money, to sort of show your good faith, if you know what I mean," he said.

"Well then I would have to have a place to put the cattle, and some place to live. It is all so complicated," she sighed, shaking her head in confusion.

He looked bemused. "I wouldn't say it's any worse than living on the prairie by yourself."

She looked at him sharply, wondering if he were being sarcastic. No, he wasn't capable of such remarks. She toyed a little with her coffee cup, feeling positively stuffed full of the steak, potatoes, and rolls that had been served. Now, they were bringing in berry pie and she wasn't sure she could eat it. But she wanted to get the Sheriff to volunteer his help without having to directly ask him. If she asked directly, she would be in his debt, not a circumstance she wanted, if she could help it. He fell for the bait.

"I might be able to help you get started. You'd be wise in finding yourself a good foreman though. One you could trust," he declared, cutting off a huge bite of pie and swallowing it almost without chewing.

"Could you recommend anyone?"

He pondered for a moment. "Not off-hand. Know some good ones, but they already have a good place and not likely to leave it. I'll think on it, though."

He accompanied her when she talked with Mr. Thomas. She had decided to start with about fifty head of good stock, hoping to build her herd the first couple of years.

"Yup, be going down to Omaha anyways, to look over the

stock. Seems the government is going to give some more bulls and cows to the Indians. Dumb bastards will probably butcher them all the first couple of months anyway."

"Mr. Thomas, perhaps it would be wise if you chose some of the best you can find," she suggested.

"Why do something stupid like that?" he wanted to know.

"Well, seeing as this is a new experiment for the government, they may be watching closely to see how it works. If word got back that you gave them inferior stock, you might lose your government franchise as the Indian's cattle agent," she reasoned.

"Hum, never thought of it that way," he said.

"It also might be wise to help Mr. Kinney distribute the animals. The poor man doesn't seem to know much about cattle, and I'm sure he doesn't want this experiment to fail and the blame be dropped on his head," she offered generously.

J.D. Thomas eyed her cautiously. She left him wondering how much she actually knew of the whole cattle business in the territory and how far her newly-bought influence would go.

She still had several hundred dollars in her satchel. The Sheriff was loath to leave her side, but she insisted on going back to the schoolhouse.

"My duty there is not yet fully discharged, Andrew. I will fulfill my commitment."

He walked with her a ways out of town. She circled back when he left her to retrieve her hidden clothes. Then she ran hurriedly to where Jason awaited her.

"What happened?" he asked.

Breathlessly, she told him of her daring deed. As she told her story, his eyes widened, and he stood up.

"I thought you were a friend of the Sheriff's," he said.

"I'm not sure 'friends' is what you would call us," she defended.

"You tricked him and you bought our land?" Jason was puzzled, trying to put the whole thing in perspective in his mind.

"It wasn't yours anymore," she reasoned.

"One person does not own such land," he growled at her.

"Well, if I didn't, many others would have."

"No one can own the land, not like one owns a blanket, or even a horse. It belongs to everyone to use. I do not understand the white man's thinking that he can own his mother."

"His mother!"

"The land, the land, the land, the land," he said, standing and stretching his arms first to north, then east, south and west. "You are no different than any of the others, then, are you?"

"Jason, if I didn't buy the land, then all those strangers would own it," she protested, not understanding why he was so angry.

"I have been generously allowed one hundred and sixty acres of my people's land, on which I am to become like a white man. I have been given no choice. They tell me I should do this."

She tried to interrupt him, which only made him wave her aside, and become angrier.

"It is not enough they do not want us to dance our dances, or sing our songs. It is not enough that they no longer let our men be warriors, and that they destroy and rape our women. It is no longer enough that they bring diseases that kill our children and make others blind. Now they must destroy the tribe itself, scatter us to the wind like the ashes of the dead."

Her heart thumped loudly in her chest. She had never

seen him so angry, nor so majestic. He stood, staring into the sinking sun, his legs apart, giving the appearance of a colossus straddling the universe.

"And now, you, you show that you are one of them. We can share a bed and eat the same food, but can we ever know each other? I thought you would come with me, to be my wife, and live with me in the ways of my people."

She was startled. It had never actually occurred to her that Jason would consider any sort of marriage. She would not, she could not, submit herself to him as such, become "his" and "part of his people." She loved him, and she loved her Indian friends, but she did not understand many things, and she was sure she could not believe in all that they believed, or live as they lived.

"I could never marry you, nor be an Indian wife," she told him softly.

"I don't understand!" he ranted. "Then why did you let me under your blanket. Why have you been with me all this time? Why?"

"Because I love you," she said simply, trying to explain the whole complex gamut of her emotions in that simple statement.

"Love me!" he exclaimed, "How can you love me and not want to come with me?" It was his turn to be perplexed.

"I cannot. I just cannot."

"Then it is better we say good-bye forever," he growled.

The statement fell like a thunderbolt between them. They had felt it the last night they had spent together. Now they knew it. He didn't kiss her, didn't touch her. She watched him swing his strong, lithe body onto his horse, look intently at her for a brief moment, and then ride slowly into the flaming red sun. She didn't cry out to him—her stinging, dry throat, and hot, tearless eyes the only response to his silent farewell.

CHAPTER FIVE

She rode the entire night, aided by an almost full moon. It was near the time that her blood should flow, and her back hurt terribly from sitting on the horse. She tried walking, but that only made the pain worse. She arrived at the cave before dawn and released the horse. She then found a safe, hidden cache for the satchel and its precious cargo of paper in one of the deep, small canyons where the cattle had stayed. It was dawn, but she did not want to go into the cave. Instead, she took the roll of clothing, and the blanket from the horse, and curled up outside the hut, the warmth of the spring sun lulling her to sleep.

She awoke to the cool evening breeze blowing across her. The sun was the same red flame it had been last night at Jason's departure. She pulled her knees up to her chin, and watched it go down. Abruptly it was dark. She knew she had better make a fire, and get something to eat. She turned to enter the hut and the cave. It would be pitch dark in there. The coals for starting the fire would glow slightly in the corner, but otherwise it was dark in the hovel and darker in the cave. She could not enter. Melinda would not be there to light the lamp for her.

Her whole body, stiff as an icicle, would not do what her mind told it to do. Enter the protection of the cave. The wolves, the cold night air, the sudden change in weather. It could all kill her in one night. There was no one, seen or unseen, here to rescue her. Jason was gone. Melinda was gone. She must enter the cave. She couldn't. She feared – something. Something. Some nameless something. She turned quickly, pressing her back to the outside wall of the hut, and stared out into the darkness.

The moon was not as full as it had been the night before, but it still cast its unearthly light, creating a collage of shadows and light, blues and grays and yellows. An owl hooted somewhere in the distance and the coyotes answered him with their mournful refrain. Creatures of the night peered from shadows and rocks. No friendly flame warmed her. She started to cry out for Jason, but his name stuck in her throat. He is not here, he is not here, she chanted the litany, to remind herself, to get herself to act.

Sounds amplified by the stillness of the night drifted to her ears. She heard the rustling of the bush as some unknown creature sought to hide itself from some more savage animal of the night. She heard the rippling, gurgling of the stream, and it slowly got louder and louder in her ears, until it reached the deafening roar of the thunderous flood. She could see Melinda, in her beautiful blue dress, her yellow hair floating across the gray sea of the prairie. She tried to call her, but the name stuck in her throat.

Twice before she had been on the brink of madness. Twice before she had come back. But the other two times, there had been someone to help her come back. This time there was no small smiling face or gentle caress. Just the cold night wind, and the dream of the little blond and blue form floating across the prairie. She reached for it. It evaporated, only to reappear again further away. Sagebrush twisted in the dark, and turned itself into all the demons of her past. The split skull of Graves grinned at her from the distance, dancing over the blue and blond ghost. She screamed.

The scream banished the other creatures. Now she only had her internal hell to deal with. She wrapped the blanket around herself, and huddled by the door of the hut. The cold sweat drenched her hair and plastered it to her face and neck. She breathed heavily, as though she had just run a long race with Raphael.

The thought of Raphael helped bring her to reality. She did not know whether what she had done was right or wrong, but it was done. She was not sure of many, many things. But she was sure that she had to live in this country, on this land, near to these people. They were not her people, but in a deeper sense, they were more her people than those which she had left back east. She had no true people of her own.

She would have to find some place to live. She could not live in the cave. Perhaps in the next light of day, she could force herself to enter the cave, and right the things that were there. But not now.

When the sun arrived, she had made her decision. She recovered her satchel from its cache. The agent's old post would now be on her land. She was sure that Kinney had already moved to his new quarters. The tribe had been shifted two days ago, Kinney busily making sure of the allotted lands. Yes, she would take up temporary residence at the old post. It already had corrals for her animals. She would not enter the cave, not until she could chase away the memories, or at the fears that now accompanied them.

She herded her cattle on ahead of her, the herd now consisting of seven. She saw that Kinney was still at the post, but apparently, it was only a visit. He would, in any case, prove no problem. While he was greedy and irritating, he was neither farsighted nor tough. She herded her cattle into the corrals, and left the horse tied to the post. She was still in her dusty dress.

She decided it would be more prudent if she did not have the satchel with her. She hid it under the stairs.

Kinney was poring over a map, standing at the counter. He frowned as she entered. Clearing his throat, he stood up straight. She sensed instantly that their whole relationship had changed. He was no longer the big boss. He had no power, regardless how petty, over her. She owned an immense amount of land. Now she was someone to be reckoned with.

"Good morning, Mr. Kinney. I thought you would be residing in your new establishment by now. You know, this building now stands on my property," she began.

"Oh, yes, quite. I was just getting my maps that show the assignments of the allotments," he stuttered, and bowed a little to her.

She looked briefly at the map and knew it would never work. The concept of the plot was bad enough, and it was even doubly worse that they had tried to eliminate the influence of the tribe, but, making the whole thing a ridiculous charade, was the fact that the map made no reference to the families. Every man, woman, and child of the tribe had been given an allotment. The children's lots were not next to the parent's lots. The wives and husbands had lots miles from each other, interspersed with three or four lots of absolutely unrelated people. It was a mess. Amanda envisioned all the pains Kinney would have in dealing with such problems, and felt a twinge of pity for the man. But only briefly. She wanted him out of her sight. And she wanted the house. She had to get her life started again, and his presence was hindering her.

Then they both heard the scraping noise in the back room. They looked at each other.

"You have someone with you, Mr. Kinney?"

"I was about to ask you that self-same question, Mrs. White," he answered. "Should we see what it is?"

Together they walked to the back of the house. Crouched in a corner, bleeding from numerous cuts and scratches, was a ragged, dirty Indian child.

"Aha, caught you, you little bastard! What are you doing here?" Kinney barked as he jerked with child to his feet. With all the dirt and blood, it was difficult to tell his identity, but Amanda recognized the beautiful eyes.

"Poor little thing. He's been hurt. Why don't you leave him in my care, Mr. Kinney?" she suggested, not indicating in any way that she knew the identity of the child.

"Have to get written permission," he muttered. "Regulations, whenever any of them leave the reservation."

"Oh, but you could just write it down."

Kinney grunted, tore a small corner of the map off and wrote down the permission, signed it and handed it to Amanda. Officiously, he rolled up his map, tipped his hat as he put it on, and strolled out of the house.

Instantly, Amanda whirled around to Raphael.

"Are you hurt?" she asked anxiously.

"Naw," he replied, his eyes wide as saucers, the whites even more intense against the darkness of his black, thick lashes.

"What's wrong?" Amanda demanded. This was not the way the usually loquacious Raphael acted.

He inhaled deeply, and then slowly let it out, studiously picking the dried blood on his arm. Then he looked squarely at her, cocked his head to one side. "They jumped," he said,

"Who? Jumped what?" she asked. He annoyed her with his obscure answer and her own thickheadedness.

"My uncle. And some of the others. They were mad at the whole deal and decided they wouldn't take it anymore. They said they were born to be warriors, and that is the way they would die," he said. "They said I was too young, and they wouldn't take me with them," he added bitterly.

Amanda scarcely breathed. "Who else, besides your uncle?"

"Spotted Owl, the one who gave you the horse. Some others. Moksois was allowed to go with them," he was even more bitter saying this.

Jason. She should have known he would go. She should have known. Once news of this was out, the whole army would be on the march to capture these renegades. For those who jumped the reservation, no mercy was ever shown, even if they did not go looting, raping and murdering. Jason had gone, to earn his name as a warrior, no longer to be called "Pot-belly" but to remembered as "Terrible Eagle."

He eyes misted and she heard and saw nothing. She was riding in the wind with Jason, running, running. She knew the desperation of his flight. She had done it once. Only her flight had been by train and stagecoach, to fly somewhere. He had nowhere to go.

She looked at Raphael through her tears. "Will you stay with me awhile?" she asked him.

"I have no one else," he shrugged.

"Neither do I, Raphael, neither do I."

"What is this name you have given me?" he asked. She laughed a little. It felt good. So concerned, were these people, about what name one had. But their superstitions gave great power to a word, so she understood.

"Raphael is the name of an angel," she said.

"Shit," he said as he spat on the floor, "I'd rather be a hunter."

She laughed.

"Let's take care of these wounds and find something to eat. Then I'd like you to watch my cattle for me. I have something very important to do."

They managed to scrounge a few roots and berries. Kinney had left two cans of beans, which they downed in a short time. Raphael's wounds were actually many superficial scrapes he had gotten while trying to escape through the bushes and rocks. He had done all right until he had to jump a ravine and misjudged and plunged to the bottom. He was totally disgusted with himself for allowing such a thing to happen.

She left him with the cattle, nursing his wounds and his pride, and galloped back to the cave. There was no time to let her fears and ghost stop her. She ran first the school and then her home. The rifle. She had left the rifle in his care. They had not taken it with them when they went to Harlan because there was too much danger of being caught with it, and that would have destroyed everything. It was not in the school. She lit the lamp in her cave. She looked under the scraps of clothing, the bits of food, and the books. But there was no rifle, and no bullets. He had taken it. She was relieved, somehow. He was not defenseless. If he had to go as a warrior, he at least went as a prepared one. Her immediate urgent task done, she looked around the cave. There was nothing of worth to save here, except her books. She would not be able to carry them all at once. She would take a few now, and return with Raphael to get the rest later.

She picked up five or six books and left the cave, and returned to Raphael. They would have to get some food, and begin the long task of building again.

The next trip to Harlan netted some very different experiences from her last visit. No children dogged her heels and called her squaw. The storekeepers and people smiled, men tipped their hats, and ladies nodded. She acknowledged them all, singled out no one. Sheriff MacGregor was with Captain Greenwood, tracking the renegades, who had given the little town even more excitement. She ignored the speculations and rumors about what had happened. If she got any news, she would have to believe only that which Captain Greenwood himself told her.

She went to Mrs. Graves' general store. The gray lady sat behind the counter, as stoic as she had been on their first meeting. Amanda pitied her. Her husband had been a louse, but he had been someone who occasionally broke up the loneliness of this life. This time Amanda had indulged in the luxury of a wagon and horses. Jacobin had tried to charge her an outrageous sum for broken nags, but when he learned she was not completely ignorant of horses, he changed his mind and began to drive a hard but fair bargain. She loaded the wagon with supplies and clothes, tossing in a few for Raphael.

"Your little girl wear those things?" Mrs. Graves finally broke her silence.

Amanda fingered the cloth. "No, they are for an Indian orphan I know who needs some clothes," she explained. Then for some reason, she wanted to share her sorrow with the gray lady in some way. "My Melinda drowned in a flash flood this spring."

Mrs. Graves looked away quickly "I'm sorry," was all she said. Amanda paid her bill and stuffed Raphael's' new clothes in one of the boxes. It had been a very long time since she had driven a team of horses. And this was not a one-horse buggy, but a wagon drawn by two draft horses. But the feel for them came back to her. It was a good feeling.

***

Raphael, ambivalent about his new clothes, delighted in their newness and their colors, but, as they were white man's clothes, he wasn't sure he would wear them. She told him it was up to him. She had just thought he might want something else to wear besides what he had on. When he was sure the decision was truly his, he chose to wear them. But he compromised. He would wear the shirt with his leggings, or the pants without the shirt, but he would not wear the shirt and pants together. He reminded Amanda of Jason and his army coat.

A wave of nausea hit her. She leaned against the wall until the dizziness went away. It was more than two weeks past the time for her blood to flow. The traumatic events of the last two months had done something to her.

Jason used to amuse her at the time she would feel the warmth of the blood between her legs. No warrior should come in contact with a woman at that time, no hunter cross her path. He would lose his power. But then he would be torn by his desire to be with her, if nothing else but to lie on her breast talking to her. She teasingly reasoned with him that since he was not officially a named warrior, it shouldn't make any difference. He would only get angry with her. But after he had curled up in a pout in the schoolhouse for one night, he would crawl back with her. And she would be prudent enough not to tease him then. Oddly, somehow the imposed chastity would bring them closer together, because he would talk of his people and their ways and she would tell him some things of her past. When she told him of her discovery of her in-laws' treatment of Melinda, he had been horrified. When she told him of John-Paul, he was entranced. When she told him of her father's lab, he was mystified. He did not understand that, anymore than she understood him when he told her the power of the spirits and the shaman.

***

Two weeks past her blood, and the nausea. Oh, no, she

thought, getting even sicker to her stomach. Jason has left me with a parting gift, after all. It just can't be, after all these months. I couldn't be.

But when the second month went by, and there was no blood, she was sure. The morning nausea came more regularly, and she had trouble hiding her difficulty from her dear shadow, Raphael.

Nights, she tossed and turned, lying on the floor of the bedroom and wrapped in a blanket. She could try to rid herself of the burden. She had heard once of a woman who had tried it, but she had died in the attempt. But even more important to her was the fact that this was part of Jason also. And she had lost Melinda. Somehow a new life in the world was good to her and made her want to keep this child and protect it. A little sister. Melinda would have loved it. The way she mothered poor Cherub, a new baby would have delighted her. She had been so distressed at the loss of Little Doe's baby. Melinda wasn't here to care and dote on it. But she would care, wherever she was, she would care. And Jason would care, wherever he was. But it was up to her for the daily living of it. What on earth could she do, with an illegitimate, bastard half-breed? She would not explain it as an orphaned Indian child. It would be hers or it would not be. She herself was dark-haired and brown-eyed, so even if this child were dark, it could be explained.

But a fatherless child could not be explained. She would have to find a father. She thought. She could shove the blame on some rider in the night who had raped her, but that would cast aspersions on the child, and some would ask her why she had not killed herself after "debasing" herself so. No, she had to find a legitimate father, and fast. The only possible candidate – Andrew. She would make another trip to Harlan tomorrow.

She rode to the town in the wagon, dressed in a new

dress, not hurrying, trying to formulate a plan. The Sheriff's receptivity to her was doubtful. He was so engrossed in his obligations and duties lately. Even if she did succeed in persuading him to marry her, it would have to be a long courtship. She did not have the time. She had to devise a way to get him to marry her immediately. She would have to twist his sense of honor and use it against him. Once she had his name, and her position as "honorable" and "chaste" were re-established, she would be able to continue the way she had been. She wanted the land, she wanted the ranch. She wanted them now, for herself, and later, for this unborn being within her, so small she could not yet feels its movement.

The Sheriff was not in. He was out at the fort, according to Jacobin, but expected in later. She stewed at the general store, fingering the cloth and looking at the goods. She sat in the makeshift restaurant at, drinking gallons of coffee. She ventured into the bar and purchased two bottles of whiskey "for medicinal purposes." Harlan was trying to take its place as a true town, and was erecting a town hall at the end of the street. Amanda idly scanned the two high cliffs on each side of the town. If a big flood came, it would wipe the entire town out, the same way she and Melinda had been caught. She shivered and sighed. The Sheriff was riding back into the town. She waited until he had entered the tiny jail, and then followed him in.

"Well, Amanda, what a surprise!" he said, genuinely pleased.

"Andrew, I'm going to have to prevail upon your good nature one more time, I'm afraid," she tried not to hurry the words, although her heart beat fast. She was glad it was a hot day, so there was an excuse for her profuse sweating.

He waited patiently for her to continue, offering her a

chair, into which she gratefully sank. She had killed a man, fought the winter weather and robbed a bank. But this was somehow very different.

"I just realized yesterday that if Mr. Thomas brings all those cattle, I have no idea where or how to keep them, or what they'll need. Taking care of the few I have is no great problem, but if he brings fifty head, what am I to do? Goodness, I don't know how I get into such predicaments. I seem to get into them. I certainly don't want to send them back, or give up the land. I mean, I have to do something, for God's sake."

He watched her through the tirade, listening intently and frowning. "Are you soliciting my advice, then, ma'am," he asked.

She blushed slightly at his choice of words.

"Well, yes, I guess I am."

"Is it that my advice has proven sound, or that there is no one else to ask?" he asked, leaning toward her.

She was taken back by his interrogations. Always before he had helped her unquestioningly. Of all times for him to get suspicious of her! She was irritated, tried not to show it, but her voice sounded edgy.

"I don't mean to impose on you, Sheriff MacGregor. It is only, well, there are few people I know or trust here."

"And you trust me?"

She swallowed hard. It was as though he knew she was up to something.

"You have never given me any reason not to," she replied.

He leaned back in his chair and put his dusty boots up on the desk. "Just what is it that you suggest we do?"

"If you would be so kind as to come to the house with me, and perhaps suggest where I could put up the fences. And then where I should hire the work done. I would, of course, pay you for your help." She had mustered her dignity and stood up. She was tall, and silhouetted again the window, and he had to squint to look up at her.

"Today?"

"Oh, at your convenience, of course."

"Today, then," he said, scooping his hat off the desk, and taking her arm. "I have no prisoners to guard and no money in the bank to guard."

She winced inwardly. She had not even considered him and his position in her plan to rid the bank of its money.

"I have my wagon," she said.

"Fine. I'll ride with you, then," he said.

He tied his horse to the back of the wagon, and took the reins from her. He had his bouts of chivalry at odd times, she observed. There wasn't much room on the wagon seat and their shoulders touched occasionally. She searched for a safe topic of conversation, not wanting to think ahead to what she would have to do.

"I see they are building a town hall," she opened.

"Right silly of them" he answered. "They think that the town will be the country seat when this territory becomes a state."

"You don't think it will be?"

He shook his head. "The new Federal marshal is being stationed in Cody. And the railroad is going that way. No railroad through Harlan. Just the stage. Its days are numbered."

She contemplated his observations. For all his simplicity and apparent lack of education, he was observant. He seemed to understand these people. She hoped he did not understand her as well, nor was as observant about her.

"A Federal marshal should be quite a help to you and the troopers," she observed.

"Too much so. They don't be needing me pretty soon."

"No? Then what will you do?"

"Oh, I don't know yet. Been a lot of things, you know."

"Like what?" she asked.

"Worked at ranchin' for a while, until the old man died. Then the bank took the ranch for the mortgage and they kicked me off. Went to work layin' railroad ties. Hard work, but I ate every day. Even tried lookin' for gold, but don't have the luck for that, I guess. I seem to be best at things that need just plain hard work."

"Where did you look for gold?"

"Around Denver."

"Did you ever find any?" she asked.

"Not me. Some was found. Mostly a lot of talk and noise, though. Denver's becomin' quite a town, I hear. Might go up there."

She had never thought of him as a person who had a beginning and a past. To her, he was just the Sheriff. She might not accomplish her task as easily as she thought she could.

"Do you want to leave here?" she queried.

"It's not a matter of wanting. It's a matter of needin' something to do. Ain't got the money to get any land," he stated flatly.

But she detected a trace of bitterness in the set of his mouth. Perhaps she had found the wedge she needed to open his armor.

They arrived at the ranch. Raphael had gone to the cave to get the books together, at Amanda's request, so they were alone.

She was uneasy about what she planned. Would it work? Odd, she hadn't had any of these doubts about the robbery. Perhaps because they were strangers, the bankers, and the money was a cold, impersonal thing. But this was not. And in spite of all her distrust, she respected this man. A wave of nausea drifted through her, making her dizzy as she stepped out of the wagon. She gripped the edge and stood absolutely still until it passed. She would have to go through with it. Why were things so complicated? What would happen if she simply went to him and told him she was pregnant and that the baby needed a father? Isn't that what Mary had told Joseph? And he had understood. But he had had an angel from the heavens to inspire him. No, it didn't work that way, not in reality.

It was later afternoon. If she made him some kind of meal first, it would relax him. If she could get him relaxed, maybe she could succeed.

"Would you like something to eat?" she asked.

"It's getting late. Maybe we should get to the business at hand," he noted, surveying the corrals and house.

"Oh, it's been a long ride. A little something to eat won't hurt a thing. Then we can look the place over, and you can tell me what you think."

He stood briefly by the wagon while she walked up the stairs. She turned and smiled at him. He followed her into the house. She had converted the store into sort of an office. She led him back into the dining room, and then into the kitchen, which had a small bedroom off it, evidently where Kinney had kept his "cooks." Amanda had deliberately left the door open, breaching every law of etiquette. She bustled about and managed to make some eggs and biscuits in spite of her shaking hands. Chattering about the ranch and what she would like it to be some day, she didn't realize herself until just now how many little dreams and hopes she had for it. She let slip the fact that she had deliberately bought the lands bordering the reservation on this side, hoping to shield her friends a little.

She set the food before him, and sat down to eat, noticing he had reverted to his more familiar way of not talking, but he did smile a little.

"It would be nice to have such dreams. You will probably see them through, too. You seem to be able to get what you want," he said.

Again, he had made a statement that made her blush. If he noticed, he didn't say anything. They had finished their meal. Both knew the sun was low, but neither made any attempt to rise from the table.

"Perhaps you would prefer something a little stronger than that coffee?" she ventured.

He raised his eyebrows and smiled. "You keep something stronger around?" he asked.

"Well, not usually. But I heard that this whiskey had good medicinal properties, so I purchased some," she said, taking the bottles from her supplies.

"Will you join me?" he asked her.

"I've never tasted it. What's it like?" she asked him,

"Doesn't really taste good, but feels good after it goes down," he explained.

She poured him a cup full, and then put a small amount in a cup for herself. She watched as he downed the entire cupful, her eyes getting wider and wider as he took the drink without a breath or stop.

"Do you have to drink it that way?" she asked.

"You can sip it, but it takes longer to warm you up, then."

She filled his cup again, and gingerly took a sip of hers.

"Would you want a ranch of your own?" she asked.

He drained the cup before answering her. She was appalled at his capacity. She had only purchase two bottles. Now she was not sure it would be enough.

"Always wanted one. Never could afford it. Couldn't seem to get it. Hard enough just to keep body and soul together, sometimes."

"What happened to your parents?" she asked.

He leaned back in his chair, hooked his arm over the back of it, and twirled the cup around by its handle.

"Killed in an Indian raid, they say. Don't know for sure. I was just a little shaver. The old man found me under a bunch of old blankets, he said. Then he took me home. Always told me whenever I was ornery that he should have left me there to freeze or serve as target practice for the Indians."

"He must have cared for you some."

"I was a damned good hand at that ranch, that's the only reason he kept me around," he slurred his words a little and took a deep breath.

He drained another cup again. She marveled at his peculiar way of imbibing. She had seen her father and his friends with their brandy after dinner, but none of them every gulped the fiery liquid. She took another sip of hers. It did seem to give a feeling of warmth from the inside.

"Are you a good sheriff?" she inquired as she filled his cup again.

"Don't know. Caught a few outlaws and jailed a few drunken Indians. More nuisance than work," he replied, gripping the cup with both hands.

The whiskey was loosening his tongue at least. She still wasn't sure how she was to proceed in this venture. She had to get him to the bed. She couldn't very well accuse him of fathering this child if he just talked her to sleep.

"Do you like being sheriff?" she asked, moving her chair closer to his and leaning over to fill his cup. Her breast brushed his hand, but he didn't move, either to avoid her or take advantage of the situation. She would have to think of something more direct.

"Don't really like it. Don't dislike it, neither," he studied his cup, and then in one slow, swooping gesture, drained the cup.

Amanda had finished her small drink. And the bottle was empty. He looked at her intently, studying her as if seeing her for the first time.

"Mrs. White," he began as he stood up with drunken dignity. "I have infringed upon your hospitality, and I have not done what I promised to do. However, I will leave you now and return in the morning." He took a step to go outside, and then to Amanda's absolute amazement, crumpled in a heap at her feet.

"Damn!" she exclaimed. How was she to seduce him if he were passed out? She stood with her hands on her hips, studying the mass of man lying at her feet. Well, she would make the accusation, even if he didn't remember the act.

She dragged his limp body to the bed. As she tried to pull him up to the bed, he fell on top of her and she had to wiggle out from under him. She was sweating and her hair was wild. She sat panting at the effort. He groaned and rolled over on his side away from her. She managed to unbutton his shirt and pants. She pulled off his pants, not having to bother with under shorts because he wore none. Next, she peeled off his shirt. He was very heavy and uncooperative, occasionally moaning in his unconsciousness. Finally she had him nude and then began to disrobe herself hurriedly. She did not want him to awaken until she was with him.

While she stripped she studied his body. It was a younger body than she thought it would be, more like Jason's than her former husband's, but much more muscular and hairy. He had masses of dark hair on his chest, his groin and his legs. It matched the dark hair of his beard, which curled slightly, as did the masses of hair on his head. With all that hair, it was difficult to say how dark his skin really was. She pulled the cover over them.

She listened to his heavy breathing in the dark, feeling cold and alone in spite of the warm body next to her. How long would he be passed out? She wanted to sleep, but knew she would have to be awake when he awoke. But the little bit of whiskey she had served as a soporific, and she drifted of to sleep in spite of her good intentions.

***

She felt his calloused hand on her bare shoulders. He was wide-eyed and confusion showed on his face.

"Amanda! What happened?" he whispered hoarsely.

"Don't you remember?" she whispered, too, burrowing further down in the covers.

His chest heaved with deep, irregular breathing.

"I remember the bottle of whiskey, but how did I get here? Did I hurt you?"

"Don't you remember anything?"

He shook his head. Suddenly he became aware of his total nudity and blushed a bright crimson. She had put his clothes in a heap by the door. In order to reach them, he would have to get out of the bed and walk across the room naked. She decided to press her advantage, in spite of the small voice urging her to be honest with him and tell him the truth. She couldn't risk the truth right now.

"It's a little obvious what happened. Why didn't you warn me what that terrible drink would do this to you?" she said.

He opened his mouth to say something, but blushed

again instead. He sat back heavily in bed and hung his head, breathing rapidly.

"My god, Mrs. White. Amanda. I didn't mean to hurt you. Can I ever make it up to you?" He put his face in his hands.

Her plan of attack at this point had called for self-righteous indignation to shame him into the "proper" action. But she couldn't do it. She didn't know the situation would upset him so. Was he really crying, or rather, trying not to cry?

Putting her hand gently on his arm, she sat up slightly, holding the cover to her front, but unwittingly baring her naked back with her long black hair trailing behind her. Softly she told him, "You didn't hurt me, Andrew. But it does put us both in an awkward situation."

He looked at her, inadvertently letting his eyes wander over her face and back. His breathing was jerky, but he didn't move or say anything.

"Andrew, marry me," she whispered.

"What!" he asked incredulously.

"Marry me. It would be the only way to make me an honorable woman again. You said last night you always wanted a ranch of your own. We could be partners. I have the land, but don't know how to use it. You know how to use it, but you don't have the land. It seems to me it's the only way."

"You want to marry me?" he asked.

She looked down and away. "Well, I think I certainly could do a lot worse. And after what has happened, it.."

"Right now?" he asked, still in disbelief.

She nodded. "Why not?"

He leaned away from her, staring at her as though she had just grown another head and he were trying to see if it matched the first one. Finally he said, in a calm voice, "The closest preacher is at the fort."

"Then we'll go there. Uh, since we're going to be business partners, too, perhaps we'd better draw up a business agreement. That way, well, we'll have less to argue about afterwards."

"Married folk do seem to argue a lot, don't they," he observed.

She laughed. "Yes, they seem to."

She pulled the sheet around her, got out of bed, grabbed her clothes and went into the next room to dress. When she returned he had dressed and regained some of his taciturn dignity. She had brought a piece of paper, and for an hour over coffee they discussed what specific details of the partnership they needed to work out. To Amanda's surprise, they differed little. Both agree that if the other should pre-decease one, the whole of the property should go to the other partner. Both agreed to allow the Indian's hunting rights on the land as well as ceremonial rites. Amanda knew of the Indian burial ground but was surprised to learn that the Sheriff did also. She also made a mental note that she had to stop referring to him as "the Sheriff."

They both agreed if any children were born of the union, that the child or children would inherit the property after they both were dead. (This particular reference brought the crimson back into the hairy tanned cheeks of Andrew.) They both agreed that any buying or selling of property, cattle, etc. would be done by mutual agreement. They also agreed that they would share equally in the profits from the ranch.

"What if we should decide later that this isn't going to work?" she asked.

"You mean, like divorce?" he said.

"Yes."

He meditated a moment. "Fifty-fifty split." It was fair. She agreed.

"Maybe we'd better wait to sign this until we have some kind of witnesses, like at the fort," she suggested.

"Okay," he replied. "Amanda, are you sure you want to go through with this?"

"I'm sure. Are you?"

"No, I'm not sure. But if I think about it too long, you might change your mind. And I'm sure I don't want to risk that," he laughed a little and rubbed the back of his neck. "Sure does seem strange, though."

Raphael returned just in time to see them leave. He promised to stay at the ranch until they returned. When he heard what they were planning to do, he gave a loud whoop and hugged Amanda. With considerably more dignity, he shook Andrew's hand and congratulated him. Amanda was glad that they got along. It meant that there would be no problem about Raphael's staying here.

They didn't talk much on the way to the fort. Amanda spent most of the time scanning the plains with her heart and eyes. This was now truly her land. She was not happy. Too many things had happened for her to be happy. She missed Melinda so that when she thought of her, her whole insides contracted, and her eyes blurred. She thought of what she was doing. Would it have been different Jason were still here? She didn't know. He wasn't here. She missed him. Yet she was content in a way she hadn't been in a long time. She needed a home, and now she had one.

Captain Greenwood greeted them at the fort. Amanda became very aware that her dress was very dirty when she saw Mrs. Greenwood in her new summer frock of bright yellow, which made her red hair look even more brilliant. She carried a parasol and wore her matching yellow bonnet.

"Well, I declare, Mrs. White. What a surprise. What

brings you away from your precious little Indians?' Mrs. Greenwood cooed.

"I'm no longer their teacher," Amanda said simply, not wanting any confrontations with anyone right now.

"Captain Greenwood, is the Chaplin here?" Andrew asked.

"Of course, I'll send for him," Greenwood responded. After dispatching the soldier, he asked Andrew, "What's the problem?"

"Oh, no problem, Captain. Amanda and I are going to be married."

"Married!" Captain Greenwood and his wife exclaimed together. Immediately, Mrs. Greenwood's attitude changed. This was in her line of endeavor and she loved any excuse for a party.

"Oh, my dear, we must find you a suitable dress. Emily Sue still has her wedding dress from two years ago. She's a bit rounder than you, but it will do. And the fiddler. Oh dear, I do hope his finger has heeled. His horse stepped on it last week when he passed out in the barn. Drinks like a fish, but, oh, can he play. You men just find the chaplain, and get the chairs into the chapel. I'll take care of the rest of the details. Come on, Mrs. White. Do you mind if a call you Amanda? My first name is Liza. You can change at our quarters. We must have to see what we have on hand for refreshments." She hollered at a woman at the end of the boardwalk who was staring at them. "Emily Sue, Emily Sue, we're going to have a wedding!"

The two women chattered on about what to do and what should be done. Amanda was grateful for not having to participate actively in any of it. She didn't care what the ceremony looked like, so long as it was legal and binding. Emily Sue's white dress was a bit big for her, but it was so full of flounces and lace that the size didn't matter much.

In the short span it took to get dressed and fix Amanda's hair, Captain Greenwood and Andrew had found the chaplain, and arranged the chairs outside, the chapel under the blazing summer sun, since, once the news had flashed through the fort, everyone had decided to attend. They all turned in wonderment as Amanda walked down the aisle. Andrew smiled down at her and handed her a bouquet of wildflowers. She listened to the meadowlark sing as the chaplain intoned his admonishments and prayers. She heard Andrew say "I do" and heard herself say it, but more she heard the wind blowing gently across the plain, bringing the smells and the sounds she had learned to love.

There were whistles and shouts from the troopers as Andrew gingerly kissed her, putting his arms around her, but not holding her tightly. The blood pounded in her temples, as she devoutly wished it were all over and they were back at the ranch.

But even after the ceremony, they were not allowed to depart. Liza Greenwood had found the fiddler, sober and with a healed finger, and had mustered up sandwiches and punch for everyone. Amanda tapped her foot to the beat of the strings and enjoyed the music. Sergeant Pepper came striding up to them.

"Everyone deserves at least one dance with the new bride," he announced, sweeping her onto the floor."

"I know your new husband don't dance," he whispered in her ear as they waltzed around the room, amid the cheers and foot stomping. "And I could see your foot atappin'."

Sergeant Pepper proved a remarkably good dance and her feet remembered all the steps from her other life. After the initial dance, each trooper and officer that could took advantage of Peppers' lead, and Amanda found herself in need of the drinks and sandwiches. She noticed that as many of them respectfully congratulated Andrew on his good fortune and beautiful bride. He beamed at their compliments. He reminded Amanda that they still had one more thing to do at the fort. To answer her quizzical frown, he replied, "The business agreement." Captain Greenwood and the chaplain signed as witnesses to their signatures, the chaplain commenting that it was a strange way to begin a marriage.

Amid shouts of congratulations and wildflowers thrown at them in lieu of rice, they mounted the wagon again and set back for the ranch. When they had ridden for a while Andrew commented that although the Captain had offered to let them stay for the night, he was anxious to get back home. It sounded strange, "home," when he said it. Amanda still had the white dress on. She made a note to return it to Emily Sue as soon as possible. She thought it ironic that she married in white again, especially in her condition.

Raphael greeted them exuberantly. Amanda hugged him and told him he was to sleep in the spare room behind the kitchen, not in the barn as he had been doing. He looked questioningly at Andrew, who nodded. Raphael was ecstatic, dancing a war dance and yipping and yelling all the way into the house.

They went to the main bedroom. Andrew sat on one side of the bed. Amanda sat heavily on the other side and sighed. She felt exhausted. Yet somehow she was reluctant to sleep beside this man, now that he was not drunk and passed out, and in full control of himself. She had married him and now had an obligation to him. And she dreaded it. She knew how it had been with her first husband, and how it had been with Aaron. That was not what it had been with Jason. But Jason was Indian. And Andrew was white. Was that really the distinction? Or was it that she loved Jason and he loved her? Did she love Andrew? She surely respected him, liked him, knew him, perhaps better in the last two days then she ever knew her first husband.

"Amanda?" he asked.

She started out of her reverie. "Andrew?"

"Are you tired?"

"Well, yes, all that dancing and the excitement. I guess I am," she replied, slowly removing her shoes. He watched her every move, still sitting on the edge of the bed.

"You sure do look pretty," he said softly.

She smiled at him. She took off her blouse and stockings and skirt until she was just in the white under slip. He looked at her.

"Amanda, I," he started to say, then looked down at his boots.

"What is it?" she asked, somewhat impatiently. She was tired, and in no mood for understanding and solicitous conversation.

"I ain't never been with a woman, least not what I could remember," he stammered.

She sat absolutely still. This strange turn of events had never occurred to her before. No wonder he was so terribly confused this morning when he awoke. She moved next to him on the bed.

"Never?"

He shook his head miserably. "I know I want you. I just don't want to hurt you."

"If you don't want to hurt me, then you won't," she said gently. "I can, well, I can show you, not that I've had that much, you know, but," she was suddenly ill at ease, too.

Always the man had taken the lead with her, well, almost

always, after a while with Jason it was difficult to tell who was the initiator. She remembered how gentle Jason had been with her. She could be no less with this man she had just married.

He hesitantly put his hand on her neck and shoulders. "I love you, Amanda. I think I have loved you from the first day I saw you," he whispered.

She kissed him on the mouth, gently at first, and then more insistently. He responded, wrapping her arms in his arms, tightly, and pulling her to him. She pulled away from the kiss and buried her head in his neck and shoulders while her fingers unbuttoned his shirt. He awkwardly pulled off his shirt and pants while she dropped the slip to the floor. Together they cuddled under the covers. Amanda kept her eyes averted from his, not knowing if he were looking at her or not. He again engulfed her in his arms, this time the urgency of his body guiding him. He wanted to take her immediately, but she pulled back.

"Gently, gently, don't hurry. I'm not going to run away," she whispered.

He controlled his body's insistence, pacifying himself by caressing her body and permitting her to touch him. He trembled at her touch. She explored the hair on his face and chest. As she touched his groin, she knew he was near exploding. She guided him into her, only to have him explode almost immediately.

He lay almost on top of her, breathing heavily, holding her, part of him still inside her, but limp and ineffectual. She was frustrated by his lack of ability to give her release. But she was not afraid or hurt. She would survive this part of their marriage. Perhaps, in time, it would get better. He had said he loved her. For some reason that she herself could not fathom, she believed him. He slept, and finally she did too, with exhaustion. When she awoke the next morning he was already up and she smelled the delicious aroma of coffee and bacon. She dressed quickly and went to the kitchen to discover her new husband fixing breakfast.

"I didn't know you could cook! I didn't think men knew how," she exclaimed.

He chuckled a little. "How do you think I survived all these years by myself? Sit down, and I'll treat you to breakfast this morning."

With exaggerated chivalry, he pulled her chair out, and placed a cup of coffee in front of her. She laughed a little, and then tasted it. It was better than what she ever made. What did he do different? She would find out.

He left to make official his resignation as sheriff. She and Raphael tended to the cattle and the horses, making sure they had enough water and grazing. Raphael showed her how to use the thistle brush to get the winter hair off the horses. She checked them for any signs of foot problems and then found it necessary to lie down. She tired so easily now. And the damned nausea was still there. It was such a nuisance. She would get so hungry, and then eat only to heave it up a half hour later.

Andrew didn't return until late in the afternoon. She rushed out the door to greet him, worrying that something had happened to him. He embraced her and kissed her.

"The townsfolk want to throw us a shindig, Amanda. I told'em we'd be in Saturday," he said gleefully.

She stiffened. She truly did not want to socialize with the townspeople. There weren't any of them she cared about. And it would be such a chore. She knew she would tire out completely. But she hid her anger from Andrew. She couldn't explain her attitude to him. She would endure it.

The three of them managed to erect a fair-size holding

pen for the cattle. Amanda could only help for so long before she felt the nausea and dizziness take over. Then she had to return to the house. Andrew had expressed some concern and had wanted to send for the doctor but she had excused herself that she wasn't used to the excitement and the hard work and all.

Saturday came. She donned the best dress she had, which was her new, though terribly practical, calico. She had been dressed in her jeans and shirt all week. Andrew had objected to her mode of dress at first, but she told him it was immensely impractical to wear a dress and try to do the things she was doing. He wanted to buy a new dress for the "shindig." She told him what she had would do fine.

Friday night she had Raphael heat water for her for a bath. It was the one concession to civilization that Kinney had left, a large, round bathtub. She chased Raphael and Andrew out of the arm kitchen, and luxuriated in the bath a full half hour. Her hair was still damp and she was brushing it dry in the breeze when they came back in.

"It wouldn't hurt you to take one either," she commented to Andrew.

"Why? I just get dirty again," he objected.

"For the same reason we wash the clothes and do the dishes," she retorted. "Besides, those clothes will rot off you if you don't."

He muttered and grumbled, but did manage to get himself bathed and into clean clothes. His clean hair was even curlier than his dirty hair had been, as was his beard. He clipped at his beard and hair with scissors.

He insisted on making love again that night. He was like a kid with candy. He just couldn't seem to get enough of it, even on the nights after they had worked extra hard all day.

He learned quickly and was always concerned that he didn't hurt her. Although he did not set off the spasms of joy and pleasure that Jason had managed to evoke, he could produce a wave of relief and contentment in her. She marveled that such a basically simple act was really so complex.

Saturday they rode into town. People she knew, and even more people that she didn't congratulated them the minute they set foot in the town. The "shindig" was being held outside the new town hall, not yet completed and with only half a roof. All the ladies of the town had tried to outdo each other with their baking and cooking. Amanda had thought about bringing something, but somehow, she didn't care to enter the competition.

After tasting some of the food, she was glad she hadn't. Some of it was delectable. Mrs. Graves had made a berry pie. Amanda recognized the berries as the ones she and the little Indians used to gather and eat. But in the pie, with the sugar and flaky crust, they took on a new personality. Amanda hadn't realized how much she had missed good gooey food. Strawberries and cream had always been her favorite and someone had managed to find some in this vast wasteland. Amanda gorged herself. Andrew teased her that if she continued eating like that she would get very fat. She laughed and blushed a little, which only seemed to add to her charm to the other gentlemen.

On the ranch, she and Andrew were equals. But here, in the town, in the strange place among his people, she played her role, and became the proper little wife and was properly demure. Actually, she was content to stay on his arm. She didn't want to have to mix among the people to try to make conversation. She listened to the talk about ranches, cattle, their disease and the market, and about the new colt Jacobin had. She listened, took it all in, and remembered it, without ever letting on she understood. Andrew seemed just as content to have her on his arm, frequently holding her hand on his arm with his free hand.

"Hate to tear you away from the little lady," Jacobin said, "but think we ought to drink a toast to your husband. How about one?"

Andrew shrugged and smiled at her. She wasn't about to be a shrewish wife in front of this crowd, so she released her hold on him and let him go. She wandered over to a group of women, including Mrs. Graves, and sat unobtrusively listening to their talk of cooking and children. She found herself interested in spite of herself.

One of the women finally noticed her and asked, "I thought you had a child?"

Amanda looked briefly at Mrs. Graves. Then she took a deep breath. Everyone would know this sooner or later. "I did. She died in a flood this spring," she stated simply.

"Oh, you poor thing. What a horrible thing to happen."

There were murmurs of sympathy, but the idea had opened up a whole new topic of conversation, and they all started talking about the various tragedies they had experienced or knew of. Only Mrs. Graves did not join in. She took Amanda's arm and asked her if she would like to get something to drink. A grateful Amanda and Mrs. Graves walked to the long tables of drink and food. There were a few flies around, but since it was still early summer, they weren't very thick. Amanda liked this woman. She saw a strange kind of courage in her.

"They never did find my mister," she was saying.

Amanda winced inwardly. Would she ever be able to tell this woman what really happened to her husband? Did she have the right not to tell her?

"Everyone said he probably just got sick of this place and took off. But I don't think so. My husband had lots wrong with him, but he wasn't a quitter. Nope. More likely the Injuns or rattlers got him. Anyway, I'm just going to run the store and wait for him. We built the place together, you know," she said.

"No, I didn't know. Had you been here long?" Amanda asked, as they sipped at their tepid punch.

"About five years. Only married six. Wished he would've stayed away from Jacobin and Kinney. Them two's always up to trouble."

Andrew had come out of the bar and came directly to her. The newly elected mayor declared he had to make a congratulations speech and wish their one-time sheriff and friend good luck. He droned on for about fifteen minutes, his speech punctuated with cheers from the crowd. Amanda felt dizzy. The nausea had come and gone without her losing her ample dinner, but she felt sleepy. She whispered to Andrew, "Do you think they would mind if we left?"

He looked at her pale face. "Nope. Now they have the excuse, they'll celebrate all nightlong. Won't even notice if we slip out." With that, they left.

They arrived in the late evening. Raphael had fallen asleep on the porch. Andrew lifted him up and carried him to bed. By the time he got back to their bed, Amanda was asleep.

***

They worked hard at the ranch to make things better. Andrew foresaw the need for more feed for the animals in the winter and had heard about a new strain of hay that would grow in this soil and climate. He wanted to plant some and try it. They would need a barn for the milking cows. He wanted to build a new house. Amanda argued against it, noting that there were many things they needed instead.

"The valley where your school was would make an ideal place for a home," he observed.

"No!" she exclaimed. "We'll never use that place, or build on it. It's," she groped for the right words to express her feelings for the place. "It's sacred."

"Sacred?"

"I, I buried Melinda there. I can't change it, use it," she explained.

"I understand," he said, brushing her hair back from her sweating forehead.

They took a break from their work. They drank the cool water of the steam and ate some beef jerky. Amanda wondered if this were the same stream that ran by the cave. She would trace its source someday.

***

Her middle grew thick. She could no longer button the buttons on her pants. She would have to tell Andrew. Tonight.

She undressed slowly that night. He was already waiting for her in the bed, watching her. At least in that, Andrew and Jason were alike. They both seemed to enjoy looking at her.

"How can you work so hard and still be so pretty?" Andrew wondered at her.

She smiled at him as she cuddled next to him in bed. He pulled her to him and caressed her back and neck.

"Andrew?" she began.

"Um," was all he answered.

"Andrew, I think I'm pregnant."

His hands stopped. "Are you sure?"

"Pretty sure."

He didn't say anything, just kissed her on the mouth lightly and held her for a long time. "Will it hurt you if we make love?"

No, I don't think so," she said. So they did, but he was very, very gentle.

***

It was a hot summer. They worked hard. Amanda's belly grew and it became increasingly awkward for her to do anything at all.

"Amanda, you can't continue to work out here with me," Andrew said.

"What would you suggest I do, then," she asked.

"Do the work in the house like a woman should," he answered.

"Do you think it's any easier to carry the water or the wood than it is to drive cows to and from the water?" she countered.

'It's not proper," he reasoned.

"Propriety be damned. I'll do what has to be done," she answered.

"You've got to take care of yourself," he replied, backing down a little.

"I will, Andrew, I will," she assured him.

She continued to work by his side during the day. At night all three of them did the household chores. Andrew more frequently than not did the cooking.

"Men do not cook," Raphael observed.

"They do if the want to eat," Andrew answered.

"Men do not carry water," Raphael stated.

"They do if they want to drink," Amanda told him.

AMANDA

So Raphael carried the water and got fuel for the stove, did dishes, and learned to cook a few basic things. He became part of their home.

***

"Where is he? " Andrew came charging in while Amanda was cleaning up the breakfast dishes.

"Raphael?" she asked.

"Who else?"

"Why?"

"He's been playing tag with the damned bull. Got it all lathered up this morning. We'll lose that animal if that damned kid doesn't stop it." Andrew was angry.

They didn't find him for two days. His hunger finally got the best of him, or maybe loneliness. He came in the evening, head hanging. Amanda rushed to him, her worry about his safety overcoming any anger. But Raphael sidestepped her embrace and he stared squarely at Andrew, who stared back at the boy.

"You know what you did wrong?" Andrew asked.

Raphael breathed in deeply, squared his shoulders, his beautiful eyes wide and serious. "Yes, sir."

"Will you ever do it again?"

"No, sir." And he didn't, at least as far as Amanda knew. And nothing more was said about it.

She saw that Andrew and Raphael had a special rapport. The boy tried to imitate everything the man did. He even scratched at his non-existent beard the way Andrew scratched at his thick black one.

***

Andrew wanted to go into town on the Fourth of July, to

celebrate with the townspeople. Amanda didn't. They debated the issue. They never truly argued, not the way she and Jason had argued. Andrew won this round. They all prepared a picnic lunch. Andrew insisted that Raphael go along with them. As long as Amanda had that slip of paper from Kinney entrusting the child to her care, they could take him anywhere with them, Andrew insisted. Besides, he would probably win all the races, the way he could run.

The townspeople reacted with mixed emotions about the trio. Amanda overheard the ribbing Andrew received about getting his wife pregnant so fast. Some of the people from the fort were there, and Mrs. Greenwood was ecstatic over the idea of a new baby on the way. In a long, confident conversation while waiting for the men and boys to line up for the races, she confided to Amanda that she probably could not have any children. She and the Captain had been married for seven years, and still no children.

Andrew and Raphael won the three-legged sack race easily. Amanda believe it was not because they were so much faster, but that they worked so well as a team that they never tripped or faltered like the others did. Once the people saw the relationship between Andrew and the boy, they accepted him, although none of the children would befriend him. This did not seem to bother Raphael too much, who simply became Andrew's shadow. The women complimented her on her boysenberry pie. Amanda smiled and accepted the compliments, not wanting to spoil their effusive comments by telling them that her husband had made it.

She overheard the conversation about the new coal company nearby and how it made such good fuel, since wood was so scarce. She wanted to hear more, but the men would not discuss business with a woman, and simply returned to idle chatter about the weather when they became aware of her presence. She wanted to find out more.

An unexpected source of information was Mrs. Graves, who used it to heat her store. She gave Amanda the name of the man who delivered it and the name of the mining company. Amanda was determined to write them and utilize this new source. It would certainly be better than what she had. She would compose the letter when they went home.

It took a month for the company to reply and then the deliveryman came out to see her. It was expensive, but she was determined to have it. Since the deliveries were far apart, she decided they should have a storage area. Andrew didn't think the idea would work too well, but he humored her by helping fix a cellar to store it in. She tried to cook with it and decided she liked it. They would use it.

***

Someone was here. She could hear him. He was very quiet. The sun was just showing on the horizon. She got out of bed and put on her sack dress. It was the only thing that would fit her. It was getting shorter as her stomach was getting bigger. She didn't remember being this big with Melinda at five months. The memory made her heart constrict. It was still painful to think of her. Time might heal a wound, but there was always the sensitive scar tissue.

The whole tribe must have been outside there, quietly, patiently waiting for them to awake. When they saw Amanda come out, Winona and Paul approached. She was delighted to see them, hugged each one. Winona had gotten even more serious, she believed. And Paul had grown as tall as she was.

"Paul, does all go well with you?" she asked.

"Oh, yes, Amanda MacGregor, I have passed my thirteenth

summer well," he replied, showing her they knew the news of her marriage. She suspected Raphael was the source of their information, but how he found the time to get it to them she didn't know.

"Every fall, we gather to dance and sing before the coming of winter, and visit our ancestors," Winona began. "The land where we used to do this no longer belongs to us, says the man in Washington. However, it now belongs to one who we believe is a friend. We wish only to hold the ceremony on the land. Then we will return to that which has been said is ours."

"Are you angry with me for buying the land?" Amanda asked her.

"No, not with you. Only that once again we believed in the word of the white man, and once again, it was broken."

Andrew had come out and stood beside her. She had no doubt of his feelings. They had agreed they would try to keep the land as open to the Indians as they could. He understood them and was also angry at the government's decision. While they worked the land, somehow, they could not believe such vastness was all theirs to keep forever.

"You hold your ceremonies. The only difficulty I foresee is with Kinney," Amanda said.

Winona handed her a piece of paper. "Paul helped me decide how it should be written. Kinney was very surprised when I brought it to him to sign. I truly think he thought that we had not learned anything from you.

The paper was written in a somewhat childishly round handwriting. It stated that the tribe had the right to enter upon Amanda's land for "Ceremonies and other such needs," providing Amanda and Andrew agree to it. It absolved Kinney of all responsibility, but left open many possibilities of just what the Indians could or could not do. Amanda smiled.

While it contained no deliberate untruths, it was deceptively simple in allowing for many contingencies.

"We will sign it. I hoped you understand that if any of you should be hunting, and the deer just happened to wander onto our land, we would understand that it would be necessary for you to purse it to finish the hunt," Amanda noted.

"I understand, and will tell the others," Winona answered. Amanda and Andrew went into the house to sign the paper.

"I hope we are doing the right thing," Andrew commented.

"We are," Amanda said. She was not sure of the consequences, but she would not deny her friends their celebrations.

"You are welcome to join us this evening, at the campfires," Winona offered.

"Thank you. We may do that."

Raphael had disappeared when the tribe left to go to the burial grounds. Neither Andrew nor Amanda commented. Andrew did not scold the boy when he returned toward evening. They simply accepted him at the supper table. He ate ravenously. They heard the drums in the distance.

"You will come?" Raphael asked them both eagerly.

Andrew ruffled the boy's hair. They had not insisted he get it cut and it hung far down his back. "Yup, I think we will for a while," Andrew told him

Raphael whooped and raced out of the house towards the campfires.

Amanda laughed. "You would think he would at least show a little enthusiasm occasionally."

"He does," Andrew replied, her witticism being lost on him.

The Indians had set up their tepees in a semi-circle, with a large campfire near the drummer and singers. The women were dancing in a circle, not touching each other, yet swaying in rhythm as though they were one. Amanda watched, fascinated. She felt her feet moving in the beat of the drum. Winona saw her and beckoned to her.

"Dance with us," she said to Amanda.

"I don't know how," she replied.

"You can learn. It's not difficult."

She joined in the circle next to Winona, watching her feet and the swaying of her body. She was awkward at first, but soon discovered the repetition of the step and felt the rhythm of the others. Some of them would sing occasionally to answer the singers. The drums would speed up and then slow down. It ended as a fast-paced stomping, moving rapidly around the circle, and then stopping abruptly, with a few whoops and yelps from appreciative bystanders.

Then a few of the men started to dance, slowly at first, then more rapidly, bending, dipping, whirling. Amanda was awed by the power of the dancer to move and turn and still maintain his balance, while the other lunged at him and withdrew.

She whispered to Winona, "What kind of dance is that?"

"It is a story dance. It tells of the last wild buffalo bull we hunted and how brave he was in spite of the many hunters."

There was dancing, food, and much talking and story telling. Amanda found Paul and some men exchanging tales near a fire. When Paul discovered her presence, he convinced her to tell some of her tales. Once she started, she found it difficult to get away from the gathering. She finally pleaded fatigue because of her condition. Winona offered to walk back with her to the house, since both Raphael and Andrew were caught up in their own groups. Raphael danced joyfully with the others, and Andrew swapped tales with the old warriors.

"It reminds me of the Fourth of July celebration," Amanda said. "It's so noisy."

"It is a good time for us," Winona said. "We don't often have a chance to get together like this since we have been forced to live on separate places of land."

"Is it working at all?" Amanda wanted to know.

"We are surviving. Many are not happy. Those who fled, many were killed," Winona told her. Amanda was afraid to ask, but she had to know.

"Jason?"

"No one knows. He disappeared the night many of the others were captured and hanged."

Amanda breathed an inward sigh of relief.

"He has the rifle, you know," Winona said.

Amanda nodded. "And the others, Paul, and the little ones. Are they okay?"

"Paul is one of us. He lives with the old shaman. He learns many things. The two who look the same have married the same man." Winona smiled. "I don't think he can tell them apart yet."

Amanda laughed. "Poor man, they could cause him much confusion."

"Yes, especially since they are both pregnant, and they will come due at the same time."

"Will you marry?"

Winona's face clouded over. "He who I was to marry was hanged. No, I will not marry. I do not wish to bring children into this world of ours as we now live."

"I'm sorry, Winona. That must be a very difficult decision," Amanda observed.

They had arrived at the house. Winona bid her good night and returned to the noise and the dancing. Amanda fell exhausted into the bed. But her back hurt so much, she finally opted to sleep on the hard floor. Andrew had strenuously objected the first time she did this. But she told him that she felt better and she would sleep on the floor if she chose. He had accepted it, but at first refused to join her. But his need for her overcame his prejudice and pride, and he threw his blanket over her and they snuggled together. When he got up the next morning, he complained of being stiff. She said she felt good. After that, they slept more on the floor than in the bed. He gradually got used to it.

***

The cattle had come. Andrew's hay had grown, but they had trouble finding a reaper and finally had to settle on the ancient way of the scythe. It took a long time to harvest, even longer to bale and put away. The first snows had come by the time they had some of it put away and stacked. Amanda could no longer help with the lifting. She was much too large and awkward. Andrew worried about her when he left her, not wanting to leave her alone, knowing he needed Raphael's help and yet wanting him to stay with her. They put the cattle out on the best ranges, which had some areas of protection from the weather, and yet would offer some kind of feed. They were not far, but far enough that Andrew would not be home until after dark when he rode to check on them. They had enclosed some of the ranges with the new wire fences. Amanda had worn gloves when she helped with it, but still, it cut into her hands.

Then the real winter hit, and they seldom went anywhere. The Christmas season was upon them. Amanda racked her brain for a present for them. There was no going to town unless it was a dire emergency. She didn't know how to knit, but she did know how to sew the skins as Winona had shown her. She took the leather from the cow they had butchered for the winter and made Andrew a coat with the hair inside so as to keep him warmer. Then she took what was left over and made Raphael a pair of warm gloves. They had made a cradle for the new one to come. The dinner was not different from what they had had many nights previously, but Amanda had remembered how they used to make taffy back home, and after two false beginnings, she managed to put some together. They pulled it between them, Raphael, Andrew, and Amanda, shaped it into fancy twists, let it cool, and then gorged on it. It used a lot of their sugar, but it was worth it. Then Andrew made some of his good coffee, and they sat huddled together around the warmth of the stove. Amanda had remembered some of the old Christmas carols, and she sang some in her deep alto voice. Andrew could join her on a few of them, as Raphael listened curiously.

"Your god came to your people as a baby?" he asked.

"Yes, but he wasn't born in a palace like a king, but in a manger, with the animals," Amanda explained.

"Our little ones are often born with the animals, especially when we were traveling. It is better for them to be born where they can soon see the rising sun," he declared.

"Why?"

"Oh, so they know they have arrived here and that it is a good place," he patiently explained. "Though, knowing what a nuisance kids can be, I wonder sometimes as to why."

"You were little, once," Amanda teased.

"I don't remember," Raphael said in all seriousness. "And I have no one to tell me what I was like."

"Do you believe in God?" Andrew asked him.

"There is a Great Spirit who is everywhere," Raphael said.

"I'm not sure I believed in God," Amanda interjected. Both of her companions looked at her sharply.

"You don't?" Andrew exclaimed. "Then what do you believe in?"

The question hung in the air. She wasn't sure how to answer, but they were both waiting for one.

"Just life, I guess," she finally replied.

CHAPTER SIX

Andrew decided he should check on the cattle. He and Raphael saddled the horses and bundled up in all their extra clothing.

"We'll be back by dark," he promised, as he kissed her, holding her as close as her distended belly would allow.

His tenderness toward her had increased and at night he would lie by her, with his hand on her stomach to feel the baby kick. If her feet and legs hurt, he would rub them gently and firmly, bringing the blood flowing through them again.

She took the bucket from the hook when they left, buried herself under a mountain of clothing, and fought her way against the wind and blowing snow to the barn where the two heifers were. They were lowing impatiently, full of milk. The two draft horses neighed a greeting. She rubbed their noses affectionately. They were big, beautiful things, roans, with white tufts of hair on their feet. For all their brute size and hard working capability, they were truly gentle souls, and Amanda could get them to do almost anything for a bite of carrot and a kind word.

As she adjusted herself on the milking stool, she felt a pain in her lower abdomen. She waited to start the milking until it had subsided. Then she milked the cow. By the time she had finished the one, the pains were becoming more frequent. She had had the pains off and on for two weeks now, but never so regularly before. She knew what was happening, and sat down to rest briefly to regain some strength. But she dozed off momentarily, only to be awakened by another sharp pain. She tried to open the door, but suddenly was seized by an overwhelming pain, one that would not be ignored. She knew she would never make it back to the house. God, it was so strong. Her whole body heaved with the force of it. It would not allow her to ignore it. She must give into it and perform the ancient rite. She had no choice. The muscles of her body relaxed for a moment. She settled herself into the clean hay, half-sitting up and half squatting.

She remembered when she and Winona had talked about Little Doe. Winona had explained that, unless the birth were very irregular, most Indian women had their babies in a squatting position, to allow the weight and position to work for them. She found it so difficult to breathe while lying down she decided to try to squat, just as the next forceful push started. She hung onto the post of the stall and concentrated on pushing the baby out of her, to start its new life. She had no idea what time it was, or how long she had been there. She only knew when the next pain came, telling her to put all her being into the task. The surge of water came, staining the floor of the barn. Then the purpose become more urgent. How could she catch the child and still hold onto the pole? She had to have its support. This position did make it easier to push the child away from her. Her only reason for existence at that moment was to push this child into the world. She felt its head begin to emerge from her. She gave one final push as she sat up on her haunches and reached down for the child. In one huge push, in one final effort, she was no longer two but one again.

She lay back, sweating and exhausted. She held the bloody, wet, crying child under her coat with the cord still attached. When she recovered her breath, since she had no sharp object, she bit the cord for the final severance from her body. She felt another surge of liquid between her legs as the afterbirth came.

The baby wailed loudly, but she didn't care. It was alive, very alive. That was all cared about. She lay for a half hour, holding the child and trying to get warm. She was so cold, so cold, so tired. She broke the layer of ice in the watering trough of the cows, wet her scarf in the cold water, and washed the blood from the child and herself quickly. Then she tucked the child under her layers of clothing. She laid one of the horse blankets down to protect her from the prickly hay and cold floor and hugged the child to her breast, making sure that it could breathe, but that it was warm. They slept.

***

The cries of the baby awoke her from her deep sleep. She was so groggy she was not at first aware of what it was. Then she knew and she smiled. She helped it get its greedy little mouth to her breast, where it sucked avidly for a few minutes, and then more lazily. Amanda watched it – her. The little girl had a big head of dark black hair, and intensely brown eyes, with golden flecks in them. She had long fingers and legs, and had wet on Amanda some time in the night. She had to get them to the house, clean them up, and restore some order in their life.

Why hadn't Andrew come in? Where were they? She hoped nothing had happened to them. She stood up stiffly as she held the baby tightly to her. There was blood all over the floor. It had stained all of Amanda's clothing. The cows complained because they were full of milk. They would have to wait.

Apparently she had been there for a full day and night. The sun was still low as it rose in the east.

"Welcome to this world, little one," she whispered to the baby.

The sun shone brightly on the snow. The glare almost blinded her. She heard the horses behind her as she was almost to the house. She turned to greet them.

"My god, Amanda! What in the hell?"

Andrew was off his horse before the animal had stopped. He grabbed her, seeing the blood and her pale face. She pulled back.

"It's all right, Andrew," she laughed. "Let's go into the house. I have something to show you."

He more carried than helped her into the house. Raphael followed, the concern showing on his face, too. When they were in the warmth of the house, she told Raphael to build a fire. She told Andrew to bring a blanket. He flew into the bedroom, and brought one of the coverlets from the bed. She then, and only then, brought forth her precious bundle for exhibition. The little milk the baby had had from her mother had put her to sleep. Amanda wrapped her quickly in the blanket to protect her from the cold.

"She's beautiful," Andrew said in awe. Then, realizing the full impact of what had happened, he gripped Amanda by the arms. "My God, you were all alone! My darling Amanda, are you really all right? I'm so sorry that you, that I wasn't..."

She kissed him lightly. "It's okay, Andrew. What had to be done, I would have to do alone anyway. Let's get her into some warm clothes and then I want to clean up."

She had left a trail of bloody spots across the floor. Andrew scrubbed the floor until they were gone. Raphael, after brief inspection of the new arrival, hurriedly warmed some water on the stove, and prepared a bath for Amanda. He made it so hot she felt like she would boil alive when she got in it. But if felt good and she soaked in it until it cooled. Then she climbed out and dressed. She felt dizzy and sat down to regain her head. Andrew had refused to leave her alone and was fixing something to eat. He picked her up and carried her into the bedroom and placed her on the bed beside the baby, who slept peacefully in her new cradle. Raphael helped bring in the dinner and the two of them sat on the bed with her and watched her eat.

"Have you eaten?" she asked.

"We will, later," Andrew said.

"What's her name?" asked Raphael.

"Well, I guess we haven't thought that far ahead," Andrew replied.

"With all that dark hair, she looks like a little cub bear," Raphael observed.

Amanda shivered. Someone had called the child's mother a she-bear, a long time ago.

"Kathleen," Amanda bestowed the name of the child.

Andrew peered over the side of the crib. "Little Katy MacGregor," he said to her, and she promptly began to cry.

"Pick her up and bring her here," Amanda said.

"How?"

"Just make sure you have her head and body supported and pick her up."

Andrew looked at her helplessly. Raphael frowned at the noisy thing. Gingerly Andrew picked her up, his big hands forming a platform for the squalling infant. He carried her to Amanda like a priest with a sacrifice. Amanda unbuttoned her blouse, and the child sucked greedily, pulling until the twinge in her breast told Amanda that the milk was coming. She had never nursed Melinda, never had the change for this close warmth and possessiveness. They all watched as the child ate her fill and then slept again.

"I suppose you will have to milk the cows, Andrew. I seem very tired. Would you?" she asked.

He put his head on her breast where the baby had sucked minutes before.

"I shouldn't have left you alone," he moaned.

"Are the cattle all right? Will we have a herd this spring?" she asked.

He laughed a little and covered her up with the blankets. "Yes, we will have a fine herd next spring."

But when he had tucked her in and left, another bout of terrible fatigue overcame her and she slept as though dead.

***

He was shaking her awake and shouting, "Amanda, Katy is crying. You must feed her. And you have to eat."

He was holding the baby in one arm, trying to rouse her with the other. She took the baby to her breast in a few, and then drifted back to sleep.

The next few days were foggy. She knew she was bleeding badly, but couldn't seem to get her bearings. Andrew or Raphael would bring food into her and she would eat it, even though she gagged at times and had a hard time keeping it down. Andrew would force her, telling her it was the only way she could keep her strength up and could feed Katy. She saw him from far away, saw him as he changed the bloody sheet, and knew he slept on the floor next to the bed. But from there, she was in a haze as to whether it was day or night.

Finally she awoke one morning to a gray, cold day. Her head was clear. Gingerly she sat straight up, then attempted to put her feet on the floor. Raphael came in and caught her trying to stand up. He firmly pushed her shoulders down, pushing her back on the bed.

AMANDA

"Andrew says you must not get up yet. He says you are very weak and we must take care of you. You stay here and I'll get Andrew."

He raced out. She heard Katy crying, and wanted to pick her up. The poor little thing was raising a ruckus. But then, the crying before had always seemed so distant. She could never remember Melinda crying much, but Katy seemed always to be crying. But then, she was never around Melinda much when she was a baby. Remembering this made her even more determined to reach the child.

But Andrew's dark form interfered with her plans. Andrew brought the baby to her.

"Can you feed her yourself?" he asked.

"Yes, of, course," she answered, irritated by his implication of her inability. But as she opened her nightshirt, and held the baby, she saw her hands shaking.

"I've been pretty sick, huh?" she asked.

"Very sick. One day you were so bad you had no milk for the baby. We boiled some of the cow's milk and fed it to her with a spoon, but it didn't satisfy her. She is very thin, too."

Amanda was weak and thin, but the bleeding had stopped and the fever and the nightmares. She could eat without gagging, and Andrew and Raphael made sure she was well fed. One or the other was constantly bringing her food. Within another week she walked about on her own and could take on some of the lighter chores of the household. Katy had managed to gain a little weight, and she was no longer the skinny little thing she was before. Her glossy black hair and bright brown eyes enchanted Raphael, who declared that perhaps children were not such bad things after all.

***

One evening, after feeding the baby, she couldn't sleep. She knew Andrew and Raphael were still up, and she wondered what they found to do so late into the evening. She stopped at the door, catching the conversation.

"It's all I know, Andrew. That's as far as she taught us before the tribe had to move," Raphael was saying.

"Well, at least I can read some, now. Before, well," Andrew replied.

"I thought all white men went to school and knew how to read," Raphael said.

"I didn't. No schools around and the old man didn't know how to read. The only thing he knew how to do was to write his name, and that's what he taught me. His name was Andrew MacGregor, too."

"I think when I become a man, that I, too, will have this name."

"You already have a name," Andrew said. "I thought your Indian name was Little Otter."

"It is a child's name," Raphael said disgustedly. "What is the meaning of your name? Why did you take the name of the old man?"

"Well, I took the name because he was a good old man and I wanted to be a good man. Meaning? Guess the only meaning it's got is that it's mine so it's what I am."

"What you are is good?"

"I guess. I'm not so sure what's good or what isn't, sometimes."

"Good is being brave, and being a warrior, and attacking your enemy," Raphael averred.

"There's more to courage than killing a man, or carrying a gun, my friend," Andrew observed.

"Have you killed a man?"

AMANDA

"Yes. But it was something I had to do. I'm not particularly proud of it."

"But a warrior should tell of his deeds and be proud of them!"

"Sometimes not killing is braver than killing," Andrew stated.

Raphael frowned. He was evidently confused by this conflict, because he changed the subject. "Do you wish to try to read some more?"

"It's be kinda difficult if neither one of use knows the words, now, wouldn't it," Andrew answered.

"But I can read them" Amanda interjected. They both looked up in surprise at her presence. "I'm sorry, I didn't mean to eavesdrop, but I didn't know how to let you know I was here. I would teach you both, if you want me to."

Andrew took her hand and led her to his chair. They sat on either side of her, and she began another school. It became their custom to read on the long evenings. She found that Andrew's ciphering was limited and so also helped him with that. Raphael's flare for the dramatic re-emerged and he would frequently entertain them by acting out some of the plays, inventing an Indian-style dance to dramatize Hamlet, who he still avowed was hesitant coward who did not understand the spirits.

***

As spring approached, Andrew decided to bring the herd closer so he could watch over it during calving. Amanda wanted to go with them, but Andrew argued about the dangers of taking Katy on such an arduous journey. So she stayed home. But the calves would not wait, and many nights, Andrew and she would wake to the lowing of a cow bearing her calf.

Andrew would check on it, watching the birth to make sure it was normal. Amanda began to alternate with him, since he was frequently up for twenty-four hours at a time. She would rouse Raphael to listen for the baby when Andrew was sleeping in exhaustion, and would pull on her pants and shirt and coat. With her hat low over her forehead and her hair tucked under the hat, she would attend the birth of a calf.

She had watched Andrew reach his arm up into one cow to turn the calf so it would come out right and the mother and little one would both live. They found that she was more adept at this, because not only were her arms long, but they were narrower, and her hands smaller and there was less danger to the animal. It was a good calving. They had added twenty new ones to their herd.

They also had another visit from their Indian neighbors. They were informed that the spring festival would be held at the warm springs, where the water bubbled out of the ground. Amanda was afraid they were referring to her spring that she had discovered long ago. But to her surprise, there were larger ones. They were asked to attend. But she asked Winona if they were being invited because they allowed the Indians to use their land or if they were being invited because they were truly wanted.

"Both," Winona answered.

Amanda was ready for a change, for a little excitement, after the long winter. She brought Katy and was ready to go. All the Indians had to inspect the child, including the fiercest-looking of the most dignified warriors. The one who had married the Gemini paid particularly close attention, whispering soft words of poetry to the child about her beauty. Paul had to touch her. He begged to hold her, which Amanda permitted with a little trepidation. He sat cross-legged with her under the tree while Amanda prepared the wagon with good things to eat. She still had bolts of cloth that she had bought last fall with every good intention of making new clothes for herself. She held them for a moment, debating. Then she came out and beckoned to Winona.

"I'd like to give you this. I know it isn't much, but I think you would probably put it to use before I will," she told her.

"All the women of the tribe like bright colors, like these," Winona observed.

Amanda, puzzled, then finally understanding, knew her friend was trying to tell her that all would share in the benefit.

"Whatever is best," she shrugged.

Winona whispered to one of the Gemini, who spread the news to the other women. They came to look at the cloth, smiling at Amanda and commenting on the beauty of the cloth.

"But we have no such great gift to give our white sister," Ruth lamented.

Before Amanda could protest that is not why she gave the gift, Naomi took a necklace from her neck and placed it around Amanda's neck. It was made of carefully and evenly matched bear's claws.

"It's beautiful. Thank you," she said to Naomi.

Her students had grown to such young women in such a short time. The Gemini were already married. Not so Winona. She wondered if such a vow of celibacy was unusual among Indian woman. Knowing how hard their lot was sometimes, she wouldn't doubt it if it were preferable. Perhaps she would ask Winona more about it sometime.

Right now they were on their way to the spring festival. She went to retrieve Katy from Paul.

"She is unusual," Paul said, handing the baby to Amanda. "She will have a gift with horses."

"Have you taken to predicting the future?" Amanda teased.

He blushed a little. "Sometimes I know these things."

"I think sometimes you see things we sighted people don't" she commented, putting her arms around his shoulders and leading him to the wagon. "Will you ride with us, or do you have a horse?" she asked.

"I would be honored to ride with you," he said.

He climbed into the back with Raphael, who rattled on to him about all the things they had done. It had been awhile since Amanda had heard the language, and she couldn't understand all that was said. Then Paul replied with the things that had happened in the tribe. She did catch the fact that they had compensated somewhat with the white man's strange way of living along by putting their homes in the corners of the quadrants, so that at least there were often four families together. They had managed to re-organize lots, so that while they still adhered to the order of so many acres per person, they put whole families together. That must have been a prodigious feat of logistics, Amanda thought, remembering the hodgepodge Kinney had shown her. She was curious as to what had happened to Kinney. Did he still try to rule like a petty tyrant, or was his power curtailed just as the Indian lands had been diminished?

"Andrew, do you come along with me on these things to humor me, or do you enjoy them?" she asked, putting her arm through his.

"Some of these people are my friends, Amanda. I like being with them, the same as I like being with some of the folks at Harlan," he answered, seemingly puzzled at her questions.

He seemed so simple in his relationships. He trusted people, something she did not always do. Did he never really question what had really happened that night?

She gasped when she saw the mineral springs. They were spread out over perhaps an acre or more. The water seeped out of the ground, sending off its steamy, odorous vapors in all directions. It then cascaded down into a pool, only to travel underground from some distance and re-appear in another amorphous pool. From there is cascaded down into the fresh water river. So that is why the water from the stream often tasted strangely. It was full of these mineral waters. Perhaps that is why these people managed to stay fairly healthy, in spite of their sparse diet. They pitched their tepees and made their camp a little ways from the mineral waters. They spent the day making preparations.

"All will fast tonight. Tomorrow morning, when the sun rises, we will go to the waters and thank the Great Spirit for his gift of the waters," Winona explained. "Then we will have the celebration."

Seeing Raphael go without eating was something Amanda never thought she would witness. But he did not eat. There was a hush over the Indian encampment. They had been offered the hospitality of Winona's tent. Amanda lay in the stillness of the night, feeling the cool air, the same kind of air she had felt when she had tried to return to the cave after Jason had left. She felt a deep chill go through her, a restlessness. She couldn't remain in the tent. Andrew was sleeping, snoring lightly. Katy slept content, the only one in the whole camp who had eaten. Raphael slept at the door. Amanda stepped quietly over him and emerged into the night. The fires were out. Occasionally a dog barked, but nothing else disturbed the air that carried the spirits. She walked to the ground between the two mineral water lakes. She breathed deeply of the sulphurous aroma, and sat cross-legged, staring at the moon. Her stomach rumbled with hunger. The moon's face came closer and closer. It was smiling and had blue eyes.

Melinda reached out to her with both hands, showing her the pretty blue flowers she had. The she turned and walked away and waved good-by. Amanda did not try to follow her. She saw no danger. Melinda was smiling and skipping away, and the moon returned. It had traveled much further into the sky, and Amanda had to lie down to see it. This time it had brown eyes with yellow flecks in them. It was smiling again, but the smile was different. The arms that reached out to her were brown. It did not wave goodbye, but this time lay down beside her. She slept.

***

The sun greeting the mineral lakes awakened her. She stood up abruptly and hurried back to the tepee, knowing her child would be hungry. Her friends were awake and quietly moved in preparation of the ceremony. Amanda fed and changed Katy, and she and Andrew watched as the shaman said his words to the waters and each of the Indians drank from a common gourd of the waters as they came off the first waterfall. The shaman offered the water to her and she drank. She winced inwardly at the taste, but tried not to show her distaste because she did not want to offend these people. Andrew also drank of it. Then they stood with the others while they danced a slow dance and sang a song of thanks. Then they filed back to the camp with dignity. The women prepared a huge feast, and as all ate, the singing and the dancing and the drums started up. Amanda knew it would continue for a long time. But they had cows to tend and cattle to feed. They had to return to the ranch. She did not look for Raphael. She knew he would return when it was done. She would not question him.

***

The fort was also holding its annual spring festival, celebrating Easter and spring all rolled into one. The ladies all filed into the church with their Easter hats and finery. Amanda again wore her old dress, but knew without him saying so that Andrew thought she could find the time to make a new one. She made a mental note that she would concede to this one idea he had about "what a woman should look like" and make one to wear for such occasions. There was a picnic afterward, with races and games for the children, and finally a dance, with the drunken fiddler a bit tipsy but still in fine form. Sergeant Pepper managed to inveigle a dance with Amanda, after which, Andrew lent her out to a few others to dance to her heart's content.

But when the dances were over, they returned to the hard work of the ranch, again sharing equally in the tasks at hand.

***

"You can't bring Katy along while we're checking the fences," he protested.

"Why not? She's perfectly safe strapped to my back like this. The Indian women do it all the time."

"You are not an Indian woman."

"That doesn't mean I can't borrow a good idea when I see one."

Thus the partnership grew. Days blended into one another as they struggled to make the existence into a living. It was a constant tension of the new and the old, Amanda often wanting to innovate, and Andrew wanting to conserve the old ways. He wanted to drive the cattle down to the stream every day. She wanted a windmill to pump the water to them. She won that round. On one visit to town, she met a man who was selling books and magazines and new cures for animals. She bought the books and devoured them and sent for more. Sometimes they would try the new way, when it would seem easier or more profitable. Other times, they decided to stay with the old ways.

***

"Andrew, when is your birthday?" she asked.

"Don't rightly know."

"Mine is March fourth."

With a twinkling eye he asked, "Are you asking me to get you a birthday present and throw a big party like we did for Katy?"

She blushed a little. "Certainly not. It's just I have no idea how old you really are."

"You've never told me your age, either," he said.

They had been married for two years and yet still didn't know many simple things about each other. They were too busy trying to live from day to day.

"I'm twenty-four," she stated.

"Not sure how old I am," he said, pulling the cinch tight on the saddle and checking the bit. "Think I'm twenty-six or twenty-seven, about there, anyways. Never did celebrate no birthday, though."

She handed Katy up to Andrew and mounted her horse. She still rode the sturdy little Indian pony, even though their herd had grown. And they had purchased of the new horses.

"Why don't you celebrate your birthday with mine? Then we could share it," she suggested.

He grinned. "So we grow old together, huh?" and galloped away with the little one holding tightly to the horn of the saddle.

She thought he was older. Maybe because she had never seen him without his beard. But when she remembered the muscled, lean body and the vigor of him, she knew he couldn't be as old as her first husband had been. It wasn't that his skin was not as white as her first husband's, where the sun did not reach, but rather that there was such life in the body. Jason's had been that way. Could she never stop thinking of him? It had been over two years. It should be done. How could she love two men at the same time?

***

"She's too young to learn to ride," Amanda objected.

She felt panic rise up in her as she watched Andrew lift Katy onto the saddle of the pony. The little mare was a gentle soul, she knew. But Katy was barely three.

"If she going to grow up in this country, she has to learn to ride," Andrew reasoned. He adjusted the stirrups until they were at least where Katy could put her tiptoes on them. She sat up straight. She watched Raphael jump on his horse and ride off. Then she held the reins of her pony just like he did.

"Take her around the corral and I'll walk beside her," Andrew instructed him.

They walked around. She clapped her hands and laughed. After two or three times, Raphael urged the horse into a faster walk. Katy sat on the horse with ease, as though she had been born there.

Now when they rode out, it was with four horses.

***

"Mommy, Mommy, come quick! Raphael's sick!" Six-year-old Katy hollered, galloping up to the milking shed and sliding off her horse before it could stop.

"What is it, child?" Amanda asked.

"It's Raphael. He drank some stuff out of a bottle and it made him awful sick."

Amanda left the buckets of milk and the cows, and threw a rope on her horse, and rode bareback to where Katy took her.

Raphael knelt on the ground, leaning over, and retching. She knelt beside him. She spied the bottle of whiskey, lying empty a few yards away. She had long forgotten about even having it around.

"You stupid kid," she said. "What have you done? Did you drink that whole thing?"

"Oh, Amanda, I hurt. My head! The ground moves. I'm going to die. I'm going to die. I will sit in the shadows and sing my death song," he moaned.

"You're not going to die. At least not from that bottle. I might kill you myself, though. Let's get you down to the water and get some cold water on you."

She helped him stagger to the spring. He was taller than she and when he leaned his weight on her, both of them almost went tumbling into the water. She knelt down to splash his face, but she decided to use more of a shock treatment. She tumbled him head over heels, into the cold spring water. He yelled as though she were torturing him. She kept him there for a few minutes, then helped him out and stretched him out under the tree.

"You are a very mean old woman!" he accused her.

"Don't you ever touch that stuff again, or it will be more than just a cold bath you'll be getting, you savage heathen," she growled at him. "Katy, go get a blanket from the house," she instructed.

Katy leaped on her pony and sped to the house. She brought back the blanket and Amanda wrapped Raphael in it.

"Stay with him until he comes to," Amanda told her six-year-old. "Then you two come to the house. Can you do that?"

"Sure, Mommy."

She didn't tell Andrew about the "firewater" incident. The threat hanging over Raphael prevented him from trying a repeat performance.

***

The stupid calf had itself caught in the bushes halfway down the side of the gorge. Andrew decided they would have to try to haul it up by ropes since they couldn't help it go down, and it would be too hard to simply carry it up. Since Amanda was the lightest, she elected to go down the side and tie it up. The thing was frightened, and fought her as she tied the ropes around its middle and neck. Andrew and Raphael began to pull it up, while Katy held their horses and slowly back them away, adding their strength to the haul. Amanda climbed down a little, staying under and to the side of the animal. The ledge over which they had to pull it hung out, and she leaned out some to help it over. Just as they pulled it over, it kicked her. She felt her foot slip and she lost her grip. She went tumbling down the side of the embankment, rocks jabbing at her and ripping and tearing her.

***

The room was dark. She heard murmurs in the next

room. Her mind was separated from her body. Someone's face appeared over her, but she couldn't recognize it. The darkness folded over her again.

The next time she awoke, a different face looked at her. She tried to say something, but couldn't. Her mouth was dry and her tongue was swollen, filling her mouth so there wasn't enough room for the words to come through. Then someone lifted her head a little and helped her drink a little. It helped.

Again she awoke and drank. The ringing in her ears and the throbbing of her legs and the pains in her stomach and abdomen told her she had returned to her body.

The fourth time she awoke, she knew some of the pain to be hunger pains. She whispered to the person that she was hungry. The person came back and fed her. The person gradually grew a face that looked very much like Winona.

"I have to relieve myself," Amanda said hoarsely.

The person who looked like Winona shook her head, and pushed her back to the bed and then helped her relieve herself into a pan.

Finally, she awoke again. She knew it was Winona with her. And she was ravenously hungry.

"How long have I been out?" she asked as she stuffed her mouth with the soup and crackers and fresh milk and strawberries."

"Five days," Winona answered.

"Is everything all right inside me?"

Winona hesitated a minute. She had always been honest with Amanda before, so Amanda waited for her answer. She knew it wouldn't be an easy answer to take, since Winona was taking so long to formulate her answer.

"You had much bleeding," she began.

"Yes?"

AMANDA

"Many times, when a woman is injured in such a manner and bleeds in such a way, it is said that she will not be able to ever have more children," Winona explained.

"I can't have any more children?" Amanda repeated, not quite comprehending.

"I would say probably not," Winona said. "I'm sorry."

Amanda sat, thinking. No children. Andrew would never get his own child. It seemed so sad.

"It doesn't matter, Amanda," he said when she told him. " I have you and you are alive. I thought you were dying. I don't think I could live without you."

She held his head in her arms and stroked his hair.

"Amanda?" he began.

"Umm."

"I have to ask you something, though."

"Yes?"

"It isn't easy to say." She waited, her hand frozen. Her heart began to beat harder. "Katy isn't mine, is she?" he asked.

Amanda swallowed hard. Andrew lifted his head and looked at her. "I love her as my own. She will never know that she is not mine. But I didn't father her, did I?" Andrew asked.

Amanda slowly shook her head. "No, you didn't," she whispered.

"But is she the reason you asked me to marry you?"

"Yes."

"If you had not been pregnant, would you have asked me?"

"No," she answered.

He caressed her face with his fingers and then kissed her fully, gently, on the mouth. Then he pulled his face away only a fraction of an inch.

"Then it doesn't matter that I did not father her. I am her

father now. And because of her, you married me. I love you, Amanda."

"You don't want to know who the father is?" she asked fearfully. She didn't want to tell him, but he had the right to know if it was important to him.

"I think I know," he said.

She shivered. He knew now. She was relieved of carrying the burden alone. She was afraid it would come between them. She was afraid it would make a difference in how he treated Katy.

But it didn't. He loved her. He loved Katy and taught her and disciplined her, the same as he always had. Perhaps he had always known, but just wanted her confirmation.

***

Kinney came to visit. It looked to Amanda as though the man had shrunk. The limp was more noticeable now and he shuffled a little when he walked.

"What do you want?" she asked angrily.

"I've come for the boy," he said.

"What boy?"

"The one you call Raphael."

"Why now? You haven't checked to see if he was dead or alive for eight years. Why now? You can't have him. This is his home.

"Well, the law says when an Indian is eighteen he's not a boy anymore. He has to come back and live on the reservation."

"Like hell he will."

"Or he can become a citizen, and give up all rights to the reservation and tribal rights," Kinney explained.

"Become a citizen? He is a citizen of this country," she stated, confused.

"No, not legally. You see, Indians are not citizens of the United States."

Amanda was astonished at the idea. "Then he'll become a citizen. What does he have to do?"

"You understand, that if he is a citizen, he will give up all tribal rights and cannot return to the reservation without permission from the agent and the council," Kinney said.

It sounded a little like being stuck between Hell and Hades, to Amanda. She rang the dinner bell until Kinney was forced to take refuge from the bedlam by covering his ears. Andrew was out riding the fences, but she knew Raphael and Katy were in the barn, caring for the new Arabian horses they had just acquired.

She explained the problem to Raphael.

"I guess I just got so used to being here, and sometimes with my people, I never gave much thought as to what my 'legal' rights were," he said ruefully, stuffing his hands in his pockets.

"We're going to have to work something out," Amanda swore. "You are not going to be forced to go away simply because some idiot in Washington doesn't know a mule from a horse. Kinney, come inside."

"Oh, Mrs. MacGregor, I have to return to the reservation. So many things to do, you know," he said.

"I know exactly the kind of things you do, Kinney, and you are going to stay right here," she ordered him, growing ten feet tall with indignation.

"Sit here," she ordered him to sit at the chair in the front office. We're going to have a private conference." When Kinney started to object, she whirled to him, glaring at him eyeball to eyeball. "He's not going to run away. Sit down. Katy, bring Mr. Kinney a cup of coffee. Then go get your father."

Raphael sat at the table, rolling brim of his hat back and forth in his hands.

"Well?" he asked her, swallowing hard, staring mournfully at her with his large liquid eyes.

Maturity had sharpened his features somewhat, but he was still her beautiful child. He wore his long hair braided down his back, and always wore a bright headband, which only enhance the liquid gold of his skin. She loved this young savage like the son that she would never have. And no halfwitted Indian agent was going to steal him away from her.

"I've never really asked you what you want to do, Raphael. I think now we'd better know."

"I want to stay here," he said simply.

"Don't you want to return to your people?" she asked.

"They are not my people, not like you and Andrew are. I'm one of them because my skin is brown and my hair is black and I talk to the Great Spirit. But I am also a rancher. I love doing what I do here, with the cattle, and especially the horses. I couldn't go back to live exactly as they do. But I cannot become like a white man and live in a city either. I want to stay here," he answered.

"I'm not sure how we can work it out. If you become a legal citizen, then every time you wanted to visit your friends, every time you went to the dances and the festivities, you would have to ask Kinney. You would have to go to the council. You would no longer own that piece of land you now have. You would not be one of them."

"Is this their decision, also?"

"I don't know. But I don't think Washington has given them any say in the matter," she said.

"And if I don't become a 'legal citizen' I can't stay here with you. You're my parents. A man doesn't desert his parents. He cares for them when they get old like they cared for him when he was young. I belong here. I love this land." The pain showed in his voice and he gripped his hat with both hands. "What can it matter to all those important people in Washington that one Indian has become eighteen? Does it really matter to them where he goes or what he goes?

There was a timid knock at the door.

"Excuse me, Mrs. MacGregor," Kinney said nervously.

"What is it? Can't you see we're talking," she was exasperated beyond any patience. Couldn't he leave them alone?

"I may have a solution," he said.

"Well?" she asked.

"Many of the younger Indians have work permits that allow them to leave the reservation as long as they have a sponsor who will provide them with work and take the responsibility for them."

Amanda raised here eyebrows. "They are then still members of the tribe?"

"Yes, but they can leave the reservation."

"How do we get Raphael one of these permits?"

"I issue them. At a price, or course, all the paperwork and all," he said.

Of course, thought Amanda. He always thought of a hundred small ways to make money off the Indians.

"And what is the fee?" she asked.

"Well, it varies considerably with the health of the worker, and his age and experience. You see, not too many people want the old ones to work for them, but some of the younger ones don't have much experience. At eighteen, with all his ranching experience and his ability to handle horses, he would be worth quite a bit," Kinney launched his pitch.

"You sound like an auctioneer at a slave sale, Mr. Kinney," Amanda said sharply.

"Oh, no, Mrs. MacGregor, it's nothing like that. It gives the Indians an opportunity to make money, and to see what the real world is like."

"How much, Kinney, would you need to release Raphael from your clutches?" she growled.

"Oh, fifty dollars ought to do it," Kinney said.

She cocked her head at Raphael, asking his approval. He nodded almost imperceptibly. She stormed to the desk and wrote out the draft. Kinney reached for it.

"Not so fast. I want the agreement in writing. Here, write it down, exactly what the terms are. We have bought the young Indian man called Raphael, or Little Otter, for the grand sum total of fifty dollars."

Kinney's hand shook as he wrote out the words, just as Amanda had dictated to him. She looked at the paper and the signature and then showed Kinney the door. After he was gone, she opened the small safe they kept at the ranch and put the document in it.

Andrew was furious with the whole situation when he came in with Katy. He stormed and paced the floor.

"And what can we do about it?" he ranted. "All these idiotic decisions start with some fool in Washington. Every time there's a new President there's a new 'Indian policy,' each claiming they'll civilize our savage brothers!" He clasped Raphael on both shoulders. "You're sure this is how you want it to be?"

"It's as close I think I can get right now, considering the circumstances and the new laws."

Andrew slapped him on the back. "Let's go finish those fences," he said.

***

It had been an unusually cold spring. The calves that came seemed to come earlier than usual, and there were many who had a hard time being birthed. They all took their turns staying up to watch, even Katy. The twelve-year-old stayed with the two mares in the barn, knowing their time was coming. It worried Amanda that she would sleep in the barn, but she slept better there because she said she could hear them and would know if they needed her help. Paul had been right. The child had a sense for horses. They trusted her, and she could ride, rope, or train any horse that walked or ran.

Andrew had left early in the morning to check the herd on the north range. He had taken blankets and supplies. They had a shack up at the range. He planned to stay there overnight and then bring the herd down in the morning. Amanda didn't like it when he was gone overnight. He had not taken Raphael or any of the hands with him, since they were needed elsewhere. He had kissed her lightly when he left and tried to soothe her worries. Her worries turned to pacing and fretting when a spring blizzard came howling down through the valley. She didn't sleep that night. She tried to read and found she couldn't. She lit a lamp and looked in on Katy. Lying there, sleeping, in the lamplight, she looked so much like Jason that Amanda's heart ached. Where would her life have gone if she hadn't had this child? Especially after losing her first-born?

The knock sounded like the wind at first. Then Amanda was sure it was a knock. She rushed to the door and flung it open. Spotted Bear carried Andrew to the couch and laid him on it.

"What happened?" she asked. Then realizing Spotted Bear did not speak English, she switched to the Indian tongue. "What happened?"

"I don't know. I found him lying beside his horse. I was out hunting and the deer came to your land. It looks as though he had been thrown. There was blood on his forehead and his arm does not hang right. I don't know how long he had been there," Spotted Bear told her.

"Where was he?" Amanda asked, as she gently pulled the wet, frozen clothes off Andrew. "Would you help me get him into the bedroom?" she asked.

She and Spotted Bear carried Andrew into the bedroom. She saw his arm. It hung at his side all askew. It was more than just broken. It was twisted and ugly. She propped the arm up on a pillow and attended to his slashed brow. His hands and feet were blue from cold. Her eye burned with dry tears as she hurriedly covered him with layers of comforters and blankets and quilts. She heated some water on the stove and in the warm water, gently bathed his feet and hands, sighing with relief when she saw the color ebb back into them.

"Spotted Bear, would you get Katy from the barn for me?" she asked.

The man left. Katy came flying in moments later.

"Mother, what happened?" she asked frantically.

"Your father has had an accident," she said calmly, trying not to show her own fear.

They stayed up with him that night and two more nights. Amanda tried to rouse him out of the coma he was in, but she got no response from him. Then the fever started to rise, and his breathing became labored.

On the third night, she sat with him, holding his hand and caressing his face and hair. She had never noticed the few gray hairs that were in his beard and hair. His face was tanned and leathery from the years in the sun. It seemed so strange to see him lie so still. He was usually always working so hard at something. Even on the nights when all the chores were done, if he wasn't fixing something around the house, he was oiling the saddles or mending a bridle. His hands were large, but he could be so gentle. He would brush her hair for her at night, his hands firm on the brush. He loved to brush her hair, and then bury his face in it and talk to her about all the marvelous things he wanted to do for the ranch. She loved him.

The wind had stopped blowing finally, outside. The air held the eerie quiet it always got just before the dawn. She heard his rasping breath, and then the rattle in his throat. His whole body tightened, and just as the sun burst upon them, he died.

She laid her head on his chest, and her hand upon his eyes, and lay for a long time, as though if she stayed as still as he was, they would still be together. She felt so cold, so very cold. The brilliance of the sun flowing in the window was so bright. She got up angrily and pulled the shade down, but still the sun persistently showed through. Then she looked at Andrew's tranquil face and lifted the shade again. On such mornings they would lay in each other's arms, to make love, to laugh at the things that had happened, to argue about what they were going to do with the ranch. He liked being in the sun, would be outdoors whenever possible. She let the sun shine in on his face, and with tears streaming unchecked down her face, went to get Raphael and Katy.

When Katy heard, she burst into loud sobs and raced to the bedroom. "Daddy, Daddy," she cried, throwing herself across the body, sobbing, hugging the body as though she could, by the sheer force of will of her youth, put life back into.

Raphael stood beside the bed, then sank to his knees and began a mournful death song. She let them alone with their grief, being alone in hers. Then she went to them and put her arms around both of them. She pulled Katy gently off her father's body.

"We'll have to bury him. I want to bury him up by the caves," she said.

Raphael nodded. Katy looked puzzled, numbed by her grief into incomprehension. "You wish to bury him the white man's way?" Raphael asked.

"Yes," she answered.

"Then I will build what you call a coffin for him" he said, but still didn't move from Amanda's arm.

She released him to his task, knowing the grief would be easier to take if he were busy.

"Then tell your people if they wish to attend the burial, they should come."

"Katy, Katy," she shook Katy gently who looked back at her with her large brown eyes overflowing with tears.

"I want you to ride into town and get Reverend Billings. He can tell the other people in the town. Oh, and also send a message to Governor Greenwood. I'll write it down for you."

She was calm in her efficiency, saving her deepest feelings for when she would be alone with Andrew. Katy did as she was told, in a trance and numbed. Amanda knew that Katy would feel better riding her beloved horse.

When she was once again alone, she returned to Andrew. The full realization of his non-existence spread through her body. She was so cold, so numb. She saw that his eyes had opened. At first, she started to speak to him as though he had just awakened. She stopped herself, and then started again, but saying different words than she was originally going to say.

"My God, Andrew, how am I going to live without you? It's going to be so lonely, so damn lonely," she said to him, gently closing his eyes.

She pulled down the sheets and covers and dressed him in spite of his increasing stiffness. She put him in what he looked most comfortable in, his work pants and shirt. She put his socks on and struggled to pull his boots on him. Many times she had helped him pull them off, straddling his leg and pulling while his put his other foot against her behind. He would always laugh and tell her it would help if she kept a little more fat there.

She managed to dress him. Then she folded the covers up and laid them on the chest. He had helped her tie the green and brown one last winter, at first awkward with the yarn and thread until he figured that they were using the same kind of knot he used to tie up the hay bales.

When the room was straight, she put the coffee on. She waited until it had brewed and settled, they poured herself a cup and returned to Andrew's body, keeping a vigil over it until it could rest undisturbed. She looked at him and rocked gently back and forth in the straight-backed chair.

"Andrew, I love you. I never told you that when you were alive. I don't know why I never told you. I wish I had, now. We had so many plans," she sighed from her soul and sipped her coffee.

It tasted awful. She hadn't made coffee since she had married Andrew. It had been his specialty. The many small things they did with and for each other were wrapped up in together. He had such a time trimming his hair and beard, she finally convinced him to let her do it for him. His coarse, curly hair was stubborn and hard to work with, but he always looked better when she was done.

And the children. The times he and Raphael had worked hand-in-hand completing some task on the ranch. When Katy was older, and when they could get the ice, they would make ice cream. Raphael insisted on turning the machine, and then they would all gorge themselves on it.

Memories flooded her mind, and she sat and watched the body without seeing what was really there through the mists of her eyes and mind.

Raphael returned, and with him Spotted Bear and some of the elders of the tribe. She greeted them quietly and with dignity. She heard the drums beginning, and the death songs and the wailing of the women. They greeted her quietly and stepped in briefly to the bedroom to say their own good-bye.

Katy returned, still numb and confused. She stopped at the room, wanting to go it, but the dawning of the full truth made her afraid to go in.

"You can go in," Amanda said gently.

"I'm afraid, mother," she said.

"Why? He never hurt you in his life. Why would he in his death?"

Katy put her arms around her mother and her head on her shoulder. Mother and daughter were the same height now. And Katy was no longer a girl, but a young woman. She was beginning to learn the pain of life as well as its joys.

"Mother," she whispered, "do you believe in ghosts?

"I believe each person has a spirit, yes," she said.

"I'm afraid of ghosts," Katy sobbed.

"But if you were not afraid of the person, why the ghost? I'm comforted by their existence. You can be lonely when someone dies, but know they are not truly gone. You can't see them, that's all."

"It's not fair mother, it's not fair," Katy sobbed, angry at life now.

"I know," Amanda said,

"Why, mother, why did he die?"

"I don't know," she replied, her tears mixing with her daughter's. "Do you want to go in to see him one last time?"

AMANDA

Katy nodded. They went in together. Reverend Billings came and asked Amanda a few quiet questions. He spoke briefly to Jeremiah Greenwood and Raphael. Then they left.

"Raphael said he knew where you wished to bury Mr. MacGregor," Reverend Billings said, "So I have sent them to dig the grave. The snow has already begun to melt. I don't think the ground is frozen."

Amanda simply nodded. People from the town started coming, each bowing his head quietly and saying a word or two to Amanda before visiting Andrew.

"Amanda, I'm so sorry," Governor Greenwood extended his two huge hands to hers, burying her hand in his. "It's such a shock. We'll all miss Andy terrible."

Andrew lay in the room for a day. The next morning Raphael and Jeremiah lifted the body into the coffin and nailed down the lid. Katy screamed as they put the lid on the coffin and tried to stop them from nailing it on. Governor Greenwood gently pulled her away and she sobbed on his chest while they finished the sealing. Amanda watched, wincing at each blow of the hammers. They put the coffin in the wagon, and rode to the burial plot, the same place where years before, they had placed Melinda on the funeral bier and set her spirit free. And that is what they would do for Andrew, in the manner that he believed in.

Amanda saw the gaping hole in the soft, still muddy ground. The sun was warm today, so strange to the terrible cold of the last few days. It sent the message that at last the spring had come. There were so many people. She didn't think they knew so many people. They stood quietly around the gravesite while Reverend Billings read over the body. Amanda heard the beginnings of the twenty-third psalm, but heard no more. She looked over the people. Jeremiah Greenwood. She had helped bring him into this life, and saw his mother die in the effort. Poor Captain Greenwood had almost lost his mind. She had still been nursing Katy some, and so just took the new infant to her breast, so that it would live. The Captain was now Governor, but she knew that his life was his son. Jeremiah would be bigger than his father when he reached his full growth, already standing eye to eye with him at the age of twelve.

Mrs. Graves. Still running the store after all these years, still alone. Andrew was the only one who could make her laugh.

Spotted Bear. They had helped to nurse his daughter back to health when another bout of measles swept through the Indian people. It had killed so many that the death chant was sung almost daily. When Amanda had seen the blue calico dress on the little girl, she vowed that the child would live, somehow. She had. Andrew and Amanda had taken turns, sitting up and bathing the fever from the child.

She could go from face to face, and in each of them was a tragedy or triumph that they had shared. They had helped build the courthouse and dance in the celebration at Harlan. They had written the petition for the Indians to revert their lands back to tribal holdings instead of individual little plots. And they had danced in the celebration when the government had agreed to the petition.

The time had gone so swiftly. What had happened? Where was she to go from here? Why had it happened? She had no answer for herself anymore than she had had for her daughter. Death simply happened. Andrew had never talked about death. He was always too busy living. Perhaps that is all she could do now, is keep busy living. She knew if it had been her instead of him lying there so quiet and serene in the pine

AMANDA

box, that she would have wanted him to go on living, to go on enjoying the life here. She took the clod of dirt the Reverend handed her and threw it on the box in the hole.

The people filed by, taking her hand, giving Katy a kiss on the cheek, shaking Raphael's hand. After they had all left except a few, Governor Greenwood and his son filled in the grave. Raphael hammered in the marker he had made last night, not knowing what else to do with his time and his grief.

Raphael drove the wagon back to the house and unhitched the team, the grandsons of the magnificent ones who had witnessed Katy's birth. Amanda had made a decision. As was traditional, the people had all brought food to eat after the funeral, picnicking quietly on the lawn, a few children oblivious to the weight of the time, running and yelling until a stern parent squelched them. Amanda entered the house and gathered up Andrew's things. She laid them out on the porch, and called her Indian friends to her. They understand that she needed to give things of life back to the living. The white folk watched curiously as she gave her husband's possessions to his Indian friends. The magnificent saddle she gave to Spotted Bear. The clothes to those she knew to be poorer and in need of such things. She gave Andrew's special rope to the husband of the Gemini, who rode in the rodeos every year. Andrew's huge stallion she led to Raphael, who accepted it with his head bowed to conceal the tears in his eyes. Then she went across the lawn to the staring white folk and gave a piece of paper to Governor Greenwood.

"I know you've been wanting to have a state park as a game reserve, but only managed to set apart a few acres in the mountains. I will give you this paper, which gives you the rest of those mountains, in Andrew's name," she said, smiling slightly, knowing this kind of gift they would understand best.

The people next to him murmured their approval. Then she left them all, to return to the house, to gather up her memories and cry away some of her grief.

***

"Andrew, Katy and Raphael want to get married," she said to Andrew's spirit as she placed the spring flowers on his grave. She always brought flowers, or would eat some lunch here, and feed the chipmunks that would gather round. She had worked out many problems, kneeling in the grass beside the stream like this.

"Katy was very angry when I tried to talk her out of it. Oh, Andrew, they will have so many problems. She is only sixteen. That is so very young. I talked to Raphael. He was upset, as only he can get. I think he was even more frustrated and angry when I asked him to wait. He said he had waited for sixteen years, and had behaved with perfect dignity and respect to her, but he couldn't wait any longer, and if they can't become husband and wife, they'll be lovers."

"I finally agreed to it. They'll be married in three weeks. I'm giving them the north part of the ranch. They both want to raise these Arabian horses. They're both very good with them, and there seems to be a market for them. And they both enjoy the rodeos so. Raphael insisted that Katy have a lovely wedding dress and that we invite guests and have a very large wedding. That way there will be no doubt in anyone's mind that they are serious and that it's right." She laughed a little. "I finally talked the Reverend into performing a joint ceremony with Spotted Bear, who will act for Raphael's people. I'm sure everyone will have something to talk about the whole year long from it.

"Perhaps they won't have such a bad time of it. The hands accepted Raphael as foreman." Again she smiled and shook her head. "Well, he did have to convince a few of them. He ended up sitting on Curly and shaving his head. Curly tried to get even, but Raphael would only laugh at the practical jokes the hands played on him. They like him, I think. And Katy is so serious and stubborn. I think it will make a good balance in their marriage. They'll move out of the house as soon as they get their own built. I'll be alone, again, Andrew."

She sat feeding the chipmunks. She heard her horse neigh and decided to go back home. She stood up and stared at the cave. The old sod entryway was still standing to the house, although the one to the school had collapsed. She had never gone back to the cave. She had sent Raphael after the rest of the books and the other things just stayed, probably all rotted by now. Then she had been lonely. Now she would simply be alone. She knew there were many things she wanted to do, and her life was not going to last much longer. She would have to return to the East to put those ghosts to rest finally. The nightmares and the hatreds were gone, but not the anger or the memories.

There was someone standing beside her horse, holding his big palomino. He wore a suit like many of the Easterners did, but did not wear a hat. He had short, black, shiny hair. She didn't recognize him, as he had his back partially turned to her and she could barely discern the profile. She brushed the crumbs off her pants and walked toward the stranger. As she almost reached the horses, the stranger turned. She stopped and so did her heart. She stared at him, breathing rapidly, her eyes wide. He came to her, and cupped her face in his hands and kissed her lightly on the lips.

"Jason," she whispered, afraid the apparition would disappear.

"It has been a very long time, my beautiful little black bear," he whispered to her, putting his arms around her and kissing her hard this time.

Old feelings poured through her, and the strange kind of excitement she thought she would never know again tingled through her.

"What happened to you?" she asked, not trying to release his hold, her fingers digging into the sleeves of his coat.

"The caterpillar went into his cocoon and came out a moth," he told her. He pushed her away to arm's length and studied her face, her hair, and her body.

As he studied her, she devoured the sight of him. His beautiful, long, black, silky hair had been cut much shorter, barely brushing his coat collar. But it was still thick, with no traces of gray anywhere. His face was not the smooth beauty of youth, the age lines around his both and eyes showing evident of sorrow and hardship. He was still very lean and thin, she could tell from when he held her, but his black coat and vest, with the ruffle on his shirt, hid much of it. He seemed so strange. She knew this was the new style of men in the Eastern cities. But it did not fit what she remembered of Jason. His suit was neat and trim, and clean, as though he had just put it on. His boots were shiny and black. His horse carried a handsome leather saddle, expensive and well made, Amanda thought. What had happened to her sensual savage to turn him into such a smooth Eastern dude? Would she still love him, like this? How much had he really changed? And what did he think of her?

"Have I changed?" she asked.

"A little. I would have thought you would be fat and content, by now," he smiled at her. "You were always a handsome woman. Pretty women fade, like flowers. Handsome women get better, like good wine," he explained.

She pulled away from him and walked down to the bank, pulling her boots off and dangling her feet over into the water. He sat beside her, his feet heading away from the bank.

"What would you know about good wine?" she asked, hoping he would explain why he was not what he used to be.

"I have tasted much of it, here in the States and in Europe," he said.

She couldn't contain her need to know any longer. "Tell me what happened to you. Why are you dressed like this? You look so different. I think you are different."

He pulled a blade of new grass and chewed on it reflectively. "It's been sixteen years, Amanda. Everyone changes in that time," he said evasively.

"Don't you want to tell me?"

"I'm not particularly proud of some of my last sixteen years."

"Tell me," she said softly. He laid his head in her lap. Even after all this time, it seemed so natural, so right, that she voiced no objections, just smoothed his hair back and then put her hand on his chest under his coat.

"Well, let's see. After I left the reservation they were pretty hot on our trail. We stood them off at one spot, but when night came, we knew we had to run as far and as fast as we could. When we first left, we had thoughts of gathering a force and defeating the whole United States Army." He saw her smile at that and smiled, too. "It sounds ridiculous, but we were all very young and very angry and very hurt." He sighed a little. "Anyway, we split up, two together. I heard later that many were killed and hanged. They cornered Circling Hawk and me. We were both shot. I think they thought they'd killed us both, because when I woke up, no one was there except Circling Hawk. When I was sure he was dead, I just took off."

"I lived off the land, running, always to the rising sun." He laced the fingers of his right hand through hers. "You have done a lot of hard work."

She tried pulling her rough, callused hand away. His was smoother and probably hadn't done any seriously hard work in years. But he would not let go of hers, but gripped it firmly, kissed it, and held it to his chest. She waited for him to continue his story. He closed his eyes.

"As I got further east, the people in the towns found me more of a curiosity than a danger. At first, I was very insulted that I did not terrorize them at the first sight of me. But then I learned how to use their curiosity to my advantage, to get food, lodging for the night. Often I made a pretense of not knowing English or how to read or write." He chuckled a little and opened his eyes. "These things that you taught me about your language and people I think save me quite often. They would say things, and presume the ignorant savage didn't understand. It gave me the advantage."

"I'm glad that my teaching you helped you, Jason," she said.

"You kept me alive," he said, sitting up and looking intently at her. "I would dream of you at night, and when I was tired, I would remember how you would work for me, for Melinda, and the others, even when you were so very tired. And when I was lonely, I would remember the nights we had together and the times we laughed together, and then I was not lonely anymore."

She looked down. She could not tell him that her thoughts were often on him, even when she lay with another man. She pulled her feet out of the stream and waited for them to dry.

"Is that how you have lived all this time, by other people's curiosity and generosity?" she asked puzzled. This seemed odd, considering his pride and need for dignity and self-respect.

AMANDA

"Only for awhile. Once, when I was going from town to town, I saw a carriage overturn along the road. I might not have stopped, except the horse was still attached to it and had fallen. It was in such pain, screaming and struggling. It had broken its front legs and I shot it to put it out of its suffering. Then I heard moans. Someone was under the carriage. As it turned out, it was a judge's wife. She was pinned under it. I managed to lift it enough to pull her out. She was still conscious and told me where she lived. Then she passed out. I carried her to her house. To make a long story short, the judge was very grateful to me for my daring rescue," he smiled at himself again. "They asked me to stay with them. They sent me to law school. I graduated third in the class. Then I joined the judge's old law firm in Boston. I was very successful at it. White men's laws are very complex and not always logical."

"Not all laws are bad, Jason," she said gently.

"I didn't say they were. No, some of them are good. I learned much about the white men, being a lawyer in Boston. I also learned that there are some good white men, a few that keep their word and live as they say they believe. There are more than I would have thought sixteen years ago."

She started to ask another question, but he put his hand to her lips to quiet her.

"I've talked to Raphael, and heard of the many things that have happened to you. I'm glad you married such a good man as Sheriff MacGregor. He was one of the few white men I knew then who I trusted. He was good to you, wasn't he?"

She nodded.

"Did you love him?"

"Does that matter?"

"Yes," he said.

"Why?"

"Then you were also happy."

"I loved him, in my own way," she replied, feeling defensive and not knowing why.

Jason had no right to ask her about her life. He had left her, not caring if she were alive or dead. She started to get up, but he pulled her down into his arms.

"You're angry. You still shoot sparks out of your eyes when you are angry," he said.

His closeness stirred her. She wanted to get away from him. She couldn't react this way to him, not after all these years, not after he left her!

"You just left me, not caring what happened to me," she shot back at him.

"If I recall, the night I left you I had asked you to marry me, and you refused my offer," he corrected her calmly.

She sank back down on the cool grass. They lay there, looking at each other, he lightly rubbing her cheek with his fingers. She heard the meadowlark. She smelled the fresh grass and the wool of his coat. She had to keep talking to avoid confronting herself for a while.

"You dress very well," she said.

"And it is very warm, in this weather," he said, sitting up and swiftly pulling off his coat. His shoulders had gotten broader, and the black vest and full white sleeves of his shirt only emphasized them.

"You never married?" she asked.

"No."

"Why not?"

"I had you. It was enough," he replied.

"I was nowhere around."

"You always were with me, Amanda."

"Is that why you came back?"

AMANDA

"I had to see you, had to know if you were well, if you were happy."

"Now you have found out, now what will you do?"

He frowned and heaved a soulful sigh. "I have to help my people," he said.

"Help them? They seem to have survived this long without you," she said.

"That's just the point. They are just surviving. They don't understand the white man's way, and they keep getting pushed into a smaller and smaller area and keep losing more and more of their rights and land. I can help them, especially now with what I know, and who I know."

"Then you will go back to the reservation?" she asked.

"Yes."

He gripped her shoulders. They were standing face to face. She saw the golden flecks in his eyes, the same ones that danced in Katy's eyes when she became intense and serious.

"Amanda, come with me," he said.

"Come with you? To the reservation?"

He nodded.

"Why?"

"I need you Amanda. I want you as much as I did sixteen years ago. Maybe more."

She pulled away from him and walked to a big cottonwood and leaned her head against it briefly and then turned to him. She looked at him, feeling the knot in her stomach. She wasn't sure she could stand losing him a second time. But there were so many years, so much had happened. She couldn't erase those years. They had remolded her. The lady of the East had died so many years ago. The girl who had emerged from the dark cave had grown and changed.

"You expect me to drop my whole life and run to the reservation and be what you think I should be?" she asked.

"I want to be with you," he said, not coming close, just standing with his hands in his pockets.

"Wanting and having are not the same things," she stated simply.

"I wasn't aware we were debating philosophy," he said sarcastically.

He stepped swiftly up to her and kissed her hard and long, his tongue playing with hers. She knew he was trying to revive the old feelings. She knew she desired him. She wanted him. But she was angry with him, for all the years he wasn't here for her, angry because he had left her with a child to care for, with no thought to it or its welfare. She tried to push him away, but he just became more insistent, pulling her to her knees with him.

He twisted her long hair in his hands and pulled her head back. "Tell me you don't want me and I'll go," he whispered hoarsely.

She couldn't lie to him. He would know she was lying. Her whole body would tell him she was lying. He kissed her throat as he released her hair. His hands explored her, freeing the buttons of her shirt. She wrenched herself free of him.

"Damn you, damn you, damn you!" she spat at him. "You think after all these years you can just come back and take me? Do you want to leave me with child like you did last time? Well, you can't because I can't ever have anymore children!" she pulled her blouse shut with her hand and glared at him. He sat back on his haunches, stunned at what she had said.

"With child?" he asked incredulously.

She instantly regretted having played her trump card, and had revealed a secret that up to now, only two people had shared. But there was no going back.

"Katy is yours, not Andrew's. But Katy doesn't know. You're never to tell her," she said fiercely.

"Why didn't you tell me?" he asked.

"I didn't know until after you had left." She waited before she continued so he could digest the full impact of what she had said.

"Is that why you married MacGregor?" he finally asked, after a long time of studying her.

"Yes. I couldn't bear a child and care for it by myself in this hard country. I was completely alone. I had to do something."

"Did he know?"

"I told him later, after Katy had already been born," she said.

"And still he stayed with you and cared for her?"

"He loved her like a father. He would never have hurt her for anything," she asserted.

"Then I won't tell her. Her remembrance of him will remain good," Jason replied. "Is this why you're so angry with me, because I left you with child? How could I have know, if you didn't even know then? Good God, Amanda, I was only seventeen, and a very confused and angry seventeen. I only knew two things. That I was an Indian and that I loved you. And both of these worlds were crashing down around my head. You wouldn't marry me. Would you have married me if you had known you were pregnant?" he asked.

She thought for a minute, "I don't know, Jason."

"And will you marry me now?" he asked.

"No," she whispered.

"Then I will leave you again. I don't stay where I'm not wanted," he said, turning to the horse.

She ran to him and stopped him from mounting the horse.

"Don't leave, Jason," she pleaded.

"What do you want of me?" he asked.

"Don't leave. Why can't you stay with me at the ranch? Why can't you take care of the ranch with me?"

"I can't, Amanda. If I am to help my people, I must try to become one of them again. I thought you respected my people and the way they live," he said.

"I do, Jason. And I love Winona like a sister, and Paul is like a son to me. Raphael is a son to me. But I cannot be one of them."

"You prefer the white man's way?"

"Not entirely, no."

He sidestepped her and grabbed the reins of his horse. "You want the best of both worlds," he said.

"Yes, why not?" she cried. "Why can't I try to have the best of both worlds? Isn't that really what you are taking back to your people? The good things you have learned in the white world? Aren't you going to try to protect them from the bad? Do you thing there is not bad in that tribe? You've been away too long. You cut your hair and you are not warrior. You are still Moksois!"

He dropped the reins and whirled to her. He grabbed both of her arms. She could see the anger in his locked jaw and stiff shoulders. His breath was hot on her face. He didn't speak but instead just glared at her. Gradually he eased his grip.

"I know the old ways are not perfect, " he said. "But I have to return. It's where I belong. I have tried both worlds. I have chosen the one into which I belong."

"Well, I too, have chosen. I live in neither world, and yet both. I want the best of them both," she said

"You are asking for an impossible perfection," he said sadly.

They were both quiet, lost in their own thoughts. She could not just send him away. He was buried too deeply into her soul to simply eliminate all thought of him from her life. There had to be a way to be with him, if only once in a while, if only for a little while.

"Jason, why does everything have to be so absolute with you? You accuse me of seeking perfection. You are, too, aren't you? It's completely either with you, or without you." She tried to feel her way with him, to find where he really was.

"And what do you suggest? That we live part time your way, and part of the time mine?" he asked.

"Something like that. I know I still love you. I would be lying to both of us to deny that," she said.

"You know, that is what you said before," he said.

"I'm not as afraid as I used to be," she leaned into him and wrapped her arms around him. He held her, putting his cheek on the top of her head. "We can work it out, somehow. I know we can. I want to be with you. But I can't marry you. I can't be wife to anyone, anymore. That time of my life is done. I have to have my freedom, for myself. I can't be an appendage to anyone."

"It wouldn't be like that," he protested.

"It would have to be if we were married. Your people have some definite ideas on how a woman should and shouldn't behave and what she should and shouldn't do. Look at the difficulty Winona has had because she refused to marry and have children," Amanda pointed out.

"Your people are the same way. Ladies don't take their gloves off when shaking hands with me, and on and on," he mocked.

"I know. That's why I can't marry you. I don't fit either place."

"Do you know what the people of the town would think if we were to simply live together as lovers," he laughed.

She smiled and laughed with him. "Oh, yes, I know. But I'm rich and own a lot of land. They would still do business with me. And the few who do count would accept it, even if they didn't like it."

"Are you sure?'

"No, but I hope that's how it would be."

"So you would live on your ranch, and I would live in my tepee, and come to visit every Saturday night. Is that the way it must be?"

She grinned at him. "Oh, I suppose we could trade off and I would visit your tepee once in awhile."

"That would give my people a chance to gossip. Have to keep it all even, you know."

She laughed. "It does sound silly, doesn't it? But I don't care. It would work for us. And that is all I gave a damn about."

"Ladies don't swear," he frowned at her in mock horror.

"I do," she told him impishly. Then, she looked serious. "Actually, I won't be at the ranch in a few weeks."

"Why not?" he asked, confused by the new development.

"Governor Greenwood has appointed me to fill the senate seat vacated when Senator Jacobin died," she told him. "It will mean I will have to be in Washington."

He studied her a long time. She would be one of the first woman senators. Then he kissed her. "That's a long way to go for a weekend with my woman."

"But isn't that where you will have to go to fight some of those complicated legal battles for your people that you were talking about?" she asked.

He nodded and grinned. "With you as a senator, and me as their lobbyist, we'll have them owning the whole damn country again."

AMANDA

"At least that," she agree. "What are you doing?" she asked, watching him take off his vest and his shirt.

"Taking my clothes off," he replied.

"Why?"

"If I'm going to be an Indian, I'm going to look like one," he explained, pulling off his boots.

"Well, your clothes don't show what you are, do they?"

"Not necessarily, but you see," he continued to explain as he loosened his belt and looked down at her with a half-grin on his face. "It's very difficult," he continued as he loosed his pants and dropped them to stand before her totally nude. He took her hand, "I don't like to make love with my clothes on."

She laughed and wound her arms around his neck and kissed him as if to kiss all the lost years away.

"Neither do I," she said. She pulled away and stripped off her clothes as he watched and they lay in the sweet spring grass together.

EPILOGUE

"We are all here to read the last will and testament of my grandmother, Amanda White MacGregor," intoned Andrew Jason MacGregor, better known as Matcikineu. "Since my parents are in Los Angeles, and would not make it back in time, they asked that I gather all of you and read the will. As all of you here know, she had taken care of most of the details contained within it before she died. The will merely re-affirms her decisions."

Then he opened the paper and read to the people gathered there. A small-wizened Indian woman leaned on her cane and listened carefully. Across the room, a very old, very short, sandy-haired man with a persistent cough shifted his eyes around the room. The old blind man sitting in front wore the marks of honor of a shaman. He would mutter to himself from time to time, when some portion of the will was read.

"My son and daughter, Raphael and Kathleen MacGregor already have their ranch and their horses and their son. They need nothing more from me. They may do with my personal effects as they see fit. Since my grandson, Matcikineu, had decided to be a lawyer and a businessman, I bequeath to him the oil fields in the eastern ranch, and all that entails. Good luck, my handsome warrior."

"To Jeremiah Greenwood, I bequeath my Arabian horses and all the headaches that go with their temperament and beauty.

"The rest of my land and cattle and all the accouterments of caring for them, I return to my friends of the tribe. Let their council decide how best they can be used for the benefit of all the people."

"My only stipulation to all this is that I be buried as Jason was buried, so that my spirit will be on the same ground as my long-lost Melinda, my beloved Andrew, and my darling Jason.

"To you, the living, I bequeath all the sorrows and joys of this life, as I look forward to whatever the next one will hold for me."

"Amanda MacGregor."

The handsome young man looked up at the gathering. His brown eyes with their gold flecks traveled from one to the other. His face was beautiful, but there was a stubborn set to the mouth that belied his twenty-one years. His hair was long and shiny black, but his beard was short.

"Does anyone challenge this will, or have any questions?" He asked.

No one spoke.

"Then this reading is ended. I will attend to the details to be sure the will is carried out."

They stood quietly and shuffled out of the cave into the brilliant sunshine.

"Silly place to hold the reading of a will," Kinney complained, painfully stooping to get out of the hole. Winona just smiled and shuffled to the waiting wagon, where two young girls, mirrored images of each other, sat waiting for her.

Jeremiah had to hunch his huge shoulders together to squeeze through the opening. He stretched when he finally reached the outside. He glanced briefly over at the grave he had helped to dig so many years ago. He didn't like this place. It was spooky. He recalled the strange Indian ritual of two nights ago, and shivered.

The blind shaman came out, not even having to feel the walls to know where he was. As usual, he was muttering to himself. Jeremiah caught a few words he was saying. "Amanda you create more problems than you solve with some of your solutions. But I think it will work." And the shaman continued on his way, wagging his head and talking until a small cherubic-looking Indian boy took his arm and led him to the wagon where the old woman sat.

Finally, after they had all left, Matcikineu emerged, holding the will in one hand and his black Stetson in the other. He breathed deeply of the crisp spring air, and listened to the meadowlark. He felt at home here. He would come here when his spirit needed guidance.

"Well. Grandmother, you have them both now, and little Melinda. I know you are happy."

He set the hat on his head and swung onto his horse. He had not allowed any cars or machines to come to this place. He would make sure that those here were not disturbed. He rode into the fiery red ball of the sunset, his long hair streaming back in the wind—away from the stream and the cave and the quiet solitude there.

ABOUT THE AUTHOR

Pamela Conrad grew up in Wyoming around the thermal hot springs of Yellowstone and near the Arapahoe and Shoshone. She brings that experience to her story of Amanda.

She has also written, *The Ancient Warrior: Return of the Gargoyle*. Her civil war series, *Michael's Song*, will be available this fall.

Ms. Conrad has her Bachelor's Degree in English and a Master's Degree in Instructional Design from the University of Iowa. She has had a varied career in business and education and is now president of her own training corporation.

She also is an artist working in pencil, charcoal, watercolors and acrylics. She finds time for fencing, SCUBA diving, yoga, tai chi, gardening, and music and is an avid reader.